# ON THE
# LINE

## Books by Fern Michaels

Fear Thy Neighbor
Santa Cruise
No Way Out
The Brightest Star
Fearless
Spirit of the Season
Deep Harbor
Fate & Fortune
Sweet Vengeance
Holly and Ivy
Fancy Dancer
No Safe Secret
Wishes for Christmas
About Face
Perfect Match
A Family Affair
Forget Me Not
The Blossom Sisters
Balancing Act
Tuesday's Child
Betrayal
Southern Comfort
To Taste the Wine
Sins of the Flesh
Sins of Omission
Return to Sender
Mr. and Miss Anonymous
Up Close and Personal
Fool Me Once
Picture Perfect
The Future Scrolls
Kentucky Sunrise
Kentucky Heat
Kentucky Rich

Plain Jane
Charming Lily
What You Wish For
The Guest List
Listen to Your Heart
Celebration
Yesterday
Finders Keepers
Annie's Rainbow
Sara's Song
Vegas Sunrise
Vegas Heat
Vegas Rich
Whitefire
Wish List
Dear Emily
Christmas at Timberwoods

The Lost and Found
Novels:

Secrets
Hidden

The Sisterhood Novels:

19 Yellow Moon Road
Bitter Pill
Truth and Justice
Cut and Run
Safe and Sound
Need to Know

## Books by Fern Michaels (Continued)

# Books by Fern Michaels (Continued)

Anthologies:

Home Sweet Home
A Snowy Little Christmas
Coming Home for
   Christmas
A Season to Celebrate
Mistletoe Magic
Winter Wishes
The Most Wonderful Time
When the Snow Falls
Secret Santa
A Winter Wonderland

I'll Be Home for Christmas
Making Spirits Bright
Holiday Magic
Snow Angels
Silver Bells
Comfort and Joy
Sugar and Spice
Let it Snow
A Gift of Joy
Five Golden Rings
Deck the Halls
Jingle All the Way

# FERN MICHAELS
# ON THE LINE

**ZEBRA BOOKS**
Kensington Publishing Corp.
www.kensingtonbooks.com

ZEBRA BOOKS are published by

Kensington Publishing Corp.
900 Third Avenue
New York, NY 10022

All Kensington titles, imprints, and distributed lines are available at special quantity discounts for bulk purchases for sales promotion, premiums, fund-raising, educational, or institutional use.

Special book excerpts or customized printings can also be created to fit specific needs. For details, write or phone the office of the Kensington Sales Manager: Attn.: Sales Department. Kensington Publishing Corp., 119 West 40th Street, New York, NY 10018. Phone: 1-800-221-2647.

ZEBRA and the Zebra logo Reg US Pat. & TM Off.

First Kensington Hardcover Edition: April 2023

First Paperback Edition: June 2024
ISBN: 978-1-4201-5427-6

ISBN: 978-1-4967-3718-2 (ebook)

10 9 8 7 6 5 4 3 2 1

Printed in the United States of America

# Acknowledgments

The author would like to acknowledge Executive Chef Nicholas Liberto, Sous Chef Pablo Toxqui, General Manager Jason Reiff, and the staff at One Willow. You make the magic happen.

Many thanks to Ashley Finamore, PharmD., Clinical Pharmacist, for her vast knowledge of oncology pharmacology.

*Bueno Apetito* . . . and be careful in the kitchen.

# Contents

# PART I
## THE MYSTERY

# Chapter One
# Blood Is Thinner

*Present Day*

"**Y**ou suffered a mild contusion to the head."
Mateo Castillo blinked several times as the man in the white coat explained. *Where was he and who was this person?* Then he shook his head.

"Do you know where you are, Mr. Castillo?" the doctor asked quietly. Thirtysomething Mateo tentatively moved his head from side to side—or as much as he could—to keep the searing pain away from the back of his eyes. The doctor, a salt-and-pepper-haired gentleman around the age of sixty, smiled down at him.

"You are in the NYU Hospital emergency room. I'm Dr. Conroy. An ambulance brought you here."

Mateo winced as he tried to speak. "Wha . . .

wha . . . what happened? Ambulance?" He could barely stammer out the words. His forehead crinkled. "I don't understand. I was in the kitchen at Le Mer."

"Evidently you fell in the kitchen. You also lost a good deal of blood from a knife wound." The doctor pointed his stylus pen at a bag with reddish-brown sludge hanging from a pole next to Mateo's bed. "It appears you cut yourself and passed out. The wound wasn't very deep for the amount of blood loss, so we're going to run some tests."

Mateo was gaining more acuity. "Blood loss?" He continued to strain his brain for some point of reference. The last thing he recalled was standing in the kitchen of the restaurant. "I was trying out a new dish for the contest." He paused. "I was slicing shallots."

The doctor looked at the chart again. "Do you remember slipping on anything? A wet surface? Oil?"

"No. No, we are very careful, and we have mats." His eyes surveyed the curtains that surrounded his bed. "I don't understand."

"A Mr. Miller found you on the floor. He made a tourniquet out of a towel and called 911. If we don't find anything abnormal, you should be able to go home in about twenty-four hours." The doctor glanced at his clipboard. "One more question—were you on anything?"

Mateo looked at him curiously. "Do you mean drugs?"

"Yes, that would be the obvious question."

"No. Never."

"Could you have fainted?" Mateo wasn't surprised at the doctor's curiosity. For a long time, the restaurant crowd had a reputation of wild nights after hours, but that had faded over the past decade. With the advent of the Food Network and other foodie channels, the industry was at an all-time high for talent. And Mateo was no exception. He was becoming the "it" boy of the culinary scene. Mateo's eyes were a blue-gray Caribbean aqua within a darker circle of blue. They stood out against his black wavy hair and golden complexion. He wasn't a fashionista, but he surely knew what looked good on him from a young age. The restaurant scene was the perfect venue for him to shine.

"It's possible, but I don't know why I would."

The doctor looked at Mateo's arms. "Have you fallen anywhere else lately?"

"No." Mateo shook his head slowly.

"How did your arms get bruised like that?"

"Clumsy, I guess." Mateo noticed the bruises on his arms and his legs but thought nothing of it. "People are always banging into things and each other in the kitchen, especially on a busy night." He continued to speak slowly, trying to shake off the fuzz clouding his thoughts. "You need to be light on your feet and have eyes in the back of your head."

"Any other symptoms?" Dr. Conroy was typing letters into the tablet that served as his medical chart. "Lightheadedness? Dizzy spells?"

Mateo thought for a moment. He recalled feeling a bit "off" a few times recently, but he chalked it up to exhaustion and exhilaration, not worth mentioning. "No. Not really."

"When you say 'not really,' you need to be more specific. Please. It's the only way we can make a proper diagnosis."

"After a long day, I'm pretty beat and sometimes have a tough time getting up the next morning. But after a cup of espresso and a shower, I'm good to go." Mateo was gaining more clarity.

"Alright, then. We'll wait for the blood work and see what's next. I will refer your case to our hematologist, Dr. Adrian Ardell. Dr. Ardell comes on duty in about an hour. Meanwhile, get some rest. We need you back in that kitchen." Dr. Conroy had finally realized who the new patient was, a rising star in the cooking scene.

"Thank you, Doctor." Mateo closed his eyes as the beeping from the monitors kept up a steady rhythm throughout the emergency room. He thought about what a noisy place the hospital was and could not understand the signs on the road that said QUIET. HOSPITAL. *It sure wasn't an advertisement.* He lightened up a bit. At least he still had a sense of humor. He settled in the bed as best he could and closed his eyes, hoping when he opened them, this crazy dream would be over.

He was startled awake by a pretty young woman who adjusted his intravenous drip, then smiled. "Mr. Castillo, I am Dr. Adrian Ardell."

*Maybe this dream wasn't so bad after all.* He realized he was finally having lucid thoughts. "Nice to meet you, Dr. Adrian Ardell. Please tell me you will let me out of here soon."

Her wide, saucer-shaped eyes were hypnotic. "I wish I could, Mr. Castillo. But I am impressed you remembered all of my name with the right consonants in order."

Mateo felt a strong pull and tried to shake it off. He wasn't intimidated by professional women, but this one had a mystique about her. Perhaps it was the tinge of an Eastern European accent. Throughout his childhood, he'd learned to recognize many foreign accents and inflections. His mother had been a linguistics teacher when she wasn't running the school cafeteria. He couldn't help but ask, "Do I detect a hint of Ukrainian? Moldavian?" Mateo immediately regretted blurting out such a personal question. To a doctor, no less. But there was something about the woman that made him feel comfortable. Maybe because she was his ticket out of the beeps, bright lights, and muffled announcements over the PA system. Not to mention disengaging him from the IV stand. And these socks? He noticed he was wearing a pair of very ugly socks. Nothing from *his* closet, that was for certain.

She seemed unaffected by the question. Mateo quickly added, "You must get that all of the time. I know I do." Mateo's voice was more of a lilt than an accent. His deep voice added to the ambiguity.

She was still looking at his chart when she answered. "Yes. I would have thought my name would have been a clue." She kept looking down. "My family escaped from a very corrupt government. We were lucky to have relatives in the United States. Brooklyn. I came here when I was twelve years old." She checked his vitals. "And you?"

Mateo briefly recounted the journey his family

took during his childhood from Texas to Tennessee, and eventually to New Jersey. "And I ended up here." He smiled at her. He wanted to continue the conversation. "Where did you study medicine?"

"I went to college in Ithaca." Dr. Adrian Ardell held up her end of the small talk. "Cornell."

"You must be smart." Mateo chuckled.

"You should hope so, Mr. Castillo. Your life could be in my hands." She gave him a sly smile.

"My apologies. That didn't come out the way I intended. Cornell is an excellent school."

"It is indeed." She reviewed his chart. "You work in a restaurant?"

"Yes," Mateo answered. He realized not everyone was a foodie. Why should she know who he was? "Le Mer."

"Ah. Fancy." She continued to peruse his information without looking up from the tablet. "How long have you worked there?"

"Almost two years. I'm the executive chef."

"Ah. Even fancier." She finally raised her head. "You serve a lot of seafood, do you not?"

"Yes. That is our specialty. Hence the name."

She gave a little guffaw. "Of course." Dr. Ardell continued to ask more questions. "How often do you eat seafood?"

"A couple of times a week. One of the benefits of being a chef."

"Not necessarily in your case, Mr. Castillo."

Mateo wriggled himself and sat upright. "What do you mean?"

"Your blood work came back with elevated levels

of mercury. Probably from all the seafood consumption. You will need to eliminate it for several weeks until we can get your level back to normal. We'll run tests again."

Mateo was stunned. It never occurred to him he could be eating too much seafood. He tried to keep a balanced diet.

"I want you to drink at least two liters of water per day, unless you want us to administer fluids intravenously." The doctor knew he wouldn't go for that option, but she had to inform him, nonetheless.

"Oh, I will take the water torture over the IV. But thank you for offering." He looked down at his socks again. "And what about these?"

"Your compression socks? What about them?"

"They don't go with the rest of my wardrobe," Mateo teased, pulling at the blue hospital gown someone had dressed him in when he was unconscious. He was unabashedly flirting with her.

"They are a precaution while you are in bed. It helps to maintain blood flow, reduce swelling and discomfort."

"But I thought my blood *was* flowing." He folded his arms and feigned a pout. "Too much, from what I've been told."

"True. So for now you will wear them until you are released."

"And when might that be?" He gave her a puppy-dog look.

"Tomorrow morning, if everything else comes back normal."

"You mean I have to stay here tonight?" Mateo was starting to whine.

"I know it's not a four-star hotel, but it's better if you are kept under observation. We'll check your blood again in another few hours. If everything looks okay in the morning, you may be able to get back to your knife-wielding occupation."

"I beg your pardon," Mateo said mockingly. "I am a craftsman."

She stifled a chuckle. "Unfortunately, your craftmanship will be on hold until tomorrow. So please sit back and enjoy the luxury of our fine ambiance and sorely lacking gastronomy." She checked the time. "It's almost midnight. Had you eaten anything before your mishap?"

"Yes, around nine thirty. We were closing." He continued sheepishly, "Linguine with clams."

"Are you sure you only eat seafood a couple of times a week?" Dr. Ardell asked with a touch of skepticism.

Mateo raised the arm that wasn't attached to the IV. "I swear."

"Alright then. How do you feel about a grilled cheese sandwich? Low-fat cheese."

"Sounds dreadful, but I'll take it," Mateo responded.

"I have my dinner break in a few minutes. I'll ask someone to prepare one for you. It's the best I can offer. And you should eat something."

"Carbs and fat. Mmm . . . my favorite cuisine," Mateo joked. "But I don't want you to go to any trouble."

"It's no trouble," she said coolly. "I will be in the

dining room and will order it for you. Someone will bring it up."

Mateo was almost deflated. He had thought for a brief moment that the doctor was flirting back. "Thank you. I appreciate it."

"Good. I shall see you first thing in the morning. Enjoy your sandwich and try to sleep." She spun on her heel and left the room.

Mateo wasn't sure what had just transpired. The more he thought about it, the more he realized the entire night had been rather peculiar.

Two very large men wearing scrubs came into the ER and pulled Mateo's gurney out of the cubby. The larger of the two looked down and muttered, "Movin' you to a room. You're lucky. We're pretty busy."

Mateo lay flat as he stared up at the passing ceiling tiles and the bright lights. They moved him swiftly into a room with a man who had every appendage hooked up to a machine, including an oxygen tube up his nose. Mateo shuddered. The guy was close to his age. He wondered what had brought him there. He was thankful his own condition would be behind him by the morning.

Mateo tried to get some sleep, but the dinging, fluorescent lights in the hallway and the constant announcements on the intercom made it impossible. He continued to stare at the ceiling, hoping he could force himself into a state of relaxation. He remembered a line from a comedian: "The hospital is no place to get well." Several minutes later, a perky volunteer delivered the grilled cheese sandwich he had forgotten about. It was actually hot and smelled pretty good for hospital food. But then again, he could be delirious. This night truly wasn't anything he had expected.

The next morning, an intern came to his room, announcing Mateo would be released in a few hours. Mateo asked about Dr. Ardell. "She's off today," the intern responded.

"Did she have anything specific for me? Instructions?" Mateo suppressed a frown.

The intern handed him a sheet of paper outlining the dos and don'ts. Drink two liters of water per day. No green leafy vegetables. No cinnamon; no ginger; no garlic.

Mateo cringed at the list. It included almost everything he worked with as a chef. "This is going to be brutal."

The intern shrugged. "The doctor wants to see you in four weeks for a follow-up. You can make an appointment with her PA at the nurses' station. An orderly will be by to wheel you out. Do you have someone picking you up?"

"Wheel me out?"

"Yes. It's hospital policy."

"So you just dump me on the sidewalk?" Mateo didn't intend to be sarcastic, but things were not going as he hoped. The mysterious doctor hadn't stopped by to give him his discharge papers, which sucked.

"Do you have a ride?" the intern asked again.

"Not yet." Mateo stared at the paperwork in front of him. He was going to have to be very creative or trust his colleagues to taste the food.

The intern reminded him one last time that, "You need to have someone pick you up or you won't be released." He turned and left the room.

Mateo reached for the blue plastic bag sitting on the foot of his bed. He fished out his cell phone and dialed his friend Roger's number. "Yo, Rog. I need a ride . . ."

# Chapter Two

# Déjà Vu

*Three weeks later*

The ambulance went screaming up First Avenue. The traffic lights were a kaleidoscope racing over him. The man in the uniform kept asking him the same questions. "What is your name? Where do you live?" His lips were trying to move, but no sound came out. He tried to move his fingers. It was as if he were a disembodied being. A spectator. What was happening to him?

The ambulance pulled into the bay of the emergency intake at NYU Hospital. The paramedics were able to stop the bleeding by applying pressure on the wound, and Mateo was in stable condition for the moment. People were bustling around him, mumbling words he could not put together.

*Poisoning. Fainting. Fracture and lacerations to the head.* It made no sense. They could not be talking about him. He was a chef, working on a signature dish at a restaurant. How did he get here? Was this a reoccurring nightmare?

He was much weaker than during the previous visit. He thought he was supposed to improve. But this was a far cry from improvement. It was worse. His hands were cold. His toes were numb. He had the shakes. He kept going in and out of consciousness. *What was happening?* The EMS people were moving him to an area behind curtains, where he was immediately plugged into a IV filled with the same brownish sludge he recalled from his last trip. The hose up his nose was uncomfortable and was scratching his throat. He tried to speak.

"Take it easy, Mr. Castillo." Someone in green scrubs spoke to him calmly. "You're in the emergency room at NYU Hospital."

Mateo blinked several times, trying to clear this nightmare from his head. But with each blink, it became more real, and the pain in his head was exacerbated by a pulling sensation above his eyebrow.

An ER doctor entered the curtained cubicle and checked the wound. "You're lucky. It didn't penetrate the skull." Dr. Conroy checked the tubes running into Mateo's veins. "This is your second visit in the past three weeks. It appears the injury to your head was the result of a fall, but we don't know what caused the fall. We had to stitch you up, so you may have a scar on your forehead. Fortunately, you didn't sustain any other injuries."

Mateo closed his eyes and managed a slight nod

in acknowledgment. He wanted to ask *why?* but the words would not come.

Dr. Conroy checked Mateo's chart. "You must have a guardian angel, Mr. Castillo. If I remember correctly, the last time, you were found by the janitor. This time, it was a couple of kids looking for a bin filled with bottles. As much as I don't necessarily approve of children having cell phones, in this case it was a blessing. As soon as one of the boys saw the blood, he dialed 911."

Mateo knew who the doctor was talking about. There were three kids around ten years old who would come by to collect bottles for the recycling center. Even though the restaurant had a service that did this, Mateo would leave a special container for the boys so they could turn it in for some loose change and raise their awareness about recycling.

"Can you try to answer some questions?" Dr. Conroy asked. He nodded to the oxygen meter clipped to the end of Mateo's finger. "Just raise it slightly if the answer is yes, and to the side if the answer is no. Do you understand?" Mateo wiggled his finger the best he could. "Excellent. I'm going to go over some of the same questions from your last visit, so bear with me. Have you eaten today?"

A shaking finger went up, indicating *yes*.

"Within the past ten hours?"

Mateo thought for a moment. He couldn't remember and had no idea what time it was. He squinted at the doctor.

"Did you have lunch?"

A wiggle up and down. The doctor checked his

watch. It was past seven p.m. He surmised it had been within the time frame he asked about.

"Have you had any shellfish since your last visit here?"

The finger went to the left.

"Do you or anyone in your family suffer from anemia? Hemophilia?"

Two more signs to the left and right.

"Have you ever been diagnosed with von Wille-brand disease?"

Mateo had no idea what he was talking about and squinted again. The doctor explained that it involved a low level of protein that helped the blood clotting process. Mateo moved his finger to the left. As far as Mateo knew, no one in his family had any blood disorders.

"All your other vital signs are stable. Dr. Ardell will be here in about an hour, so sit tight." The doctor patted Mateo's arm when he realized what a ridiculous remark it was. "Not that you're going anywhere." He smiled. "At least not until we can figure out why you've become a regular in my ER."

Mateo managed a thumbs-up.

The doctor grinned. "That's what I like in a patient. A positive attitude. I will check on you later. Meanwhile, we are going to admit you and get you into a room."

Mateo lay there in a state of disbelief. He had felt fine earlier that day, but when he started fileting the Dover sole, he started to feel a little light-headed and nauseous. He remembered walking out the back into the alley to get some cold, fresh air and saw the kids at the far end of the alley. That was all he remembered as he drifted into a semi-conscious state.

His eyes flew open when two aides began to move him down the hall. He wracked his brain, trying to put the pieces together. The familiarity of it all was eerie. Lights were swiftly moving above his head. He could hear clamoring bells, beeps, and garbled voices. They wheeled him into an elevator, brought him into a room, and he drifted off into a restless sleep.

Mateo felt the presence of someone lingering over him. He slowly opened his eyes. It was that striking doctor with the mysterious accent again. Mateo knew it was Eastern European. She had mentioned her family escaped from a country with a corrupt government, but that covered a lot of geographic locations in that part of the world.

"Hello, Mr. Castillo." Dr. Ardell folded her arms. "I said I wanted to see you in four weeks. You must be a glutton for punishment—or you really enjoy our food." She made a valiant attempt at humor. It worked. He was able to crack a smile. "We are going to run more extensive tests on you. I suspect it's mercury again, but you told Dr. Conroy that you hadn't had any shellfish."

This time, he was able to shake his head slightly.

"So you are going to be a big mystery for me to solve." She tapped her tablet several times. "We are going to draw blood. I know you've lost quite a lot again, but I think there is still enough for us to run some tests."

Mateo managed another very weak smile.

"I am a very good detective," Dr. Ardell said with a straight face. "Plus I do not like to lose. I treat the symptoms like they are the enemy. I seek them out and then get rid of them."

Mateo wasn't sure how to interpret what she'd just said. It seemed a bit militaristic. She chuckled when she saw the look on his face. "Believe me, we will win this together." She made a few more notes on the tablet. "The phlebotomist will be in shortly and will send your blood to the lab. I'll read the results in the morning. Meanwhile, we will do chelation therapy to try to clean out any additional heavy metals in your system. I'll see you tomorrow." She turned and glided out the door.

A nurse's aide entered the room and was greeted by Mateo's roommate. "Hello, gorgeous!" a youngish man's voice boomed. "Come keep me company."

There was a feminine giggle. "Oh, you behave. We need you up and running for the collegiate football tournament."

Mateo managed an eyeroll for no one but himself. The curtain was swept open, and the aide introduced herself. "I'm Becky. I'll be on duty tonight. If you need anything, just push this button." She handed him the trigger that would send a signal to the nurses' station. "Meanwhile, I am going to need a urine sample from you." She noticed both his arms were attached to devices.

The idea of having a total stranger touch his private parts was humiliating. Mateo managed to squeak out a few words. "I think I can do it myself." His eyes were pleading.

"Okay, Mr. Castillo, but if we don't get enough for a sample, I am going to have to help you."

Mateo was more determined than ever to pee in

the oddly shaped bottle she handed him. Becky looked the other way as she lifted the sheet. Mateo jerked his head and squeaked out another few words. "Privacy, please?"

Becky chuckled. "Mr. Castillo. You are in a hospital. This is no place for modesty."

From the other side of the curtain that separated him from the college athlete, a voice boomed. "Oh, let her grab it, pal. It might be the only fun you have." He laughed in a mocking and annoying way.

Mateo wished he could cough up the words "Shut up, dumbass." But the look on his face signaled Becky to step away and give him some privacy. Mateo could hear her and the dude next to him snickering. He wondered if he had been that obnoxious when he was younger.

Never in his life had the ability to urinate been more challenging. He struggled to maneuver the bottle among the tubes and under the sheets. Knowing there were people within earshot who were keenly aware of what he was attempting made the job more intimidating. He soon realized Becky was right—the hospital was no place for modesty or decorum. You did what you had to do, even if it would take a yoga master to bend certain parts of their body the right way.

When Mateo finished, he was relieved in more ways than one. "Becky?" he whispered. She flung the curtain open and retrieved the container from Mateo.

Mr. Snarky Athlete put in his two cents. "See? That wasn't so bad, was it?"

Mateo didn't know if it was the fact he was feeling better or the idea a snot-nosed jock was invading his personal space with his mere presence, but he said, "Oh, yeah. It was great. Can't wait to do it again." He felt smug, firstly because he was able to speak properly again, and secondly because he was able to muster up a little sarcasm.

"Someone will be here shortly to draw your blood," Becky said as she left the room—but not without blowing a kiss to Mateo's irritating roommate first.

The sound of whining wheels was getting louder, suggesting another visit from the staff. At least it wouldn't be an embarrassing situation this time.

"Good evening, Mr. Castillo," a woman said as she entered the room. "I'm Terry Stenhouse. I'm here to draw your blood."

Mateo had enough strength to push the button to raise his bed so he was more upright. Too bad he hadn't thought of that half an hour earlier. It could have made his gymnastic attempt to obtain a sample a little easier. He surmised Becky hadn't thought about it because she was too fascinated with the other guy in the room. Ms. Stenhouse rolled the cart close to the bed. Mateo spotted five empty vials on the cart. He was doubtful he still had that much blood left. "Not sure if I have enough," he joked to the tall woman who was tying a rubber hose around his bicep.

"Don't you worry, Mr. Castillo. I know how to get every drop." She winked at him. "I am going to insert a Mediport in the back of your hand so we don't have to keep poking you. This way, we can draw the blood from the port."

Mateo was already feeling like a pincushion. His

voice was coming back even more. "How many times do you think you'll have to do this? Take blood?"

"As many times as your doctor asks. Tonight I'll be taking a lot of samples so we can run a series of tests at the same time. We need to try to eliminate possible causes."

Mateo didn't want to think about "possible causes." Maybe he just needed a vacation. He knew he was exhausted and stressed. He was having trouble sleeping. He had been getting dizzy. He was anxious all the time and getting more headaches than he ever had before. A week under a palm tree, coupled with a colorful cocktail decorated with a tiny umbrella, might be the remedy.

After several minutes, Ms. Stenhouse declared, "All done. Now that wasn't so bad, was it?" Mateo wondered if that was standard hospital lingo. That, along with *this won't hurt a bit.*

"No, it's fine." Mateo thought it was a heck of a lot better than his earlier "wasn't so bad" incident.

After that, Mateo drifted in and out of sleep. He had a recurring nightmare. The same sounds, the lights, the voices in the background. *Why was this happening to him?* He thought about asking for something to help him sleep, but he never took drugs. Only aspirin, when necessary. Besides, he didn't want to contaminate his body any further if there truly was something wrong with him. Around two a.m., a nurse came in to check his vital signs and his IV. *No wonder he couldn't get any sleep.* This was worse than pulling an all-nighter when he was in culinary school. He recalled one particular assignment. He had to come up with a dish with a base of beets. He worked on his beetroot pasta sauce all night until he perfected it. The instructor was impressed with the outcome with the exception of the color. It was pink. The next time, Mateo made it with golden beets.

Eventually the sun was climbing over the horizon, bringing new light to the day. The halls were bustling again. Shifts were changing, medications were being handed out, and breakfast was being served by the kitchen porters. Mateo thought about the grilled cheese sandwich from his last visit. He dreaded what might be hiding under the plastic dome covering the plate placed before him. He raised the bed so he was upright, careful not to pull any of the tubes out, and thanked the orderly who delivered his breakfast. As he suspected, it was room-temperature toast. Dry. There was a yellow mixture that resembled scrambled eggs, and a few pieces of melon. A pint-sized milk carton was his beverage. He didn't suppose they served cappuccino or espresso. He chuckled at the thought.

Perky Becky stuck her head in to tell Mr. Romeo that she was ending her shift. He gave her the obligatory, "Okay, gorgeous. See you later."

Again, Mateo reached back into his memory, trying to recall if he grew up with anyone as full of himself as that guy. There were one or two in his high school, but he had only spent two years in a community college, so he had little interaction with collegiate sports. He dabbled in a little soccer, something he and his father would play when he was growing up, but now he simply wanted to cook. He was teased at first by some of his friends, but when he showed up at school with the most interesting and delicious sandwiches, he became the local hero. His mother taught him authentic South American recipes, and he learned dozens along the way from Texas to Tennessee to New Jersey, always trying to put his own personal spin on them.

Mateo fidgeted with the eggs on his plate when a disembodied voice from the other side of the curtain spoke. "Man, this food is the worst." Mateo chuckled to himself. If anyone knew the difference between good food and bad food, he surely did.

Mateo was going to decline responding but reconsidered. "Did it occur to you that the cafeteria has to provide meals for over three hundred patients per meal, and most are special diets?"

"Whoa, dude. You an expert on food or something?"

"Yeah. Or something." Mateo's mood suddenly lifted.

After the trays were cleared, another nurse came in to take Mateo's vitals and check the leads from the IV. "Dr. Ardell is making her rounds. She should be here shortly."

Mateo reached for the TV remote and turned on the news. More riots, more homeless, more shootings. And that wasn't even in New York. He shook his head. He thought about his life, his upbringing. He was grateful. His parents were loving and supportive. They taught him how to be a man of good character. His father told him at a very young age that "Life can bring you many challenges. If you meet them with integrity, you will always win. At times, it may not seem that way, but at the end of the day, you will be able to put your head on your pillow and know you did your best."

The restaurant business was filled with people from all walks of life. Some good. Some not so much. Could he be having second thoughts about his life's work? No! He chalked it up to being disoriented.

The sound of footsteps grew louder as Dr. Ardell entered the room. "Good morning, Mr. Castillo. How are you feeling today?" she asked with her almost imperceptible accent. Mateo was glad she didn't use the plural, "How are *we* feeling today?" He never understood that question. How would *he* know how someone else felt? As horrible as he felt physically, her presence brightened his mood. He had thought about her several times since his last visit to the hospital, but he had mostly been engrossed in his work. The time moved by quickly, and he hadn't formulated a plan to try to meet her again. *This* was not what he had in mind.

"Aside from the mean cuisine, the lack of sleep, and the tubes connecting me to these things," he said and pointed to the IV, "I'm okay. But I believe you would know more about that than I do."

Dr. Ardell moved closer to Mateo's bed. "I have some disconcerting news."

Mateo sat up taller.

"You have an extraordinary level of mercury in your system."

"How can that be?" Mateo was baffled.

"I was hoping you could tell me," she continued. "If you haven't had any seafood for two weeks,

I cannot understand why your levels are even higher than they were several weeks ago. We call it 'idiopathic.' I'm afraid you are going to need another transfusion. Perhaps a series of them. Your red blood cells and platelets are extremely low. You are going to have to stay here for several days until we can ascertain if the transfusion improves your blood work. But before we put good blood in your body, we are going to do a procedure called chelation therapy. We will introduce Dimercaprol into your system intravenously. It acts like a sponge and absorbs the mercury and is expelled through your urine." She stopped to allow Mateo to digest the information. "If these don't work, we will need to do a bone marrow biopsy to seek out the origin of your condition."

The words were reverberating in his ears. "Biopsy?"

"It's protocol, but let's see how you respond to the treatments first. Is there someone we can call for you? Family? Friends? Associates?"

Mateo began to think. He didn't want to alarm his parents, and he had no siblings. "My parents are in New Jersey, but I have a couple of friends I can call if necessary."

"You should tell your employer you will not be going back to the kitchen for at least several days. Do you think they can manage without you?"

"We're closing for a few days for some renovations in the dining room. That's why I took the opportunity to work on a dish."

"I see. You should let someone know your whereabouts. We wouldn't want anyone to call the police and file a missing persons report." That was her best attempt at humor. She knew how frightening the word *biopsy* could be.

"I'll call Nora, the hostess. She can let the owners know. I'll also call my friend Roger so he can feed my cat, Newman."

Dr. Ardell chuckled. "That's a funny name for a cat."

"It's a *Seinfeld* thing," Mateo said. "I was around twelve years old when it went off the air, but you can see episodes on some of the streaming networks." He wasn't sure how much this doctor knew about pop culture or if she even cared.

"Oh, I am familiar with *Seinfeld*. My family arrived here the same year the show ended." She stopped herself from revealing any further personal information. "But your cat? Newman?"

"He's a good cat. Not at all like Newman, except for his girth. He's a bit rotund."

"Bringing home leftovers from the restaurant?" Dr. Ardell was much more relaxed at this point.

"Guilty." Mateo grinned. Then he caught himself. "You don't suppose Newman can get mercury poisoning, do you?"

"It's possible. Has he been showing any signs of distress?"

"No. Not that I'm aware of." Mateo thought hard. "But I will definitely ask Roger to keep an eye on him."

"That sounds like a good plan." Dr. Ardell entered a few more notes into her tablet. "All right, Mr. Castillo. I will have them run more tests tomorrow to see if the transfusion helps. Meanwhile, you try to rest."

"Thank you, Doctor."

"You are very welcome." She turned to walk away.

Mateo stopped her. "Doctor? You can call me Mateo. Mr. Castillo is my father." He grinned. She returned the smile and left the room.

# Chapter Three

# Dr. Adrian Ardell

Dr. Adrian Ardell was born Adrianna Ardel–lyanu in 1986, in a landlocked country surrounded by strife and political tension. Her father, Petro Ardellyanu, had been held as a political prisoner from the time Adrian was eight until she turned twelve. During that time, her younger brother Victor was diagnosed with hemophilia, but the health service denied him treatment because of his father's incarceration. Victor died after a car accident left him bleeding to death on the side of the road. He was only six years old. Petro was grief stricken, blaming himself for his son's death. He thought about suicide, but that would have left his wife and daughter to fend for themselves in a nation where, if you spoke against anything or anyone, you became a pariah of the state. A nation that jailed a man for protesting the rationing of milk by oligarchs who hoarded it and then sold it back to citizens on the illegal market. A nation that would allow a child to die because of politics.

Petro's imprisonment got very little press coverage, except from an international group for ethical treatment who filed a petition on his behalf. The government wanted to avoid further interference and attention to their corrupt system, so they ultimately released him. To their way of thinking, he was a petty criminal. The agreement was no publicity, no press, no fanfare, and the family was to leave the country and never speak of the incident, whether about Petro's incarceration or losing a child to bureaucratic tyranny. Some thought it was a serious punishment and a disgrace. Others thought the contrary—it was a free ticket out of a suppressed nation.

With the assistance of the international group and their legal team, Petro changed the family's last name to Ardell and relocated, along with his wife and twelve-year-old daughter, to America. New York. Specifically Brighton Beach, Brooklyn, long an enclave of Eastern European settlers. Adrianna thought her first name was a painful reminder of her past, so she asked to be called Adrian. No one in the family objected, although her mother pointed out it was more of a boy's name. Adrian said she didn't care and rather liked being different. And so she was.

After several years of working in America, Petro and his wife applied for citizenship. He wanted his family to live the American dream. A world of opportunities and democracy.

Petro worked in a local butcher shop, and his wife cleaned rich people's homes. Their daughter was about to turn thirteen, and they were concerned about her future. Too many young girls were lured into prostitution or pornography at incredibly young ages. Making the most amount of money in the shortest amount of time was a way of life for many immigrants. But Petro was an upstanding member of his community. And the American dream meant sending your children to college.

Adrian had a rigorous schedule as a teenager. Her parents believed if they kept her busy enough, she would be able to avoid peer pressure. They instilled the necessity of a good education. Adrian was tutored by the son of one of her mother's wealthy clients. Each day, after school, she would take the forty-eight-minute ride on the Q train from Brighton Beach to the Park Slope brownstone where her mother worked the afternoon shift. Adrian would spend the time on the train reading and preparing for her tutor. Adrian knew Kyle had a bit of a crush on her, but she wasn't interested. Some of her friends encouraged her to "go for it," but she didn't want to marry someone who came from money. She wanted to earn it herself. On her own terms. Not only was Adrian book smart; she was also street-smart. She was astute. She saw the direction many young women were heading, and she wanted none of it. She wanted to become a doctor and find a cure for the horrible disease that took her brother's life.

By the time she finished high school, she was at the top of her class, winning awards for chemistry, physics, and biology. She earned a full scholarship to Cornell University. From there, she moved on to their medical college and finished her four-year residency in Manhattan. She was the first in her group to be offered a full-time job at NYU Langone Tisch Hospital. Her work was her life. When she wasn't on duty, she was working in the research labs.

Adrian was a stunning woman. She had big, saucer-sized brown eyes and golden hair, and a voluptuous figure with lips to match. And they were real. Every inch of her. Once you got past her natural beauty, it was the intensity in her eyes that drew you in. When she spoke, you listened. You listened carefully.

Today she was listening to a little voice inside her head. *He is quite a handsome man. Alluring.* Dr. Adrian Ardell hadn't been on a date since . . . since she couldn't remember when. She was engrossed in her research and her work at the hospital. There was no time for romance. It was almost sad. Getting married and having children was never on her radar, and now, going on thirty-seven, her days for having a baby were numbered. The few friends she had kept reminding her about the ticking biological clock. She would respond with, "Even if the alarm goes off, I am hitting the snooze button." That was usually met with laughter, but lately, not so much. She wondered if she was having a life crisis, though she wasn't quite at mid-life. Yet.

\* \* \*

Mateo was absorbing the possibility of a bone marrow biopsy. He couldn't wrap his head around it. *Why?* He was never sick as a kid. He'd had the usual things: measles, mumps, chicken pox, an occasional cold. There were never any red flags indicating he might have a life-threatening condition. Maybe he should discuss this with his parents. Maybe they could shed some light on it. But not right now. He would wait until the results of the chelation therapy and transfusion.

The following morning, Dr. Ardell came into his room wearing a slight smile. "Mr. Castillo—excuse me, Mateo—it appears the treatments are doing their jobs."

"Does that mean I can leave?" Mateo suspected the answer would be "no."

"Not today. Perhaps tomorrow. We will do another blood test before we release you."

"Okay." He sighed. "Any chance you can find me another grilled cheese sandwich? These unidentifiable meals are far from appetizing, and I need to build up my strength." He gave her a boyish grin.

Dr. Ardell's slight smile deepened. Her patient was flirting with her. Something she wasn't accustomed to—she tended to be rather intimidating—but found charming. "I'll see what I can do." She turned and walked away without saying another word.

Once again, that annoying voice boomed from behind the curtain in Mateo's room. "Oh . . . doctor's pet. How did you manage that?"

"Like you said, I'm an expert on food. Or something." Mateo smugly folded his arms across his chest and got his tubes tangled again. He didn't dare hit the call button for help. The bozo next to him would never let him hear the end of it, and the last thing Mateo wanted to hear more of was that guy's voice.

The day seemed endless. Mr. Big Man on Campus had a dozen visitors. They were either gushing cheerleaders named Muffy or Bitsy, or fellow athletes named Chip and Wells. The roommate's name was Coleman. That was his first name, and if Mateo heard the words "Cole, my man" one more time, he was going to rip the tubes out of his arms and strangle all of them. That's when it dawned on him that his anger was highly elevated. This wasn't like him; he was generally an easygoing person. He wondered if it had something to do with his blood. But that would mean there was something terribly wrong with him. Something he kept denying, hoping it was an anomaly and would simply go away after the transfusion. An hour later, he was distracted from his dark thoughts by a special delivery from the kitchen: another grilled cheese sandwich. The sight of the ooey-gooey mess brightened his mood, and he settled in.

The following morning, a nurse took another sample of Mateo's blood. He was feeling much more like himself and was anticipating being discharged. Now he had to figure out a way to find out if the meticulous doctor was available—as in not having a significant other. And if so, would she consider having dinner with him? The two big questions floated through his head as he ate what he thought would be his final hospital meal of lumpy yellow stuff and cardboard toast. Within the hour, Dr. Ardell arrived with a troubled look on her face. Mateo knew it wasn't good news when she addressed him as "Mr. Castillo." That was patient-speak, not possible date-speak.

He attempted a positive demeanor. "Good morning, Doctor."

"I'm afraid I have some disappointing news."

"Seriously?" He was taken aback. "But I'm feeling much better."

"That is quite possible, as your mercury levels declined, but not enough. You are still very much at risk."

Mateo was stunned. "Wha . . . what . . . do we do now?"

"We'll need to do a bone marrow biopsy." Her face was expressionless.

"Is it really that serious?" Mateo was incredulous.

"I'm afraid so. The sooner we can get this done, the sooner we'll know what other steps need to be taken." She checked her tablet. "We can prep you for the biopsy, but I strongly suggest you contact your family. If we discover you need a bone marrow transplant, they would be the first we would test for compatibility."

"Bone marrow transplant?" Mateo said blankly.

"We're not there yet, but it's something you should be prepared for." She moved closer to him. "I know this is shocking news, but you are young, fit, and otherwise in good health. You may get through this easier than most."

"Well that's reassuring. I think." Mateo was completely deflated.

"As I said, I'm a good detective. I will solve this mystery."

Mateo winced. "Thank you. I appreciate it."

"Now, I think you should call your family before we do the biopsy. You'll be a little loopy during and after. We'll give you a local anesthetic and a sedative."

Mateo looked at his cell phone, which had been charging on the table next to him. "What do I tell my family?"

"Tell them we are doing a bone marrow biopsy to see why you are experiencing this condition and that you want to make them aware that you may need a marrow transplant. As I mentioned, the family is who we assess first." She looked him straight in the eye. "I am quite serious. Your life may be on the line."

He did a double take and let out a snort. "A little double entendre."

"Excuse me?" Dr. Ardell looked puzzled.

"On the line? You know that's what they call the area in the kitchen where the magic happens?" Mateo was almost teasing her.

"I am not familiar with the workings of a restaurant kitchen," she replied stiffly.

"The kitchen line is the heartbeat of the restaurant. At least that's what I believe, since that's where the incredible food starts."

"So the dining room would be the brain?" Dr. Ardell was teasing back now.

"I suppose you could say that. And the waitstaff are the arms and legs," Mateo added with a smirk.

But Dr. Ardell could hear the passion in his voice. "Each chef manages individual stations to prepare the various parts of each dish—grilling, frying, saucing. The sous chef is kinda like the captain of the line."

"And you are the general?" Ardell said with a straight face.

"I hadn't thought about it, but yes, I suppose I am." He hesitated a moment. "I would be happy to give you a tour once I get unplugged and sprung from here." There. That was the opening he had been hoping for.

"Sounds interesting. But let's get you healthy first. I do not want to perform CPR in a restaurant kitchen. Heartbeat or no heartbeat." Dr. Ardell was feeling a little cheeky, as well. She wasn't used to this type of banter, but it made her feel good. She picked up his cell phone and stretched out her arm in Mateo's direction. She wasn't going to leave his room until he spoke to someone in his family.

"Got it." Mateo reached for his cell and pressed the button to his mother's phone number. It rang twice before he said, "Mamita?"

As Mateo explained the situation to his mother, he could hear the panic in her voice. Instinct told him it wasn't only about his health. He could sense it. It was something else. Something dark. Something very few knew about, including himself.

# PART II
# THE HISTORY

# Chapter Four

# How It Began

*1988*
*Cali, Colombia*

From the mid-1970s until early 1993, Pablo Escobar built the world's biggest drug empire, known as the Medellín Drug Cartel, taking in over 450 million dollars a week—over twenty-two billion dollars a year. His enterprise was responsible for eighty percent of the cocaine smuggled into the United States. And he was ruthless. He had to be in order to have reached that level of control and maintain it.

Escobar began his career as a petty criminal known for stealing gravestones. He would remove the names and sell them. He moved on to robbing cars and fake lottery tickets, but in 1975, when

Fabio Restrepo was murdered—some say at the command of Escobar himself—Pablo found a great opportunity for wealth and power. Drugs. Specifically cocaine, or "nose candy," as it was known on the streets. His connections in Bolivia would supply the coca paste, and his people in Peru would refine it.

For almost two decades, Escobar made billions, ruled over a personal empire of mansions, and planned the murders of hundreds of politicians and journalists, with his own army of criminals carrying out his orders. At one point, he was the seventh richest man in the world.

In 1984, he ordered the assassination of the Minister of Justice, followed by a Superior Court Judge in 1985, the attorney general in 1988, the governor of Antioquia in 1989, and Luis Carlos Galan, a presidential candidate, also in 1989. Although Escobar's targets were obvious threats to his kingpin status, many other people died as a result of collateral damage. Some say Escobar was responsible for the death of over 4,000 people. But whenever he or a member of his organization were arrested, they would either bribe the official or kill them. Escobar was fearless with the exception of extradition to the United States, which he did everything in his power to avoid at all costs. All. Costs.

By the end of the decade, Escobar and his cohorts rained terror down on the citizens of Colombia. And now another cartel was gaining power and was very close to home. The Cali Cartel, operated by the Orejuela brothers and José Londaño.

The country was rife with drug dealers, filling the cocaine pipeline to the United States.

Elena Espinosa finished her classes that afternoon and walked the ten blocks home. She was learning to teach English as a second language. At twenty-two years old, she hoped she could get a job outside of the family bakery.

Elena's maternal grandfather and grandmother, whom she called Papito and Abuela, started the Lozano Bakery many years before Elena was born, and it remained as a family business carried on by her mother and father, Gabriel and Sylvia Espinosa. Lozano's Bakery had remained the same over several decades. And so did many other family traditions. Elena's mother would do the baking, and her father made the deliveries across the growing town.

Elena enjoyed baking, but she was positive she did not want the lifestyle of getting up at three a.m. to start the bread or being on her feet in a hot kitchen for ten hours at a stretch. She was twenty-two years old, studying English, and working at the bakery after her classes. There had to be more to life.

Elena and her parents lived in one of the small apartments above the bakery. As a little girl, she would listen to her parents rustling around before dawn, and then two hours later, the aroma of fresh-baked bread would engulf her. It was a wonderful, warm feeling. Back then. But now, she was restless and didn't want to face the same grind, day after day, catering to the international nouveau riche. And then there were the criminals. There was a hierarchy of drug dealers, whether they were producing it or smuggling it or laundering it. The city was thriving and so was crime. In some way, everyone was connected to the cartels, whether it was directly, indirectly, or simply from fear.

The residents of Cali kept their heads down and proceeded with their lives, pretending there wasn't a narco-terrorist looming in the shadows. It meant living in a constant state of denial. And fear. And angst. They saw and knew what kind of destruction Escobar could impart. No one would or could save you. Escobar's army killed anyone who stood in his way. "Be invisible" was the best advice given to the populace.

Elena's father feared for their lives, but he couldn't show it. No one was allowed to show fear—or resistance. Just complacency. He thought of moving, but where? They had a successful business. Where could they go? Perhaps another town farther away? He and Elena's mother would discuss it in whispers late at night, but Elena could feel how unsettled people were becoming. She would lie in bed, straining to decipher their hushed words.

She understood her father's concern was for her safety, and why her father didn't want her going out after dark. He was strict with her as a child, but he was usually fair. He tried to safeguard her, whether it was from some greasy drug runner or a scoundrel looking to have some noncommittal fun. They weren't rich by any means, but the bakery was solvent, making Elena a good catch for a resourceful young man. No, Gabriel had to protect his family. He knew the streets weren't safe, but Elena protested. She wanted to have a social life.

Up until the past year, Elena was a bright, cheerful soul. She would sing and dance to the music of Aniceto Molina, rocking back and forth as she set the table or folded laundry. But lately she had grown sullen. Elena's mother, Sylvia, observed her daughter's somber expression as she entered their apartment.

Concerned that Elena may have overheard their latest late-night conversation, Sylvia had to ask, "What is it, *mija*?"

Elena shrugged her off and turned away. "Nothing, Mami."

"Do not lie to your mother. You have been very quiet lately. Mopey, in fact." Sylvia folded her arms.

Elena sighed. "I want to do something."

"What?" Sylvia asked in a calm voice.

Elena spun around to face her mother. "Something! Anything!" Her frustration was on the rise.

"I can only help you if I know what you need."

Elena plopped down on her bed. "I saw a flyer on a pole when I was walking home from school. It was for salsa dance lessons."

Salsa. It had become all the rage. But salsa in Cali was different from other salsa dances. Brought to Colombia in the 1960s via the US Navy, it was a mix of New York City and Havana. The rhythms of Cuba crossed the Caribbean, and local musicians blended several cultural influences, creating their own up-tempo subgenre. By the mid 1970s, Cali was considered the salsa capital of the world, with its own distinct style called "Cali Pachanguero."

Elena's mother squinted in confusion as she took the flyer from Elena's clenched fist. "But you already know how to dance." She was relieved it wasn't something more serious that was bothering her daughter.

"But Mami, I have no social life. Ever since Lorenzo and I broke up, I've only been going to school and working here. I'm twenty-two years old! I need to meet people, and I do not want to go to a club by myself."

"I understand, *cariña*. You dated Lorenzo for several years, and yes, he was your whole social life. But what about school? You have friends there, no?"

Elena propped herself up on her elbows. "Yes, but it's different. There aren't very many people I would want to spend time with."

Her mother smiled. "I raised you to be very particular."

"Which is why Lorenzo and I broke up. He had no direction. He thought he would marry me and inherit the bakery."

"Your father would never have let that happen." Sylvia patted her daughter's hand. "We hoped you would grow out of that puppy love."

Elena sat up taller. "Yes, and now I do not want to grow old alone."

Sylvia took a seat next to her daughter. "You are beautiful and smart. You will not grow old alone. Many men will want the pleasure of your company." She paused. "And you are right. You've been working very hard the past three years. Maybe dance lessons could raise your spirits and open a new world for you."

Elena turned to her mother. The gleam was back in her eyes. "It would only be two nights a week, and you and Papá can count on me to still work in the bakery."

"I think we can manage." Sylvia was delighted her daughter had an interest in dancing and promised they would discuss it when her father got back later that evening.

Even though Elena was twenty-two years old, out of respect for her father, a family discussion was expected. In her heart, Elena knew her mother would make sure it happened. Later, Sylvia made her point to her husband. "Better she learn it from an established teacher than some thug on the streets." Even if Gabriel tried to argue, he wasn't going to win. One man up against two women was never a winning formula.

The next day, Elena slipped the flyer into her jacket pocket. She was going to sign up for the lessons as soon as she finished her class. She promised she would continue to help out at the bakery—up until her life would change forever. She just didn't know it would be so soon.

Elena was pleasantly surprised to discover the dance instructor was an attractive young man, close to her age. He wasn't ruggedly handsome. Instead, he had fine features and a warm smile that softened his dark-as-coal eyes. Deep eyes. Eyes that seemed to be able to see directly into one's soul. Elena almost blushed when she shook his hand.

"Dante Castillo," he introduced himself.

Elena stifled a giggle. She had been expecting a middle-aged woman wearing entirely too much rouge and blue eye shadow, with big-puffy-teased-bleached-blond hair, pants that looked like they were spray-painted on, spiked high-heeled sandals, and enough jewelry to sink a small boat. Or an older man with a bad toupee or badly dyed black hair, wearing tight pants, a gallon of cologne, and an overabundance of gold chains that could also sink a small boat. She chuckled to herself. It was true: in Colombia, your age didn't matter. You danced. You danced in the kitchen. You danced in the living room. You danced on the street corners. She was also pleasantly surprised to find that Dante the instructor wasn't full of himself like many young Colombian men.

In the beginning, Elena was a little intimidated. She was the newest in the class, but she had a natural rhythm that took her hips to great salsa heights. Dante was very impressed after her first lesson. "You are a natural." He nodded to her as she changed back into her street shoes.

Elena looked up. "Thank you. It was a lot of fun. I like to practice to Aniceto Molina." As she bent over to tie her laces, she felt his eyes still upon her. She had a dual reaction: it was both creepy and exciting.

"I apologize." It was as if Dante were reading her mind. "I didn't mean to stare. I like your shoes." He snickered and pointed down.

"My sneakers?" Elena said, looking at her Nike Air Trainers. "They're not very fashionable." She chuckled.

"Not if you are going to the opera," Dante

quipped back. "They are the latest sneaker style, are they not?" He paused. "I am, after all, a dance instructor. Feet are part of my business." Then he snickered again. "But not in a creepy way. I promise."

Elena giggled. He *was* reading her mind. But she felt comfortable around this new acquaintance. "I help out at my parents' bakery. They're good for my feet."

Dante held out his hand to help her up. Not that she needed it, but in 1988, some of the pleasantries of courtesy had not yet died out.

Elena gripped his hand as she stood. "Thank you for a wonderful class. I will be back the day after next."

"I am glad you enjoyed it. I look forward to seeing you. By the way, I too am a fan of Aniceto Molina." He smiled. Have a good evening."

"Adiós!" Elena gave him a short wave and left.

Dante watched her as she disappeared onto the busy sidewalk filled with people heading home from work.

Elena was elated. Wearing a Cheshire Cat grin, she glided through the throng as if she were the only person on the street, her long, sleek black hair flowing to her tempo. No wonder people were gawking at her. She was probably the happiest person on the block. It was true what they said about endorphins. They gave you a feeling of euphoria, although how that and jogging could be combined, Elena could never understand. But dancing was another subject altogether.

As Elena entered the shop, her mother was bringing out a fresh tray of pan de queso, a cheese bread. The aroma was intoxicating. It was Elena's favorite. She grabbed her apron and gave her mother a kiss on the cheek after wiping away a few flakes of flour. "Mami! I had the most wonderful time. The teacher is very, very good. And handsome."

Gabriel overheard the conversation and came out of the kitchen "Handsome?" He was half-teasing. "I thought you were going for the lessons. What is his name? Does he have another job besides teaching dancing lessons? How old is he?"

Elena wrapped her arms around her father's waist and rested her head on his chest. "Oh, Papá. You ask so many questions. His name is Dante Castillo. I heard him mention he had a class tomorrow."

"Class? What kind of class? Not more dancing, I hope." Gabriel was well aware that his daughter was more than old enough to have a boyfriend, but she was also cautious, probably because of her upbringing. And then there was the growing concern about criminals. It was hard to tell who was on whose side.

Sylvia snapped a towel at her husband's behind. "Leave the girl alone. She is happy today."

Gabriel kissed his daughter on the cheek. "I am glad you are happy. And yes, I worry."

"We raised a very good daughter with a good head on her shoulders. I don't think she will be running away from home with a dance teacher."

"And if I do, I will take both of you with me!" Elena chirped back.

Several people stopped in the bakery on their way home from work to pick up fresh bread. Lozano's pan de queso was known throughout the area. The recipe had been handed down for generations, with a few simple additions to set it apart from other cheese breads. And the recipe had never been written down. It was passed on only by word of mouth. "So no one can steal it," Elena's abuela once explained. At one point, Sylvia had thought of writing it down, but she knew her mother would know. Somehow. The woman had a sixth sense about her. The recipe wasn't very complicated; some simple additional amounts of a few items was what made it different. It was easy enough to remember.

As soon as the last loaf was gone, they began the ritual of cleaning the kitchen, sweeping and mopping the floors, and shutting the iron gates. Sylvia had a stew simmering on the stove all afternoon. The aroma was competing with the smell of baked cheese bread. Beef stew for dinner along with the one loaf of pan de queso Gabriel saved behind the counter. "I think we should charge more for this." He pulled out his secreted loaf. "We run out every day."

"And I cannot make any more than I am. We don't have the space, and I have other breads to make," Sylvia reminded him. This was an ongoing issue.

"I know, I know. What if we find a bigger place?" Gabriel broke off the end of the bread and popped it in his mouth. "And what about that machine I bought?"

Sylvia slapped his hand. "That is for all of us, Señor Espinosa." She tugged the remaining bread from his fingers. "And that machine? Abuela would be horrified if she knew I was making her special bread with a machine. It's all about kneading the dough. By hand." She pulled off another piece and continued. "We would have to hire more people."

Elena got a chill. She hoped that her parents were not expecting her to step into the business, even though it was tradition. Elena's goal was to become a translator for one of the big international companies, and her parents encouraged her by helping pay for her schooling. She reminded herself it was almost the '90s. These were more modern times. The city was growing. Industry was expanding. Tourism and commerce were flourishing. And many spoke English. She had her own plan. It wasn't an option. She started to feel pangs of guilt. Could she really put her career aspirations ahead of her family's legacy?

"Elena?" Her mother pulled her from her musing. "Your father wants to expand the business."

"Yes. I heard him. What about Claudia?"

"What *about* Claudia?" her mother asked quizzically, referring to her brother's daughter. Out of her three siblings, Sylvia was the only one who showed an interest and an art for baking bread, but her niece would always help out around holidays and worked part-time at the bakery before she got married.

Elena proposed that Claudia expand her hours at the shop. Her kids were now in school, so Claudia had more time to devote to the family business. Elena would campaign for Claudia until she was absolutely certain a change of *her* plans was not an option.

"That's a wonderful idea," Sylvia said. "Your father can't expect either one of us to work more hours. There are none!" Sylvia chuckled. "Gabriel, I think expanding the business could be a good idea. I stress the word *could,* but it will take careful planning. We were lucky to take over this place. It was established over many years."

"Exactly. We just double everything!" Gabriel snickered. "I know, *mi amor.* It is a big undertaking, but we can continue to think about it. Now what do you say we go upstairs and have some of that delectable-smelling stew?"

"And what's left of the pan de queso!" Elena laughed, removed her apron, and hung it on the peg with the initial *E* stenciled above it. She wondered how long that peg would remain hers.

Gabriel went to the bathroom to wash up from the "day of dirt." It was his expression for when he had to drive out to the farms where the roads were just dust and gravel. Some were surrounded by barbwire and guards. He suspected those areas were part of the cartel, so he kept his head down when he delivered the baked goods to the menacing man at the gates. No one was allowed on the premises, and you couldn't see the buildings from the gates, as they were at least a mile from the main road. Gabriel would only admit to himself that he was scared witless every time he had to go to one of these three farms that were steady customers.

In the beginning, he thought of saying no to the orders they placed, but you did not say no to any of *those* people. Besides, they bought a lot of bread every week. Enough to feed a small army. *But whose army?* Another chill went up his spine. Then he thought about his trip the week before and the duffel bag one of the guards had tossed into the back of Gabriel's van. The guard gave him simple instructions: "Leave the van unlocked when you return." More chills. He hoped it was a one-time thing, since it hadn't reoccurred. He splashed cold water on his face. Maybe it was time to think about relocating. Not expanding.

He looked up from the sink and into the mirror. "You have to take care of your family," he whispered to himself. What that entailed had yet to be revealed to him. He just knew something had to change.

During dinner, they had casual conversations about dance classes, English classes, and a new recipe Sylvia wanted to try. Gabriel pressed the thoughts of the farms out of his head. It was a relaxing, enjoyable dinner. Each of them treasured the time together.

For the next several months, life was consistent and held a lot of optimism for the world. The weather brought no surprises; Nelson Mandela was released from prison after twenty-seven years; East and West Germany reunited; President Bush and Gorbachev signed a treaty to end the development of chemical weaponry. Overall, things in the world seemed to be settled. For the most part. But the Colombian government was hot on the heels of Pablo Escobar. The United States wanted him back.

Elena was wrapping up her final semester of university and continued to dance. She could have become a professional, but that was not the life she wanted. It was a wonderful hobby. A way to let off steam. She and Dante would salsa long after the classes were over, and they had developed a fondness for each other. A crush, to be more exact. Both on each other. Even though it was 1988, Elena was still a bit old-fashioned. She wanted something real. Something permanent. Dante hadn't even kissed her yet. He never even tried, but the thought ran through her head. More than once.

One night, when he was walking her home, she casually looped her arm through his. It felt natural. She wondered if he would ever kiss her. Elena became a little jittery. Trembling. Dante instinctively wrapped his jacket around her, and she came very close to nuzzling him. Close. Very. And that made her more nervous.

Dante's thoughts were not very far from Elena's. He thought about kissing her on more than one occasion, but she never gave him "the green light," so to speak. She could have leaned in at some point, no? Maybe after the dance party the local radio station was sponsoring. There was some competitive dancing involved, and Dante asked if she would be his partner. Elena was more than flattered. Yes, after the party, he would try to read any signals she might be sending.

Gabriel and Sylvia approved of the budding friendship. Dante was a gentleman, responsible and enterprising. Secretly they hoped Elena and Dante would become romantically involved. Not sexually, but romantically. They wanted grandchildren but wouldn't push the issue with Elena.

She was smart and could often be headstrong. If they pushed more, she would push back. They wanted her to find her own way. But quickly.

The night of the dance event was glorious. Elena could not remember the last time she felt so free. She and her mother designed a dazzling outfit with purple sequins, creating a light-show of sparkle as she shimmied across the floor. Her long black hair was pulled back in a tight ponytail that whipped around her head along with the feverish moves of the dance. The applause and cheers from the crowd brought Elena a new level of confidence. Dante was very proud of his student, and it was at that moment he knew he was falling in love with her.

Not to anyone's surprise, Dante and Elena won the competition. Some jeered, saying it was rigged because Dante was a dance teacher, but the judges decided if anyone knew how to dance, it was Dante, and the contest rules did not specify whether professionals were ineligible. Almost everyone in town knew how to salsa. It was nearly a requirement, so if there was someone better than Dante, let *him* get on the dance floor. And Elena held her own, keeping up with every step, swing, and dip.

Elena was happy in many ways. Over the past eight months, she developed a deep friendship with Dante; she was a natural talent on the dance floor; she was finishing up her studies and about to start a new job. A real job. One that didn't leave her covered in flour by the end of the day.

As the evening was winding down, both Elena and Dante were dripping in sweat, laughing as Elena's hand slipped from Dante's grip. But his quick moves prevented Elena from a faceplant onto the dance floor. He spun her around and made it look like it was planned, both chuckling as he dipped her dangerously close to the ground. The crowd went wild, and they took a final bow. The two retreated to a table and chairs where the other dancers were sitting. Some were jubilant, slapping Dante on the back, while a few others glared. There was an undeniable chemistry between Dante and Elena. It was the envy of many who watched.

Elena handed Dante one of the towels she had packed in her tote. "I am such a mess!" she exclaimed as she wiped her forehead and rubbed the towel at her hairline. She graciously nodded to those who congratulated them.

"You look beautiful." Dante reached for her hand and kissed the back of it. Then he took her towel and finished wiping the perspiration from her upper lip. Elena was glad she was sitting down, or she would surely be on the floor. She grabbed her tote. "I am going to change into something less soggy." After months of dancing, Elena knew she would need a fresh, dry outfit. She had packed a simple floral sheath dress that was easy to slip on once she wiped herself down. If she kept up this pace, she could eat a half dozen of the pan de queso without worrying about gaining weight.

But soon she would have less time for dancing, when she started her job with the foreign exchange service at the bank. She was relieved Dante had one more year of school before he completed his course in project management. He already had a job lined up with one of the major oil companies, but that also meant the company could relocate him anywhere. Neither brought up the subject. After all, they were not a couple. Not for at least another hour until he walked her home.

They said their good nights to the judges and their fellow competitors and draped their ribbons over their shoulders. As they passed a café, Dante suggested they stop for some coffee. He wanted to stretch out the evening a little longer. Elena turned to him. "Honestly? I'd rather have aguardiente," Elena said, referring to local favorite alcoholic beverage.

Dante laughed. "I don't recall you having a drink before."

"It's a special night." Elena tugged him into the café. Dante was glad she suggested the distilled beverage. It was the shot of courage he needed.

"It *is* a special night." Dante locked eyes with hers. "Elena, I have to tell you something."

Elena's mind went to something horrible. "What? What is it? Is everything alright?" There was panic in her voice.

Dante smiled. "*Princesa.* Everything is fine. Wonderful, in fact." He paused. *Get it over with,* he told himself. *What's the worst that can happen?* Thankfully, *his* mind didn't go to something horrible. "Elena, these past several months have been a joy for me. You are witty, talented, smart, and pretty."

Elena was trying not to blush. She couldn't remember the last time a man spoke to her with such tenderness. Dante continued. "And I think I am falling in love with you." There. Done. Out.

Tears welled up in Elena's eyes. She took Dante's hand. "I think I'm starting to do the same." She chuckled. "I mean you, not me." She was totally flustered. She was also over the moon. The dance lessons had truly been divine intervention. She knew it was meant to be.

They sat for another hour and sipped their cocktails, talking about the evening and if they should continue to sign up for dance contests. Elena had some reservations because of her responsibilities, and Dante also had much on his plate. Finally, they decided they would take each opportunity as it came along. If they were available, then why not? They seemed to be in sync with each other. Both had goals of finishing school, both had a love of music and dance, both had mutual respect for each other, and both possessed deep values. For the first time, Elena believed her parents would not have any objection to her dating this fine man. After Lorenzo, there had been a few dates with some of the local young men, but none measured up to what Elena expected in a partner. Until now. Yes, it was a night to celebrate.

They casually strolled down the streets, zigzagging through the crowds gathered on the sidewalks as music blared from boom boxes. It was a cacophony of Latin music. Even though there were several different songs emanating from the street corners, there was no dissonance. Just a joyful sound of people letting loose and enjoying each other's company.

When they reached the rear door of the bakery, Dante felt confident that it was finally time to kiss Elena good night. He took her face into his hands and tenderly brushed his lips against hers. She eagerly reciprocated, feeling the blood rush to her cheeks. She gently pulled away, the heat rising to her head. "Dante, this has been one of the most incredible nights of my life." She placed both of her hands on his chest. "But it's time for me to go inside." If not, she feared she would rip the clothes off both of them and ride him on the nearby picnic table. True, she was a young woman at twenty-two, but family traditions were still in place in the Espinosa family. As long as you lived under your parents' roof, you were expected to behave a certain way.

Dante's ardor was becoming obvious. "I think it's best we put some air between us before my father comes out with a gun!" Elena joked.

"That would be a most embarrassing situation." Dante snickered. He kissed her on the nose. "Adiós, *princesa.*"

"Adios!" Elena turned and went inside. He watched until she flicked the light two times. It was their signal she was okay.

Both of Elena's parents were sitting in the small living room. Each was reading a book. "Elena! How did it go?" Sylvia sprang to her feet, while Gabriel looked up from his tome.

"Mami! Papá! Dante and I won the contest!" Elena twirled her ribbons around.

"I should hope so, given how much you've practiced," her father said teasingly. "Where is your friend?"

"He went home." Elena was self-conscious, hoping her glow wasn't too obvious.

"You should have invited him in for a coffee," Sylvia said.

"We stopped for a drink on the way home. Besides, it's late. He has to study for exams." She secretly thought what he really needed was a cold shower, but the smirk on her face belied her words.

"Are you blushing?" Gabriel asked. "I think you may have a crush on that young man," he teased.

"Don't embarrass her!" Sylvia jumped in. "He's a *fine* young man."

"Yes he is, and I expect you to invite him to dinner," Gabriel announced matter-of-factly.

"I will, Papá." Elena turned to her mother. "You tell me when."

"How about this Sunday?" Sylvia offered.

"Wonderful!" Elena responded while looking at the clock. It was well after midnight. "I will call him tomorrow."

The next morning, Elena phoned Dante and offered the invitation, which he gladly accepted. On the big day, Dante wore a pair of gray slacks and white shirt with a black and gray houndstooth blazer. He arrived bearing two luscious bromeliad plants, one a deep fuchsia, the other a fiery red. There were also several Cuban cigars for Elena's father. The relationship between Cuba and Colombia was like a couple that kept breaking up and getting back together again. At the moment, they were in the process of making up, so getting Cuban cigars wasn't as difficult as it had been the preceding decade. But they were still a little pricey. Dante hoped he hadn't gone overboard. But then he shrugged to himself. *How can generosity be bad?* Plus, this was going to be the beginning of a long-term relationship. With Elena *and* her parents. He hoped.

Dante rang the bell for the apartment. He was buzzed in and trotted up the flight of stairs leading to the second floor. Lots of *hello*s echoed through the hallway, plus handshakes and the usual kisses on both cheeks. That, too, was a tradition. Even though they had met on many occasions in the past, Dante had always been "Elena's friend" and not a prospective boyfriend. Now there was a sense of jubilation in the air. It was a special occasion. Dante was a dinner guest of the family of the woman he wanted to marry. He just hadn't told anyone yet. Gabriel explained that they spoke English in their household as much as possible. The world was becoming much more international, and knowing the English language was a benefit.

Gabriel ushered Dante into the sitting room. Sylvia and Elena had spent the morning preparing the dishes they were going to serve. They would start out with a platter of picada, Colombian appetizers. Dante's eyes lit up when he spied the sumptuous and colorful display of the round, salted, yellow plantains; the strips of yucca fries paired with a smoky chorizo; beef empanadas; and pandebono, another type of cheese bread. "It looks and smells delicious!"

"Elena did most of the work." Sylvia was telling a half-truth. It was pretty much even. "Please sit." Sylvia motioned to a large, overstuffed chair, while Gabriel sniffed one of his cigars.

"Very nice." Gabriel nodded to Dante. "What would you like to drink?"

Dante wasn't sure if asking for a glass of wine

would be appropriate. Instead, he answered, "Whatever you are having, thank you."

Gabriel went to the side table, where a small display of carafes sat on a silver tray. He began to pour a cabernet sauvignon. "This is from Villa de Leyva. Everyone thinks La Union produces the best wine, but I disagree. They have good grapes, but they haven't perfected the fermentation, so I prefer this instead." He poured four glasses and served one to each of them. "I hope you like it."

Elena was all atwitter. This was a side of her father she rarely saw. He was gentle when necessary, but the opportunity didn't present itself very often. He would go to work early in the morning and return just before they closed the shop. For Sylvia, Sundays were for church, and then back home for dinner. Gabriel would work on the machinery in the bakery kitchen or fix pipes, painting, and all the things requiring maintenance. Elena's parents didn't have much of a social life, either, and she was happy to see her father enjoying playing the host.

Gabriel raised his glass. "*Salud!*" Elena, Sylvia, and Dante echoed his toast, each looking the other in the eye, as tradition demanded.

After a few sips, Sylvia and Elena excused themselves to check on dinner. Neither was sure who was giddier. Sylvia wrapped her arm around her daughter. "I said this to your father and I shall say it to you: Dante is a fine man. He would make a good husband."

Elena gently poked her in the ribs with her elbow. "Oh, Mami!" Then she lowered her voice.

"Let's give this some time, okay?" Deep in her soul, Elena knew Dante was the right man, the right person for her. They partnered well on the dance floor, and more importantly, they partnered well as friends.

"Of course, *mi amor.* I guess what I am trying to say is that we approve of Dante." Sylvia caught herself before Elena could react. "What I mean is, you don't need your father's and my approval, but it can make life a lot easier!" Sylvia chuckled.

Elena leaned in and continued to whisper. "I like him very much." She hoped the soft music of Pepe Romero's classical guitar playing on the stereo would muffle anything she might say.

Sylvia responded in the same hushed tone. "And I think he likes you, too." She slipped an apron around her waist and handed one to Elena. Then she made her way to the stove and checked the sobrebarriga sudada, a slow-cooked flank steak served with rice, potatoes, and arepas, the South American version of a tortilla. When the steak was tender enough to pull apart, it was ready for the finishing touches of chopped coriander and sliced avocados.

Gabriel poked his head in the kitchen. He was wearing a huge grin. "What is taking so long, *queridas?* We have a guest who is about to faint from hunger!"

Sylvia immediately began to protest. "But there is a huge platter of picada patacones! Don't tell me you ate all of it?" Sylvia prided herself on her hostess skills. She would often help with the church luncheons and cater various private parties.

Gabriel's smile widened. "I am teasing you, *mi amor.*" He patted her on the bum. "It smells delicious." He picked up a serving spoon and dipped it into the saucy mixture covering the beef.

Sylvia slapped his hand away. "Not before the guest!" The mood was bright and cheerful.

"Speaking of our guest, you left him alone in the living room?" Elena shook her head and wagged a finger at her father.

"You are correct. I am being a terrible host." He turned on his heel and scurried back to the room, where Dante was standing in front of a bookcase, checking out the framed photographs. "My apologies, Dante. I was seduced by the food in the kitchen, which my wife would not let me touch. And then my daughter admonished me for being a bad host, so they threw me out of the kitchen."

Dante turned and smiled. "You and your family are wonderful hosts." He gestured to a picture of a young girl with long black hair sitting on a burro. "Elena?"

"No. That's her mother," Gabriel said with pride. "Though there's a striking resemblance. I am a lucky man to have two beautiful women in my life."

Dante nodded. "I agree. You are a lucky man." He took a taste from his wineglass. "Someday I hope to be as lucky as you." His eyes glistened.

Gabriel could not have been happier at those words. "Perhaps you shall." He patted Dante on the shoulder. "Come. Let's sit. I was promised dinner would be served shortly."

As was traditional, Gabriel gestured for Dante to sit immediately to his right. Elena would sit across from Dante, and Sylvia would be seated across from Gabriel.

Several minutes later, the two women exited the kitchen with trays of steaming platters, the hints of garlic and onion filling the air along with the warm aroma of comfort food. Dante closed his eyes and inhaled the savory combination of meat, potatoes, and bread. He was in heaven. "Señora Espinosa, I cannot tell you what an honor it is to be invited into your home and for you to share a meal with me."

Gabriel raised his refilled glass, and the others joined him. "It is a pleasure to have a good friend of Elena's at our dinner table. *Salud!*"

Everyone responded in kind.

"This smells delicious. I cannot remember the last time I had a home-cooked meal." Dante's eyes glided from one luscious dish to another.

Sylvia handed the platter of meat to her husband, who turned to Dante. "Please."

"Most gladly." Dante pitched a fork into the moist, tender beef.

Gabriel then held it in front of Sylvia, who portioned out the beef on her plate. She then held it for her daughter. The large platters of food were passed around the table until everyone's dish was brimming.

"*Buen provecho!*" Gabriel exclaimed, announcing it was time for everyone to eat.

Sylvia passed the arepas around the table. Dante could barely keep from licking his fingers. "Señora Espinosa, I am a very lucky man tonight."

Elena chuckled nervously. She had been rather quiet since Dante arrived. She was giving him and her parents space to get to know each other without trying to force the conversation. "We are all very lucky." Elena raised her glass. *"Gracias por la cena!"* A toast of gratitude for the dinner. The others joined her.

The conversation over dinner was mostly light, but at one point the topic turned to the growing concern over the drug cartels. It was inevitable. It haunted everyone.

Dante rose to help clear the dinner dishes. Dessert would be served a half hour later, with a glass of Mistela de Café, an after-dinner drink usually made by hand. It was not complicated to make but took two weeks to ferment. Gabriel was glad he had stored an extra bottle in the refrigerator earlier in the month; otherwise, there would be none for this particular occasion. Gabriel ushered Dante back into the sitting room, where the guitar music continued to play.

"This is beautiful music," Dante noted.

"It's Pepe Romero. An international hero of classical guitar." Gabriel took another pull from his wineglass. "Do you know the story about his family?"

"A little. But please—tell me more." Dante was surprised by Gabriel's knowledge of wine and music. He was embarrassed to have thought this man would not be cultured. After all, Elena was his offspring, and clearly she was cultured and sophisticated but in an innocent way. He felt terrible that he had prejudged Gabriel based on his trade as a bakery owner. He would remember to never do it again.

Gabriel continued. "Pepe's father, Celedonio,

was a poor Spanish guitar teacher. He fled the oppression of Francisco Franco in the nineteen-fifties and went to America. He, with his sons Pepe, Angel, and Celin, formed the first classical guitar quartet. They were virtuosos and eventually performed with the greatest orchestras in the world. They became a phenomenon. They made classical music popular. Had he not had the courage to leave his homeland, we may never have had the joy of his and his family's music." Gabriel paused and looked squarely at Dante. "Do you think you would ever leave Colombia?"

Dante was stunned by the question. It came right out of left field. He cleared his throat. "I have not thought of it, to be honest. But I suppose there is a possibility with the company I will be working for."

"Yes, tell me more about that." Gabriel wanted to squeeze as much information as he could from his daughter's suitor without making it sound like an interrogation.

Dante explained he was finishing up his studies to be a project manager for one of the major oil companies. They were paying for his education and giving him a small stipend, with the understanding he would work for them upon completion. "I naturally assumed I would be stationed here." Dante paused and then went into deep thought. *What if he had to move far away? Away from Elena?* "But, sir, you pose a serious question."

Elena overheard the last few words as she carried a tray of coffee cups into the room. "What's a serious question?"

The men looked up at her. Gabriel spoke first.

"Dante is telling me that he would have to move if the oil company sends him elsewhere."

Elena stiffened. The thought had occurred to her a few times, but the words had never been spoken aloud. She hurried to place the tray down on the sideboard before she dropped it.

Dante could sense her apprehension. "But I still have one more year before I am certified, so I will be here for at least that long." He said it gleefully enough to ease any tension it could have caused.

Elena loosened her grip from the tray. She told herself, *A year is a long time. Anything can happen.*

Sylvia entered with an array of pastries she had made that morning. The bakery was known for its bread, so pastries were reserved for holidays and special occasions. And she believed *this* occasion was special. She placed the assortment of milhojas con arequipe, also known as dulce de leche, torticas, sweet mini cakes, and torta negra—"black cake" with its aromatic bouquet of dark rum, port, figs, prunes, cinnamon, and cloves. Once again, Dante went into sensory overload. He was grinning from ear to ear.

Finally, Sylvia and Elena could relax with the two men and enjoy dessert and libations. Sylvia sat back in her chair and observed the handsome young man who was courting her daughter. She liked him. He was generous, polite, and intelligent. He also had goals, one of which was clearly to impress her and Gabriel. *Bravo. He was doing well.* She continued to listen intently and realized he hadn't spoken of his own family. Not even a reference. "Dante? Where is your family from?"

He glanced down. "I have no family." Then he

cleared his throat. "I was raised in an orphanage run by the Sisters of St. Margarite."

Sylvia put her hand up to her mouth, stifling a gasp. "I am so sorry. I didn't mean to pry."

Dante smiled. "It's fine. Really. I had a good education, three meals a day, always had a clean set of clothes. Obviously I went to church, and I helped the sisters with the garden, played baseball. It wasn't so bad." He looked at Elena, then Sylvia, and then Gabriel. "Honestly, I feel blessed. Truly. I was surrounded by nurturing women, and I did not want for anything. Because they were very strict about studies, I was able to go to college, and now I am in a management program to work for a large oil corporation. Most children don't get those opportunities, even if they have parents." He chuckled softly, which lightened the mood.

Sylvia wanted to ask more questions. She knew there were many orphaned children in Colombia. She just never expected her daughter to fall in love with one. Not that it mattered. She smiled to herself. *At least we won't have to deal with in-laws!*

As if reading her mind, Dante continued. "I was an infant when I arrived at the orphanage in Medellín. From what they told me, a police officer brought me there. I don't know who my parents were or the circumstances. And no one ever spoke of it. But here I am now in Cali." He broke into a wide grin. "After I graduated from university, I moved here to study for the management program at International Oil Exports. The sisters from the orphanage arranged for me to live in the student housing near Iglesia de la Merced. I help with maintenance when needed and do errands for the nuns."

Sylvia nodded at his ease of conversation and felt more comfortable asking more questions. "So when you were growing up in the orphanage, how many other children lived there?"

"It varied. Most of the time, there would be a dozen of us, sometimes more, sometimes less. Some got adopted, others aged out. But it was usually an average of twelve."

"And the sisters? How many of them?" Sylvia pried a little deeper.

"At least twenty," Dante replied.

"What about meals?" Sylvia asked.

"We all ate together. Everyone had their job. I'd be in charge of gathering the vegetables from the garden, peel the potatoes, chop the celery." He shrugged. "You know. Kitchen duty."

Gabriel chimed in. "So how was the food?"

"In the morning, we would have oatmeal, lunch was sandwiches, and then a hot meal for dinner." Dante relaxed farther into his chair. "Certainly not as good as Señora Espinosa's cooking!" He laughed out loud. "Not even close! It was much like a cafeteria. Wholesome, but not overly exciting."

*No wonder he appreciates home cooking,* Sylvia thought to herself. *No wonder he's so well-mannered and respectful, too.*

The rest of the banter flowed easily and the time slipped by. Dante glanced at his watch. "*Dios mío!* I have been here for almost four hours! I hope I have not overstayed my welcome."

"Certainly not."

"Of course not."

"Don't be absurd. It has been a pleasure to have your company today," Gabriel immediately followed his wife and daughter.

Dante stood and put out his hand. "I appreciate this entire day, but I know we all have to go to work tomorrow." Gabriel shook the young man's hand; then Sylvia offered hers and kissed Dante on both cheeks.

"You are always welcome in our home," she added.

Elena could not help but blush. Her parents were close to embarrassing her. She then took her turn shaking Dante's hand and kissing him on both cheeks. "I'll walk you down the stairs." The goodbyes went on for a few more minutes as Elena and Dante moved to the stairwell that led down to the back door.

Dante began the descent, and Elena followed. They both stepped outside to avoid any eavesdropping from her parents. Dante placed his hands on Elena's shoulders and pinned his eyes with hers. "This was very special, Elena. I never had a family like this. I am filled with gratitude to have been welcomed into your home."

Mist clouded Elena's eyes. She could not remember the last time she felt this happy. She was seeing her future. She began to feel whole.

Dante kissed her softly. "Marry me, Elena Espinosa?"

Elena's knees turned to noodles. "Yes. Yes, I will."

They wrapped their arms around each other. Dante held her like a beautiful piece of porcelain. Firm enough to keep it safe, but delicate enough to appreciate its greatness.

Elena rested her head against his chest. Out of the corner of her eye, she spied her mother behind the kitchen curtain with Gabriel looking over her shoulder. She started to giggle.

Dante put her at arm's length. "You are laughing at my proposal?"

She nodded toward the window, where her parents sidestepped out of view, but not before Dante got a glimpse of the nosy couple. He, too, laughed. "Your parents love you very much."

Elena looked up at the now-empty window and smiled. "They truly do." She kissed Dante on the cheek. "I must go back inside."

"See you tomorrow?" Dante asked.

"You can walk me home from class." Elena waved and then disappeared behind the door. She ascended the stairs, knowing she was about to be quizzed.

Dante watched until Elena gave him the "all clear" by flicking the light.

Inside, Elena took a deep breath before she entered the apartment. As she predicted, both of her parents began tossing questions and comments at her.

"He is wonderful," Sylvia gushed.

"A fine young man," Gabriel added. "What are his intentions?" came next.

Elena couldn't hold anything in. She began to

squeal. "He asked me to marry him!" She took her mother's hands as they began to dance around in a circle, bumping into Gabriel over and over until he stepped aside.

Gabriel held up his hands. "I hope you said yes!"

"Of course, Papá! Why do you think I am dancing?"

# Chapter Five
# The Wedding Plans

*Cali, Colombia*

Over the next few months, preparations for Elena and Dante's wedding were underway. They would be married in six months when the weather was dry. Elena wanted to secure her place with Dante should he be transferred. She could teach English anywhere, so her options were many. But if they weren't married and Dante got transferred, it would be difficult to maintain a relationship long distance, and she didn't want to leave her family and live with him without being husband and wife. As modern as things were in the late 1980s, Elena was traditional at heart. And she knew in her soul this was the right thing to do.

One Saturday afternoon, Elena and Sylvia took

a drive to see a florist several miles away who was well known for his creativity. Gabriel had hired two more people to work in the bakery, allowing Sylvia and Elena to have time to plan the festivities. Elena was being very cost-conscious and for her flowers chose the popular Cattleya trianae orchid in white with a purple bell. She liked the idea of purple; it was the same color as the magical dress she wore on the night Dante told her he loved her. On their way home, they chatted about who would attend the wedding and who wouldn't if certain other people were there. Elena and Sylvia cackled at the idea of Sylvia's feuding aunts seated at the same table. Sylvia finally spoke the words she had thought the night they had Dante over for dinner. "At least we don't have to deal with in-laws!"

Sylvia paused for a moment. "Elena, why didn't you tell us Dante was an orphan? I know it doesn't matter, and I probably should have asked you sooner. But then again, I didn't want to be nosy."

Elena smiled at her mother. "I didn't want to put any ideas in your head until you really had time to get to know him."

"Oh Elena, your father and I aren't like that." Sylvia was saddened that her daughter felt that way.

"No, you are not, but Papá is always thinking about my future, and if I had said the man I love was—is—an orphan, who knows what would have gone through his head!" Both women laughed at the idea.

"True. He only wants what's best for you." Sylvia patted her daughter's hand. "And so it has worked out." Before Sylvia could speak another word, they

heard a loud explosion that shook the ground.
Both gasped, fearing it could be an earthquake.
Colombia was considered a high seismic risk. In
less than a minute, the sound of sirens screeched
through the air. Another minute later, a half-
dozen fire trucks, police cars, and several ambu-
lances came blaring into view. Elena pulled the car
over to the side of the road and waited until the
last emergency vehicle passed their car. Dark
plumes of smoke were filling the air. It was much
too close to home. Elena slammed her foot on the
gas pedal, whizzing through traffic in the direction
of the bakery until coming to an abrupt halt. The
streets were blocked off with police cars and people running to and from the scene.

Elena inched closer to an officer directing traffic when he put his hand up for her to stop. She
stuck her head out of her car window, trying not to
panic. She pointed several times in the direction
of the smoke. "Our place is down the street."

He shook his head and kept waving. Elena
found a spot to park, and the women scrambled
from the car. Elena ran back to the police officer
to ask what was happening. He told her there had
been an explosion. It was a car. Probably a bomb.
She tried to maintain her composure as she explained who she was. He told her she was not allowed near the site. Elena began to hyperventilate
as her mother ran up next to her. Sylvia was also
pleading with the officer and kept asking if anyone
had been hurt. She, too, was close to hysterics.
Then the officer recognized her from the bakery
and changed his stance from authoritative to com-
passionate. The explosion had caused damage at

the bakery. They did not know if anyone was hurt. Or alive. Or dead. Sylvia began to sob uncontrollably. Elena grabbed her mother to steady her from falling. "Where is Gabriel?" Sylvia shrieked.

The officer pulled out his walkie-talkie and engaged in a quick conversation with someone closer to the scene. He turned to Sylvia and Elena and told them that two women at the bakery were hurt. Fortunately, they were in the back of the building, and had suffered only minor scrapes and bruises. They were more in shock than injured, and the ambulance was going to take them to the hospital. There was no sign of any other people.

Sylvia cried out. It still didn't mean Gabriel wasn't buried under the rubble. As the officer began to comfort Sylvia, Elena dashed past him and ran toward the smoldering ruins of an automobile. Scorched pieces of metal that were once part of a van were scattered on the sidewalk. Shrapnel was everywhere. Elena could make out the charred *L* that used to spell out *Lozano Panadería*. She tried to rush through the rubble but was stopped once again. This time, it was a firefighter. She tried to wrangle herself from his grip, begging him to let her go. "My father!" she cried. "Where is my father?"

The firefighter told her the same thing the police officer told her. There was no sign of anyone else.

"But how do you know?" Elena demanded. He pointed to a German shepherd wearing what looked like an official vest. The firefighter explained to Elena that the dog was a new member of their team and was trained to find people. It was a program they had been working on with a former US Navy Seal who was training specialty dogs to sniff out drugs, weapons, and people—dead or alive.

Elena began to breathe a little easier, hoping her father had been on a delivery run and wasn't present when the incident occurred. Elena looked past the firefighter and spotted a small strongbox buried under broken glass and splinters. She pointed to it and pleaded, "May I please have that? It might be the only thing we have left in this world." The firefighter took pity on the young woman. He too was familiar with the bakery that had stood for more than half a century. He told her to wait as he picked his way through the wreckage and returned with the precious box. Elena was sobbing. They were tears of shock, despair, and a hint of relief, as she hoped the box still contained the few thousand dollars her father kept under the stairs. She brushed off the ash and opened it. Thank God it was all there. After that day, nothing would be the same, but together, they would find a way to rebuild and renew. They had no other choice.

She thanked the firefighter profusely and made her way back to where the officer was still standing guard next to her mother. "Papá was not there," Elena assured her and showed her the metal box.

"How do you know?" Sylvia was still crying.

"A dog told me." Elena wrapped her arms around her mother and wept with her.

Within the next few minutes, Gabriel's pickup truck appeared. He practically jumped out before it came to a complete stop. He ran toward his wife and daughter and hugged them as tightly as he could. Now he was certain; there was no other way around it: they needed to, had to, must relocate. He suspected the bomb was the work of one of the cartels. Medellín or Cali? It didn't matter. He had become an unwitting man in the middle, and he would have bet his life that the duffel bag he had been forced to transport had something to do with this horrible situation.

The family clung to each other for what seemed like an hour, crying and hugging. Gabriel finally broke free from Sylvia's grip and spoke to the officer. "Do you have any information about the two women who were taken to the hospital?" The officer spoke into his walkie-talkie once more and contacted the paramedics who had taken Carmen and Lucia to the hospital. Gabriel could hear the nurse on the other end saying they had a few cuts but were otherwise fine. The doctor had treated their wounds and given them each a sedative. They would be released as soon as someone could take them home.

Sylvia was trembling. She made the sign of the cross twice. Thank God they were alright.

Elena was wiping the tears from her face when she spotted Dante riding up the block on his bicycle. His legs were pumping with great ferocity. He skidded to a stop and dropped the bike on its side, running toward Elena and her parents. "What happened?" he asked breathlessly.

Gabriel looked down at the ground. "Someone blew up the bakery's van."

"But why?" Dante was completely baffled but continued before he got his answer. "Is everyone alright?"

"Carmen and Lucia were taken to the hospital but they are alright. Just a few cuts," Gabriel explained.

"Are you alright?" Dante turned to Elena and Sylvia, wrapping his arms around both of them. Elena began to sob. Sylvia was spent.

The police officer spoke to Gabriel. "You should take them home."

Gabriel looked back at the man. "That *was* our home."

The officer shook his head. "I am so sorry."

Dante immediately took control of the situation. "Come. We will go to the church." Dante put his bicycle in the back of Gabriel's truck. "I'll drive Elena's car. Sylvia will ride with you."

Gabriel nodded and escorted his wife to his truck. She was shaking uncontrollably. Dante took the keys from Elena and helped her into the passenger seat of her car. The motor was still running from when she had abandoned it almost an hour ago. He checked the gas gauge. They would be fine. He helped Elena with her seat belt as she continued to clutch the carbon-covered metal box. Dante fished around for his handkerchief and began to wipe Elena's hands as she stared straight ahead. "It's going to be alright." He brushed more soot from her cheek. Elena did not reply. Her world had literally blown up.

Dante motioned for Gabriel to follow him. It took around twenty minutes to arrive at the massive church complex. Dante pulled the vehicle toward the back of the building. He knew if it was indeed a car bomb, it was a warning. A severe warning. There could be more to come. For now, his instincts were to protect his soon-to-be family, and he knew this was the safest place for them to be at that moment.

Gabriel parked next to his daughter's car. Elena got out and handed the metal box to her father. "Papá. I was able to retrieve this from the explosion." She handed him the metal box now wrapped in Dante's soiled handkerchief. "A fireman pulled it out of the pile."

Gabriel looked at his daughter as tears formed in his eyes. "My beautiful daughter. You should never have gone through all of this. It is all my fault." His shoulders shook as he attempted to stifle his emotions.

"No. This is not your fault. This is some horrible person's fault." She gripped her father in a tight hug.

Dante looked around the parking lot. It was dusk, and there was no one in sight. School had ended several hours earlier, and the extracurricular activities were over. He motioned them to quickly move to an entrance with a sign above that said: ÁREA RESTRINGIDA—SOLO PERSONAL AUTHORIZADO.

Dante pulled out his keys and unlocked the steel door. He looked both ways again, then ushered Elena, Sylvia, and Gabriel into the building. The lights were dim as Dante led them down a long corridor. "This way." It had that distinct smell of a school, and the hallways of door after door indicated they were probably classrooms. All empty at the moment. No one spoke as they scurried ahead, following Dante's lead. They finally came upon a reception area, where a nun sat at a desk grading papers.

"*Buenas noches,*" Dante addressed her.

The nun looked up and smiled. "English, my son. Remember? Good evening, Dante. We weren't expecting you until later this evening." The conversation continued in Spanish and English. The words were pouring out of his mouth.

"Pardon my manners, Sister. This is my fiancée Elena, her mother Sylvia, and her father Gabriel—" He stopped himself before he uttered their last name. He wasn't sure how far the news had traveled about the car bomb several miles away and did not want to cause any further alarm.

Sister Adele knitted her eyebrows. "Is everything alright?" She couldn't help noticing the tear-stained faces of the two women. The man, Gabriel, was pale and had a small metal box tucked under his arm. His expression was strained.

Dante smiled at the nun, avoiding her question. "Is Father Bruno available? I know it's last-minute, but it's rather important."

Their distress was easy to see and feel. It was palpable. The nun nodded, picked up the heavy black phone, and dialed a number. "Good evening, Father Bruno. This is Sister Adele. Would you have a few minutes to see Dante Castillo? He has some friends with him." She continued before he had a chance to answer. "It seems rather urgent, Father." She nodded at Dante and the others. "I will. Thank you, Father."

Sister Adele hung up the receiver and smiled at the others. "He'll be right out." There was only one chair in addition to the one she was sitting on, so she offered hers. She motioned to Sylvia. "Please sit." Then she motioned to Elena to take the other chair. Gabriel resisted the urge to pace. Dante placed his hand on Gabriel's shoulder. "We will figure this out."

Gabriel took a long look at Dante and mouthed the words *thank you.* He was used to being the man in charge, but in this case, he could not be happier there was someone who could manage this terrifying situation. A few minutes later, which seemed like an eternity, Father Bruno entered the small area.

"Dante. What a pleasant surprise." He nodded at the forlorn-looking family in front of him and offered his hand. Dante proceeded with introductions. Father Bruno knew immediately this was something that required a private space and instructed everyone to follow him. He nodded at Sister Adele. "Thank you, Sister. Have a good evening."

"You do the same, Father." She smiled at the family. "God bless you."

"Please, this way," Father Bruno said.

The group entered another hallway of classrooms that exited into a large, stone courtyard landscaped with tropical plants. Several benches surrounded the walkways to various buildings. On the far side of the courtyard was another mission-styled building with a sign that read PARISH above the front door.

"I'm the only one here this evening, so we will have privacy." Father Bruno unlocked the front door as he made the sign of the cross. "Please." He motioned for them to enter the vestibule. "Dante, please bring them into my office. I will fix a pot of tea. Excuse me for a few minutes." He walked toward the other side of the entrance into the kitchen area.

Dante showed them the way to the office. Two walls were lined with carved mahogany bookcases brimming with first editions, journals in various languages, photos of revered priests and cardinals, and hand-painted ceramics. A large desk of Mediterranean design faced the room filled with beautiful antique furniture. Plush rugs covered the tile floors. On the far end was a massive stone fireplace, casting warmth and a glow across the room. A settee with two armchairs and a low coffee table faced the fireplace. The beauty and serenity of the room went unnoticed. Everyone was on edge, not knowing what would come next.

Dante broke the silence. "I don't think it's safe for you to be out in public tonight. We don't know why the van blew up. It could have been a car bomb, or just an accident. We won't know until tomorrow. Gabriel, you have an appointment with the police in the morning?"

Gabriel nodded. "They want to take statements from all of us."

"Us? But why?" Sylvia finally spoke. "We weren't even there."

Gabriel folded his arms and leaned against one of the massive wooden bookcases. Surrounded by all this reverence, he knew he had to tell them about the duffel bag. He knew instinctively it was related to the explosion. But he didn't know the reason. He had nothing to do with the cartel. He took in several deep breaths, anticipating the reaction he would get from his family. He hadn't mentioned the duffel bag when it was given to him, and it had only occurred once. At least to his knowledge. They could have stashed something in his truck or van without him noticing. But how often? Was he an unwitting accomplice? Who would believe him? The country was rife with criminals. He hoped the priest wouldn't take much longer. His anxiety was growing, and he knew neither Sylvia nor Elena were in any state of calm. Not even close. Even in the refuge of the priest's office, the tension still filled the air. On any other day, it would have been a welcoming retreat, but that evening would prove to be a turning point in their lives, and they knew it. But turning to where?

The priest returned, carrying a tray with a pot of tea, cups, and some cookies on it. He set it down on the long, low table in front of the sofa where Elena and Sylvia sat, their arms linked together. He looked over at Gabriel. "Sit. Please."

"Thank you. But not yet." Gabriel still had the metal box in his hands.

Dante sat in one of the large armchairs. Father Bruno poured the tea and handed it to the women first, then to Gabriel, and Dante. He then took the other chair across from the table. He looked at Gabriel. "Can I offer you something stronger for your tea?" He smiled. "It's alright. I usually enjoy a little brandy with my tea at night. It's made in one of the monasteries in the mountains, but don't tell anyone!" He chuckled, hoping it would ease the tension.

"Yes, please. That would be very good." Gabriel's shoulders began to relax as the priest rose from his chair and moved toward a hand-carved cabinet. He pulled out an unmarked bottle of golden brown liquid and proceeded to pour some into Gabriel's cup. Sylvia and Elena held up their own cups in unison, which caused Father Bruno to give a slight guffaw. It seemed as if everyone had started to finally breathe again.

After taking a few sips, Gabriel cleared his throat. "Father, you may know our bakery. Lozano Panadería."

"Yes, I do. Dante spoils us with your wonderful pan de queso."

Sylvia nodded in acknowledgment. "Thank you."

Gabriel looked around for a place to set the metal box. The priest pointed to the raised hearth, where Gabriel put what was left of their livelihood. He then began his account of what he had experienced and what he suspected. "There are three farms on the outskirts of town. I deliver bread to them once, sometimes twice, a week. They order over a dozen loaves for each delivery." He took another sip. "The farms are surrounded with barbwire fencing, and there are guards at the gates. The buildings are not visible from the entrance."

The priest bobbed his head. "I understand. There are, shall we say, rumors, about the farms."

"That is correct," Gabriel replied. He looked at Sylvia. "My wife and I discussed that possibility and whether or not we wanted to sell them bread. But as you know, you cannot refuse their business."

Elena turned toward her mother. "Mami? You knew about this?"

Sylvia bowed her head. "We baked it; Gabriel delivered it." She then looked up at her husband with a puzzled look on her face. "You didn't do anything else, did you?"

"One time they threw a duffel bag in the back of the van and told me to keep the van unlocked when I returned to the bakery. The next day, the bag was gone. I thought that was the end of it."

Sylvia was now becoming agitated. "You mean you were working with them?" She was on her feet now.

"No! *Mi amor*, please let me explain," Gabriel pleaded.

Elena pulled on her mother's hand to encourage her to sit down.

"I said I thought it was the end of it until today," Gabriel continued. "They never said or did anything again, after that one time."

"So why would you be a target?" Dante asked. Father Bruno listened silently.

"That is what I do not know." Gabriel took a pull of his tea.

Finally, Father Bruno spoke. "Do you think they may have been stashing it in the wheel wells of your vehicle?"

"It's possible." Gabriel pondered the question and then replied, "I have made hundreds of deliveries. It was always the same. I pull up to the gate and roll down my window. The guard would check to see if it was me, while another one would go to the back of the van and take out the bag with the name of their farm. Then the first guard would hand me an envelope. I would turn the truck around and leave."

"But you said one time they gave you a duffel bag?" Dante asked.

"Yes. They left it in the back, and I never touched it."

"And they never asked you again." Father Bruno said it as more of a statement.

"No."

Dante stood and began to pace the floor. "So they never asked you again, but that doesn't mean they hadn't planted anything in the van, as Father Bruno suggested."

"This is very true." Gabriel sighed. "But why blow up my vehicle? I hadn't stolen anything."

"Let's say they were using you as a mule. What if their enemies found out and took it from your vehicle? That would cause very serious trouble. For you." Father Bruno seemed to speak from experience. "It would not be the first time the cartels waged war against each other through innocent bystanders. They will stop at nothing."

The room fell silent. Elena broke the stillness. "What can we do?"

Father Bruno's face saddened. "If you go to the police, the cartel will find out. They have spies everywhere, and they have their own people in high-ranking government places. That is how Escobar can get away with so many heinous crimes."

Sylvia began to tremble again. Elena put her arm around her mother. Reality was setting in. They could not go back to the bakery—their home. Someone knew where they lived, and that someone was evil.

Father Bruno waited for the reality to set in. "I

think all of you should stay here tonight. Gabriel, you can stay in Dante's studio. Elena and Sylvia can stay in the convent. First we'll get you settled, and then we shall have some dinner."

"Thank you, but I don't have much of an appetite," Sylvia replied.

"We cannot let you go to bed with an empty stomach," the priest insisted. "Besides, I have a nice bottle of homemade wine that promises to soothe your nerves."

Sylvia gave a slight chuckle. "I thought the brandy was supposed to do that."

"And did it?" Father Bruno smiled.

"I must confess, it did." Sylvia finally smiled for the first time in the past several hours.

"Good. I'll call Sister Margaret Mary. She will show you to your rooms and give you a chance to freshen up." He picked up a black phone and dialed. "Good evening, Sister. We have two guests who will be joining us for dinner and spending the night. Could you please come to my office and show them to the guest quarters? Thank you." He turned to the two women, who were now standing together in front of the fireplace. "Sister Margaret Mary will be here momentarily. She will show you to your room and get you some fresh linens."

Elena looked down at her soiled dress. She had clutched the metal box for well over an hour, and the ash and dirt was all over the fine linen she wore. *At least my hands are clean*, she thought. The priest took pity on the young woman. "I am sure they will find you something suitable to wear." Elena looked up at the kind man, her face flush with embarrassment.

Gabriel's voice cracked when he spoke. "Thank you, Father. I don't know what to do, but being here has given me hope."

Sylvia stood and walked over to the priest. She took his hand and thanked him profusely. Elena did the same.

"Things may not turn out the way you had hoped or planned, but God will help you find your way," Father Bruno said.

A light knock on the door announced Sister Margaret Mary's arrival. Father Bruno introduced her to everyone, and she led the women down the hall, back through the courtyard, and into the building where the nuns lived.

Gabriel retrieved the box from the hearth and followed Dante to his studio apartment situated on the opposite side of the campus. As they walked the winding, brick-lined garden path, Gabriel spoke in a soft hush. "Dante, you have been so strong. You have much courage. I am happy you will marry my daughter."

Dante paused. "Yes. But when?" He was half-talking to himself. "If we cannot go through with the wedding, it will break Elena's heart."

"Elena is a strong woman. As long as she has you by her side, she will be happy." Gabriel had settled into future-father-in-law mode. "You know, Sylvia and I had discussed moving many times, but we wanted to wait until Elena finished her studies. After many discussions, we decided to look for another town to move the bakery. Elena was going to start an internship at a local bank, and once she went to work full time, we would have to hire someone else, so why not start something new?"

He slowed his pace. "Then when you and she developed a strong bond, we knew it was time for us to move on. I researched newspapers and read many articles to see where there was less strife and more prosperity. I thought about Palmira. The coffee industry has had enormous growth, bringing more people to the area. That meant more people would also need more bread."

Palmira was considered the agricultural capital of Colombia, with huge economic growth not only in coffee, but also sugarcane.

"And what goes best with coffee and sugar?" Gabriel continued. "Pan de queso. And it would be less than an hour away, from Elena, should she decide to stay in Cali." He sighed. "But now?"

Dante gave Gabriel a slight tap on the back. "We will figure this out. I know we will."

They came upon a two-story stone building that must have been well over a hundred years old. Dante fished a large set of keys out of his pocket and opened the main door. A hallway led to the left, and a staircase was on the right. Dante's studio was on the first floor near the front entrance. He unlocked the old wooden door. "It's not much, but it's home."

It was an L-shaped studio apartment. A small galley kitchen faced the living space. The alcove served as Dante's bedroom, outfitted with a small dresser and wardrobe cabinet. A bathroom that could barely hold the narrow shower, sink, and toilet was adjacent to the sleeping area. The rest of the furnishings included a futon sofa, upholstered chair, coffee table, study desk, and two floor lamps. "Not very chic or glamourous," Dante joked. "It's very similar to the place where I grew up minus the kitchen equipment and the single bed. We had bunk beds. Usually four sets per room."

Gabriel surveyed the simple space. "You have learned to live modestly."

"That would be an accurate description." Dante thought for a moment. "But please don't think I want or expect Elena to live this way. I want only the best for her. Whatever her heart desires, I will try to make it so." He motioned at Gabriel. "Please sit. I'll get you some fresh clothes and towels. I think you might fit into my slacks and a sweater."

It had not occurred to Gabriel that he and Dante were similar in height and build. He had only been concentrating on the man's integrity over the past several months. He thought again about the wedding that would most likely never happen and felt a pang of guilt.

Dante offered Gabriel a pair of chino pants and a cotton-blend sweater. "I'm afraid you are on your own when it comes to underwear." Both men let out a huge guffaw.

"I shall keep my pants on and wash them out in the sink later," Gabriel said. They were almost giddy. The events of the day had them wound tight.

Dante gave a mocking cringe and handed him a bath towel. "We have dates tonight. Go get cleaned up."

Gabriel saluted and moved toward the bathroom. It was good to feel the warm water against his skin.

\* \* \*

Sister Margaret Mary was a joyful bundle as she waddled into the foyer of the convent. She reached for a bell that was sitting on a table and rang it like the town crier. "Sisters! We have guests!" she announced with enthusiasm. Whispers and murmurs were heard in the distance as a half dozen women, dressed in habits, greeted them. "This is Sylvia and Elena." The nun looked at both women. "I'm sorry, but I don't know your last name."

Sylvia looked at Elena. Their name was common enough, so Sylvia replied, "Espinosa." Besides, it wasn't the same name as the bakery, just in case the sisters had heard about the explosion.

"Welcome. Welcome." A tall, honey-toned woman extended her hand. "I am Mother Philomena. Father phoned ahead and said you would be spending some time with us. Perhaps two, maybe three days."

*Two, maybe three days?* Both women hadn't thought about how long they might be there. It caused both of them to shudder.

Sylvia responded quickly. "We do not want to wear out our welcome."

"Nonsense. We are here to do God's work, and if you need God's help, then we are happy to oblige." The nun placed her hands in a prayer position and bowed.

"Thank you very much," Sylvia replied. She and Elena didn't know what to do next and waited for their cue from Mother Philomena.

"Now, let's get you settled. Perhaps a quick shower? You will be refreshed for dinner. It will be served in an hour."

"That sounds wonderful." Elena spoke with ease. "I could certainly use one." She glanced down at her soiled clothes.

"And we'll get you something to wear." Mother Philomena looked at Sylvia. "Both of you." She turned to one of the other nuns, who seemed to instinctively know what needed to be done and disappeared down the hall. "Come." Mother Philomena guided them down a corridor that appeared to be a dormitory. All the doors were open, and each room looked identical: a single bed, small altar with a kneeling pad, a nightstand with a lamp and a copy of the Bible, a short dresser, and a hardback chair. *Austere* would have been an apt description. It was the opposite of the warm atmosphere of Father Bruno's office. Elena wondered if his residence was as humble as the convent.

At the end of the hallway was a larger room with two single beds. "This is for when we have visiting nuns." Mother Philomena swept her arm through the doorway. "And tonight we have visiting friends." She turned when she heard scurrying behind her. It was Sister Bernice with a bundle of clothes and towels. "We have a common bathroom, but the shower stalls are private, as are the toilets."

Elena hadn't thought about a group lather, but she figured she and her mother would be the only people using the shower at that time of day. Then she wondered exactly what time of day it was. She hadn't paid attention. Everything was a blur. She also realized no one had checked the news. Maybe it was for the best. Everyone could move about without the world imposing itself. It was one of the advantages of living a cloistered life. "Thank you, Mother Philomena. Sister Bernice."

The two nuns gave a small bow. "It is our pleasure."

Elena and Sylvia removed their soiled and wrinkled clothes, wrapped the large bath towels around them, and briskly walked toward the showers halfway down the hall. It reminded Elena of the bathroom in the high school locker room. She was a little apprehensive.

"No time for modesty," Sylvia said, and chuckled at her daughter. "We must make the most of this. We don't have a choice."

Elena pulled her hair up in a bun and stepped into the tepid water. It wasn't as hot as she was accustomed to, but it was water. Clean water. As she soaped her body, her mind replayed the events of the day. It had started out so joyfully—going to the florist, making plans, and singing in the car with her mother. And now the day was ending with them as refugees, showering in a convent. "Mami? Are you okay?" Elena called over the shower stall.

"I am as good as I can be under the circumstances." As shocked as she was, Sylvia knew this would be a turning point in their lives and she'd better be prepared for whatever came their way. "We are very lucky to have Dante and these fine people looking after us."

Elena thought about what her mother just said. "You are right, Mami. As bad as the day was, we still have each other, and a safe place to stay." She made the sign of the cross and said a prayer of thanks. She could hear her mother doing the same. After a good scrubbing, Elena felt she had washed most of the day's grime away. The emotional toll would take much more than soap. She wrapped the towel around her and met up with her mother near one of the sinks. She put her arm around Sylvia. "I love you and Papá so very much. I am so grateful we are okay." Tears began to roll down her face.

Sylvia took a washcloth and dabbed Elena's cheeks. "Come. It will be okay. You don't want your future husband to see you with bloodshot eyes and a sniffling nose."

"Mami. You always say the right thing." Elena twisted to give her mother a hug, and Sylvia lost the towel that was covering her body. As she bent over to pick it up, she spotted her buttocks in the mirror and pointed. "Now *that* is something to cry about!" The moment of levity left the two women doubling over in laughter, as Sister Margaret Mary sailed into the bathroom.

"Is everything alright?" She gasped.

Elena and Sylvia couldn't stop laughing. The sister thought they might be delirious. Sylvia caught her breath. "Sorry, Sister. My daughter and I were having a laugh over something silly." She didn't know how else to explain it to a nun. *We were laughing at my ass!*

Sister Margaret Mary sighed with relief. "You both seemed to have had a very troubling day. When I heard the hooting, I thought something had gone awry."

"No, not at all, Sister. I apologize for causing concern." Sylvia avoided looking at Elena. She knew they were having the same thoughts, and she would burst out laughing again. How *do* you tell a nun you were laughing at your ass? Sylvia wrapped the towel tighter around her body.

The women splashed cold water on their faces as Sister Margaret Mary guarded the doorway. She peeked up and down the hall. "You can go back to your rooms now. The sisters are used to living this way. I am sure you are not."

"It's alright. Really," Elena assured the fretful nun. "We appreciate the shelter and the care."

"Bless you both. I am going to my room now. Dinner will be ready in about twenty minutes. I shall come for you then." She bowed and shuffled to her personal space.

Elena and Sylvia scooted back to their room, where they found two long black skirts and two white blouses laid out on the beds. The women donned the clothes and once again stifled a laugh. Sylvia was a size twelve, and Elena was a size eight. The two of them could have fit into one skirt together. Elena removed the belt from her dirty dress and wrapped it around her waist. She sat on one of the wooden chairs. "Mami, how did we ever end up here?"

Sylvia wasn't sure how to answer the question. Elena sounded more philosophical than quizzical.

Elena continued. "We were living a normal life. You and Papá had a business; I was graduating from school. And I was planning a wedding. All of that changed in less than a day."

"I know. One has to wonder why. You ask God, 'Why?' But here we are, in a convent, being looked after by people doing God's work. I think this is a lesson. What will happen next is not up to us. We must have faith. Trust. And optimism. We cannot survive without them."

Elena stood and put her arms around her mother. "You are so wise."

Several minutes later, Sister Margaret Mary's familiar soft knock sounded at their door. "Please. Follow me."

Sylvia and Elena hiked up their way-too-big skirts and followed the nun. They continued down a long corridor as the aroma of something cooking wafted through the air.

"Something smells delicious," Sylvia commented.

"Chicken stew," the nun explained. "And we have some wonderful pan de queso that Dante brought by yesterday."

Elena and Sylvia stopped in their tracks. Sister Margaret Mary turned to look at them. "What is it?"

It was at this moment when the two women realized it may be the last of the pan de queso from Lozano Bakery. They grabbed each other's hands.

"Is everything alright?" the nun asked again.

Sylvia couldn't hold back the truth any longer. Not that it mattered. Who would the nuns tell? And for what reason? "That bread came from our bakery," she said solemnly.

"Do you not own it anymore?" Obviously, the news of the car bomb hadn't traveled to the convent yet. Or, if it had, Sister Margaret Mary wasn't aware of it.

"Sister, there was an accident today. An explosion," Sylvia said.

Sister Margaret Mary's hands flew to her face. She made the sign of the cross. "*Dios mío!* When did this happen?"

"This afternoon. That is why we are here." Sylvia touched the sister's arm. "And we are so very grateful."

The nun nodded, and they continued to walk toward the dining hall. The familiar aroma of bread being warmed in the oven was surreal. It smelled like home.

The dining hall had a long, twelve-foot table surrounded by wooden chairs. A fire was roaring in an open stone hearth. In spite of the stern environment, there was still a softness, a sense of peace within the walls.

Dante and Gabriel were standing close to the hearth, talking to Father Bruno. Sylvia was anticipating a bizarre reaction to their outfits. She was not disappointed. Gabriel bit his lip, and Dante raised his glass so neither would reveal their amusement. Conversely, Father Bruno burst out laughing. "You will never be in a fashion show wearing those."

Sylvia and Elena were surprised at his cheekiness. But then again, he, too, was human. And had a sense of humor. It was a welcome addition to a very serious and trying day.

Father Bruno poured each of the women a glass of wine. "This should warm you and calm your nerves. I'm sure the effects of the brandy have worn off by now."

"Thank you, Father." Sylvia took a sip. "Your special vintage?" she teased.

"It is indeed." He raised his glass. "To new friends. May God help clear your way for better days ahead."

They responded with a traditional *"Saludos!"*

"Come. Sit. The sisters have prepared a wonderful stew. We shall enjoy dinner with no conversation about the incident until later. We must eat in peace and enjoy the blessings of the table," Father Bruno instructed and then said a prayer of thanks, followed by an "Amen" from everyone.

The sisters helped dish out the stew as Father Bruno broke bread. *Their* bread. Sylvia choked back tears. Her family's heritage had gone up in smoke. Granted, the building was still intact, but she knew they could never return.

About an hour later, the dishes were cleared, and words of gratitude were shared with the sisters. Father Bruno stood and instructed the family to follow him back to his office in the parish house. As they walked through the garden, the bells from the church signaled it was eight p.m. Elena finally had a grasp of the time of day. Had it only been twelve hours before when she was in a totally different frame of mind? A different life ahead of her? She kept repeating her mother's words over and over in her head: "We must have faith."

When they entered the priest's office, a tray of coffee, cakes, and brandy was waiting on the table in front of the fireplace. Sylvia thought about how the sisters moved inconspicuously throughout the mission. It seemed that whatever was needed miraculously appeared. She chuckled to herself.

*Isn't that what faith is about? Miracles?* Because right now, they surely needed one. Probably more than one.

Elena hiked up her skirt again and sat on the sofa beside her mother. Gabriel remained standing in front of the mantel next to Father Bruno. Dante leaned against one of the bookcases.

Father Bruno began. "Before dinner, Gabriel, Dante, and I were discussing your situation. We agree that it is not safe for you to stay in Cali."

Gabriel chimed in. "Since I do not know the reason for this assault on our business, I can only assume it is related to the cartels." He lowered his voice. The mere mention of the word *cartel* could bring a hell storm upon anyone who uttered it. "Thanks to Elena, we have some cash. It should be enough to help us get out of the country."

Sylvia gasped. "Leave the country? But why?"

"Because we don't know if these people are finished with us or not. It may have been a warning. We don't know. We cannot take any chances. I'm sorry."

Father Bruno underscored Gabriel's concern. "I have seen this before. If they are not satisfied, they will return. Your lives are in jeopardy now."

Elena stiffened and looked at Dante. "What about the wedding? Does this mean we won't be married?" She absently twisted her engagement ring around her finger.

Father Bruno smiled. "I am a priest. I think we can work something out."

"But we don't have a marriage license!" Elena exclaimed.

"It won't matter once we are out of the country," Gabriel noted.

Sylvia was getting lightheaded. This was all too much to absorb. First their property was attacked, and now they had to leave the country? She thought she was going to vomit. Dante immediately went to the sideboard and poured her a glass of water. Her hands were shaking as she took the glass from him.

"These people are violent. They do not care about human life. To them, everyone is expendable," Father Bruno continued.

"Must we decide all of this now? Tonight?" Elena asked with trepidation. Looking at everyone's faces, she already knew the answer.

"We must make plans. It will take a day or so to work out the details. I will admit, this is not the first time I have had to assist a family in a similar situation," the priest explained.

Sylvia stared at the fire, clinging to her mantra of "faith and hope."

Gabriel cleared his throat. "I know this is a terrible shock to everyone, but we must think about our future and our safety. Father Bruno explained how this can be worked out, but it isn't going to be easy."

He nodded at Father Bruno, who continued with the plan. "There is someone who has a large fishing boat in Buenaventura. He has done this before. There are two small cabins you can stay in. I will have the sisters fix baskets of food for you to take with you. The boat will bring you to Puerto Vallarta, Mexico. It takes about four days."

Sylvia was turning green from the thought of being on a fishing boat for four days. Elena was only a few shades of chartreuse away.

Father Bruno waited for it all to sink in. Dante went over to the sofa and stood behind Elena and Sylvia. He put his hands on each of their shoulders and could feel the women quivering. Father Bruno also couldn't help but notice their shaking and pulled a blanket from an armoire and handed it to Dante, who wrapped it around the women's shoulders.

Father Bruno spoke slowly. "When you arrive, my contact will give you directions to another church, where you will be met by a family. You will stay with them for two days. Then you must decide if you want to continue to the United States. If you choose to do so, we will help arrange for transportation by bus to a US border crossing." He paused. "That can take another one to two days, depending on where you go."

"But how will we get into America?" Sylvia asked. "We have no documents, and you said we shouldn't go back to the bakery."

"I will give each of you a letter asking for asylum and stating that you are victims of narco-terrorism. While it isn't an official government document, a plea from the church can go a long way."

Sylvia clenched her hands. There were too many questions. She didn't know where to begin. She was calculating the number of days it would take, provided they kept moving. At least six. Then she began her barrage. "It will take us about six days. How much will it cost? Where will we get clothes? Food? Shelter?" She was close to shrieking. "What about the bakery? Our money? Our things?" She burst into uncontrollable sobs. The reality was finally hitting her. Gabriel went to the sofa and put his arms around his wife. He started rocking her back and forth. He held her head close to his chest and stroked her hair and whispered whatever words he thought would comfort her.

Elena walked over to where Dante was standing. His face was blank. The weight of their situation was slowly pouring over him, as well. He had heard about families fleeing from Colombia. He often wondered if that's what had happened to his own family. Elena looked into his face and asked helplessly, "What are we going to do?" She turned to her father.

Gabriel held Sylvia tightly as he offered his thoughts. "First we will need to close our bank account and the safe deposit box." He looked up at the priest. "How can we do that, Father?"

"You still have your identification on you?" Father Bruno asked.

"Yes, I have my wallet with my driver's license." Gabriel pulled it out of the pants he had borrowed from Dante. "And a little cash."

The priest looked at each of them. Elena was the next to speak. "I have mine in my purse."

Gabriel tilted Sylvia's chin toward him. She nodded.

"Good. Tomorrow, Gabriel and I will go to the bank together. I don't think anyone will bother a priest and his companion."

"But we are supposed to go to the police station and give them a report," Gabriel reminded everyone.

"You can't do that." Dante repeated what Father Bruno had said to him earlier. "Escobar has his people firmly planted, and so do the Orejuela brothers. That is how they keep tabs on one another's activities. Who better to keep them informed than the police?"

"But won't they come looking for me? For us?" Gabriel asked.

"They have much more important things to do than look for someone who had a bomb planted in their car in front of a bakery. Unfortunately, it's not an unusual circumstance, and not very important to them. Between the warring cartels, it has become all too common," Father Bruno explained.

Gabriel admonished himself. "I should have moved all of us sooner. Then this would never have happened."

Father Bruno spoke compassionately. "We do what we can do when we can do it. Today and tomorrow, I can help you and your family move to a safer place. Or at least out of harm's way here. What you choose to do after that is entirely your decision."

Sylvia began to regain some self-control. Her sobbing had abated, and now she was wiping her face and blowing her nose as ladylike as she could, apologizing with each snort and grunt. It brought a touch of lightness to the very heavy situation.

Father Bruno continued. "While Gabriel and I are at the bank, Elena and Sylvia can go to the parish thrift shop and pick up some clothes. I wouldn't suggest you buy anything new until you get settled. No sense on spending money that you will need later." He saw the look of trepidation on the women's faces. "Most donations come from very wealthy families. Some still have the original price tags on them. And the sisters and volunteers make sure everything is cleaned before it goes into the shop." He was being as reassuring as possible.

All eyes fell on Dante. He wasn't in jeopardy. He had a new job he was about to start. He didn't have to flee.

He looked back at everyone. "What?"

"What are you going to do?" Gabriel asked.

"I don't understand. What else am I supposed to do?" It hadn't occurred to him to abandon the Espinosa family. Even though he was only an infant when he was brought to the orphanage, his soul was marked with the scar of desertion. "I mean, what do you *need* me to do?"

Father Bruno handed Dante a pad and pen and suggested he go to the scene of the crime and try to find out more information. Was it roped off? Were the police still investigating? Was there anyone near the premises? Dante nodded as he jotted down the questions.

"Meanwhile, I will contact the ship's owner to arrange for passage for . . ." The priest paused.

Dante pointed to each of them in turn as he spoke. "Gabriel, Sylvia, Elena, and me." That answered everyone's silent question. One could feel the sense of relief in the room. He looked around. "You didn't think I would stay here and leave the three of you to go trotting off to places unknown? I have every faith we will be able to manage. We are educated, speak fluent English, and are quite personable, if I say so myself." That brought a little chuckle from Sylvia.

"Let's go over everything before we go to bed. You will sleep much better if you have a plan." Father Bruno poured some of the homemade spirits into beautiful cut-crystal cordial glasses. "This will help, too."

In the morning, Gabriel and Father Bruno were to go to the bank and close the account. Dante would bike over to the bakery and casually assess the situation, while Elena and Sylvia picked out a few items of clothing from the thrift shop. Sylvia gave Gabriel a list of toiletries they would need, such as toothpaste, toothbrushes, deodorant, and shaving cream. She would ask the sisters about feminine products. She didn't want to dump that embarrassing job on Gabriel.

Once they finished their errands, they were to meet back at Father Bruno's office around noon. Then they would have some lunch and go over the next segment of the plan. Everyone seemed more relaxed in knowing they were doing something. *Anything.* Sylvia smiled, remembering the conversation she had with Elena almost a year ago, when Elena was frustrated with her life and first decided to take salsa lessons. How much had changed in such a short time. And how much more would change still? That was yet to be seen.

They said their good-nights to the priest, and Dante and Gabriel walked the women through the courtyard to the convent. The four stood in a tight circle while Dante offered a prayer. They kissed and hugged each other and retreated to their quarters.

Elena and Sylvia walked silently arm-in-arm down the hallway to their small, meager shelter. Two plain white nightgowns were laid out on the beds. Neither was up for much conversation at that point. What was left to say? The women were exhausted. They said their good nights and climbed into the cot-like beds. Elena could still feel the tension coming from her mother. "Mami? It's going to be alright."

"Yes, my dear daughter. Sleep well." Sylvia thought back to when she was Elena's age. Nothing could intimidate her. She was fearless. Invincible. She married a man whom her parents did not approve of who then became one of their biggest heroes when he offered to pay them for the bakery and develop it into an even bigger success. Because of Gabriel, the family legacy had continued. Now, with age fifty looming on the horizon, Sylvia had learned that life wasn't always easy. Life had many challenges, and there were no guarantees. Certainly not after today. It was good that Elena had that same spirit of courage. It would get her far.

Everyone was up with the sun. Partly because the sunrise was before six a.m., and also because the chapel bells signaled it was time for morning vespers for the sisters. Sylvia and Elena were looking forward to shopping in the thrift store. Anything would be better than what they were wearing. But when they got out of bed, they saw their clothes from the day before hanging on the back of the door, cleaned and pressed. It was as if little angels were working in the wings. And in many ways, they were.

The put on their fresh clothing and walked down the hallway to the kitchen area, bowing and nodding to the sisters as they passed by in silence. Father Bruno, Dante, and Gabriel were sitting at the long table with plates of sweet rolls, fruit, and scrambled eggs wrapped in soft tortillas. Juice and coffee were in insulated pitchers. The men stood and greeted their partners with hugs and kisses while Father Bruno looked on.

Light conversation about how each of them slept followed, and a recap of the morning assignments. Neither the bank nor the thrift shop opened until ten o'clock. Father Bruno suggested they attend the eight a.m. mass while they waited. Gabriel was never very religious and only went to church for the big holidays. Sylvia was much more devout. But today, Gabriel thought it was a good opportunity to show his gratitude for the shelter and support, and most importantly, their lives. Thankfully, no one had been killed or severely hurt. He reminded himself to ask Father Bruno if he could use the phone to call the hospital to check on their two employees who had been injured. With some luck, they would have been released last night. Gabriel felt guilty that the two women had suffered because of him. He should have moved when he first thought of it. Now he had to move as a matter of necessity. He sighed deeply.

Father Bruno placed his hand on Gabriel's shoulder. His experience and compassion made for a good combination in how to comfort people in distress.

"I know this is a very heavy burden for you, but if you can forgive your past, you will make better decisions in the future."

Gabriel nodded. His eyes were about to well up with tears. This had been the longest and most frightening twenty-four hours of his life.

After breakfast, they followed the priest to the small chapel at the far end of the courtyard, away from the residences. It was a sunny day; flowers were in bloom, and birds were singing. Elena smiled. The sky was clear enough to see the statue of Cristo Rey in the far distance. She thought it was a good sign and squeezed Dante's hand, nodding in the direction of the statue.

The chapel was part of the historic mission that began construction in the 1700s. It wasn't until almost another hundred years before the Spanish-style architectural structure was completed. Father Bruno led them to the first pew; then he retreated to the vestry, where he changed his clothes for the service. A young boy around eight years old lit the candles on the altar. It was serene. Peaceful. Within a few minutes, about a dozen people entered. Most were older women dressed in the classic black garb of widows, veils covering their faces.

A few minutes later, Father Bruno appeared and began the service in Latin. Gabriel hoped he wouldn't be struck by lightning. It had been a while since he'd attended mass. Sylvia knew what he was thinking, for she was thinking the same thing. She smiled and took his hand in hers.

Because of his upbringing, Dante knew every

word in the service. When he realized he was mumbling the words, he became self-conscious and stopped. Elena restrained herself from a giggle.

Dante, Elena, and Sylvia got up for communion, leaving Gabriel sticking out like a sore thumb. He bowed his head, hoping he could disappear for those few minutes. If what they said was true—that God forgave all—he would be absolved.

Another fifteen minutes passed, and the service was concluded. The altar boy assisted the priest with the incense, snuffed the candles, and disappeared behind the altar. Shortly thereafter, Father Bruno reappeared in the clothes he had been wearing earlier. The five of them left the chapel and began their appointed rounds.

Sister Bernice met up with Sylvia and Elena in the courtyard and escorted them to the thrift shop. She waved at one of the volunteers. "Eleanor, this is Sylvia and Elena. Please show them some of our special ladies' clothes, and something for a man."

"Right this way." Eleanor led them into a room in the back, where the walls were filled with racks of women's clothes. Very nice clothes; it looked like a boutique. "We are very fortunate we have wealthy donors. Many of the items have never been worn, or only worn once or twice. Their extravagance is our gain." She gave a little shrug.

The items were arranged by style and then size. "We should probably get pants." Sylvia frowned as she fondled a beautiful beaded dress.

"One day you will wear an even more beautiful dress." Elena was being her best optimistic self while picking out jeans and chino pants. A couple of plain blouses and T-shirts were next. She was struck by her next thought: *What about underwear?* "Mami?" She lowered her voice. "What about underwear? We can't keep washing out the same pair every night."

Sylvia thought about it for a moment. This was no time to be proud. "Eleanor? May I ask a big favor? I know this may seem very unusual, but if I give you cash, do you think you could walk down to Palmetto and buy us some underwear?" She almost started to laugh at the suggestion. Eleanor did a double take.

"You see, we have had some unforeseen circumstances," Sylvia explained. "Our home was destroyed, and we have to leave town in a day or so."

Eleanor's expression changed from shock to sympathy. "Oh, my. I am so sorry. Of course we can send someone. Just tell me the brand and size." She scurried to the counter and brought back a spiral notebook and a pen and took down the information. Elena gave the women the equivalent of fifty dollars. No fancy panties for either of them. After they had settled on some very casual clothes, Sylvia found two pair of pants and shirts for Gabriel. Sylvia spotted a small overnight bag. It was one of the few things in the shop that actually looked worn, but the iconic logo of Disneyland was still visible. Elena chuckled at the irony. That was certainly one place where they would *not* be going. By the time they finished a young woman came into the shop with a bag marked PALMETTO SHOPPE. Sylvia didn't think she would ever be so happy to see a shopping bag filled with underwear.

"Thank you so much," Elena said. Sylvia echoed her gratitude.

Eleanor began to put their items into a separate bag when Sylvia pulled out her wallet. "Oh, no. I cannot take your money," Eleanor insisted.

Sylvia didn't know what to say. True, they had to be prudent with their funds, but she wasn't expecting any more charity than they had already benefited from. "Please. As a donation to the church."

Eleanor wrote something on a store business card. "Here. When you get settled, you can send us a donation."

Sylvia was overcome with emotion. On so many levels. The generosity and compassion they were shown was the polar opposite of what she'd felt the day before when her family's business came under assault. The pendulum could surely swing from one extreme to another. "Thank you so very much. We will never forget the kindness everyone has shown us."

Elena wiped a tear from her face. The dream of her wedding would have to wait. For now. Getting the family away from fear and potential harm was the most important thing. And even if she and Dante got married in the chapel of the mission, that surely would be a wonderful story to tell their children and grandchildren. She became more resolute. She was going to take every positive piece of energy from this situation. And then she felt a huge weight lift off her shoulders. No longer would she think about what they had lost, but only of what they gained and what the future could hold.

They carried their new–used clothes back to

their room in the convent and laid everything out
on the bed, including the new underwear. Elena
checked her purse. She still had lipstick and lip
liner, mascara, and some blush. Not that they were
going anywhere where they would need it. It was
simply a comfort knowing they had the basics on
their person. It was a woman thing. Sylvia was
happy she had also picked out the travel tote bag.
They could carry their toiletries and underwear in
it. They would have to share one of the duffel bags
with Gabriel. They knew it was important they
travel light.

Dante pedaled his bike twenty minutes to the
former Lozano Bakery. The yellow tape was still
draped around the broken mess of a vehicle.
Wood had been placed over the shattered windows
and a sign that announced: LA POLICÍA—NO EN-
TRAR. He wondered how long that would be there
before it was painted over with graffiti. In some
way, he was happy none of the family would see the
heartbreaking remains of their legacy. He looked
around, and there were no police officers in sight.
It wasn't surprising. The police also did not want
to tangle with the known and unknown unscrupu-
lous members of the cartels. *Better to let the building
rot,* was the way the authorities would look at it.

Dante walked around the perimeter and peered
through a space between the plywood that covered
one of the windows. The concussion from the blast
had propelled the shards of glass through the
opening between the shop and the kitchen. He
thought about the two women who had suffered

minor cuts. They were very lucky. The outcome could have been much more disastrous, even fatal. He pulled on the knob of the back door but reconsidered his plan to enter. It could be too dangerous. The structure was decades old, and an explosion like the one that occurred could compromise the safety of the building. As much as he wanted to scale the staircase to the second floor, he knew he would be putting his life in peril, something the family would never be able to overcome should something horrific happen to him. No, it was best to view it from the ground. Such a sad ending to a family's hard work, passion, as well as the community they served. But there was nothing left for anyone to do, at least not in the foreseeable future.

Dante got back on his bicycle and pedaled into the small village. He had to make one very important stop before he returned to the mission.

Around noon, Elena and Sylvia walked to Father Bruno's office, where they met up with Dante and Gabriel. "Mission accomplished. All of them," Gabriel said as he handed the bag of products to Sylvia. She peered inside. It contained everything on her list. "And we closed out the bank account. There was three thousand dollars in it, and another five thousand dollars in the safe deposit box. Father Bruno was right—no one approached us or looked at us sideways."

"I don't believe there is a manhunt out for any of you, but you don't know who put the bomb in the van. Therefore, you don't know who to be leery of. I am happy we were able to get it done quickly," Father Bruno said.

"That gives us about eight thousand dollars. Will that be enough to get us to Mexico and then on to America?" Sylvia asked pointedly.

"Plus the two thousand dollars that was in the strongbox from the store," Elena added.

"It will give you safe passage to the borders, but I cannot guarantee anything further. Too often, the border guards are crooked and expect financial compensation. And yes, it is illegal. However . . ." Father Bruno's voice trailed off as Dante broke into the conversation.

"I have about five thousand dollars. That's fifteen thousand between the four of us. That should get us to safety—don't you agree, Father?"

"It should." The priest nodded. Unbeknownst to all—including the Vatican—Father Bruno and his band of sisters had done this over a dozen times, assisting families to safety. It was his own underground railroad to help people escape from the narco-terrorists. He had to keep it on the down-low so as not to inflame Escobar, his rivals, and of course, the church.

Dante gave a brief report on the bakery. "It is cordoned off with police tape, and the windows have been boarded up."

"There is this." Gabriel pulled out the deed for the property. Silence fell across the room. There was no way they could sell the building or the land without someone finding out. Perhaps someone tied to the cartels. Gabriel handed the deed to Father Bruno. "Father, Sylvia and I spoke about this.

The insurance company will not pay for damages. Bombs are not included in their coverage. And we don't know where we will go or what we will do. Therefore, we are turning over the property to you and the church. Maybe you can convert it into housing for underprivileged children. No matter what, I know you will use it for good things."

Father Bruno was struck by Gabriel's generosity, especially given the sentimental value of the gift. "But this belonged to your family for decades."

"And now, the time has come for us to leave it behind, in your capable hands," Sylvia reassured him as she choked back her tears. The magnitude of what had happened and the unknown future ahead made her feel as if the bottom of her world had fallen away. Gabriel took her hand and kissed the back of it.

The Espinosas were returning the favor they had been so graciously given. Another moment of silence fell across the room, but it was more of a pause of acceptance than of defeat.

Father Bruno continued to go over the details of the journey. He explained that Sister Bernice would drive them to Buenaventura, where they would meet the boat captain. They would pay him 4,000 dollars. Once they arrived in Puerto Vallarta, he would give them an address where they could stay for no more than two days. The family would bring them to the bus station, where they could continue to the US or find work and lodging in the area. The underground had a few connections, so they would not be completely abandoned. They wouldn't be coddled, either. They surely wouldn't be looked after like they had been at the convent.

Instead of eating in the kitchen, Sister Margaret Mary brought in a platter of arepas covered in shredded beef and cheese. They ate quietly while pondering their next moves.

Sylvia was the first to speak. "Do you think we could find work in Mexico?"

"It is quite possible, especially with your experience at the bakery. I will include a letter of recommendation with the other documents." Muffled *thank you*s were offered between bites.

"The boat will set sail first thing in the morning," Father Bruno continued.

Elena wiped her mouth. "Will it stop during the night?"

"No. They don't anchor unless it's an emergency. They want to get to Puerto Vallarta as quickly as possible. Much of their freight is perishable."

"And smelly." Dante laughed. Everyone stopped eating. "What?" he asked quizzically. "It's a fishing boat. Not a pleasure cruise."

"And that is why you will find Dramamine in my duffel bag," Gabriel said with a grin.

Sylvia's coffee almost came up out of her nose. "Please stop about fish and being seasick. You're making me queasy already."

The energy in the room was a mix of excitement and apprehension. They were on the verge of delirium. Gabriel then spoke again, holding up several boxes of Dramamine. "I bought enough for all of us. Do you want to take it now?" He teased.

"I would suggest you take it before you get on the boat. It takes a little time to get into your system, and you want to take it *before* you get nauseous," Father Bruno offered. "It will take about three hours to get to the boat. We should get there by five o'clock so you can get settled before you ship out. It can be a little chaotic the night before a trip."

Sylvia was feeling queasy again and let out a big sigh. "*Ay caramba!* Maybe I should take that pill now!"

"You can take it when you get on the boat. It will be docked until just before sunset. That is plenty of time for it to take effect," Gabriel recommended.

Dante snickered. "One time I was going on a deep-sea fishing trip. We were moored at the dock and having soup. I didn't feel anything at the time, but when I looked down at my bowl, the soup was swishing slowly from side to side." He stopped abruptly before he finished his story.

All eyes turned to him. "And then what happened?" Elena pressed.

"I turned green and had to leave the boat," Dante answered sheepishly.

"Oh, this is going to be even worse than I imagined." Sylvia hung her head.

"Let's look on the bright side. Maybe we will all learn to fish," Gabriel said lightheartedly.

"I am not touching any kind of bait. Not even if you beg me," Sylvia joked back.

Father Bruno held up his hand. "There will be no baiting lines or fishing for any of you. The less you are seen, the better. It would be preferable if you weren't seen at all."

"Like stowaways?" Elena gasped.

"More or less. You don't want to have any inter-action with the crew except for polite salutations. No conversations. If anyone asks, say you missed the cruise ship and you are hitching a ride."

"Is that believable?" Sylvia asked.

"Not particularly—therefore, the less said the better," Father Bruno warned. Everyone nodded, indicating their understanding. "The captain will give you instructions. He knows his crew very well. He wouldn't use them if he didn't trust them, but as the old saying goes, 'loose lips sink ships.' "

"We must start getting ready, but before we do that, I think there is one very important service we must participate in." Father Bruno had a slight gleam in his eyes. "Follow me." Everyone shrugged and joined him as he walked outside toward the chapel. Gabriel didn't think he could enter the church again without something falling on his head.

When they entered the chapel, the first two rows were filled with the nuns. There were bundles of flowers hanging on the edge of the pews. Three sisters sat to the right of the altar. Two held violins and the other, a cello. They began to play Pachel-bel's Canon in D Major. Sister Margaret Mary walked up to Elena and handed her a beautiful bouquet of flowers. Elena was bewildered. She turned to her parents and then to Father Bruno. He nodded and gave her the brightest smile. Gabriel put his arm through hers and walked her down the aisle as Dante escorted Sylvia. It has been long known the groom was not to see the bride before the ceremony, but this was truly a time for exceptions. Father Bruno led the procession as the nuns stood and turned toward the bride-to-be, each beaming with joy.

Elena leaned in and whispered to her father, "Papá, did you know about this?"

He squeezed her arm. "Of course. I know it's not what you hoped for, but it is your marriage that is important. Not the wedding." She squeezed back. "Father Bruno thought it would be easier for you to travel as husband and wife, and your mother and I agreed. I hope you are not angry or disappointed that we did this without consulting you."

Elena kept smiling at the nuns as her father continued. "This is a wonderful surprise." She meant every word of it. For the past two days, she had been anxious, upset, disappointed, angry, and distraught, not in any particular order. This beautiful ceremony set all of those emotions aside. At this moment, she was ecstatic, knowing she would be married to the man she loved that very day. The party could come later, once they got through this nightmare. There would be even more reason to celebrate.

Father Bruno took his place inside the sanctuary and began the ceremony for marriage. The light filtering through the stained glass, the music, and the smell of the fresh-cut flowers was intoxicating. Magical. It was more than Elena had hoped or planned for. When it came to exchanging rings, Elena was at a loss until her mother handed her the ring her mother's father had worn. Ever since his passing, Sylvia wore it on a chain around her neck. Now she was able to pass it along to her daughter, who would place it on Dante's finger. It had always been her intention to hand it down to Elena, but there hadn't been time to have it sized. She secretly prayed it would fit. Elena giggled as she shoved the ring over Dante's knuckle. Once she got it on, she knew it was never coming off.

Next it was Dante's turn. Everyone knew he was going to buy a wedding band on his way back from the bakery. Everyone but Elena. Even though he knew her size, the small jewelry store didn't have anything suitable. He wasn't going to buy something cheap, so he settled on a diamond band two sizes bigger than he wanted. He shuffled it from one of Elena's fingers to another; the only way it would stay in place was on her thumb. This brought several snickers from the onlookers, but it did not damper Elena's mood. She would wear that ring on her thumb forever. Someday they would buy one that fit. True, nothing had gone as planned, including the ring, but it would be another story to tell their children and grandchildren.

After Father Bruno pronounced them husband and wife, the spectators applauded and shouted with joy. One of the sisters gave a wild whistle. Elena's entire family was surprised at the raucous behavior from the women who had been so quiet since their arrival. The procession retreated to the entrance to the chapel as the nuns followed, throwing flower petals at them. In spite of how they got there, Elena, Dante, Sylvia, and Gabriel could not be happier at that moment.

There were hugs and well wishes as the couple dodged more flower petals and the group dispersed. Elena was overcome with emotion. Sylvia wasn't far behind. Even Gabriel had to stifle some sniffs. Dante was the only one who took it all in stride. Because of the life he had led, he knew the only way to get through the day was to move ahead with whatever was placed in your path—or taken away.

Father Bruno gently reminded them they had a boat to catch. Everyone retreated to their quarters to prepare for their voyage. Sylvia packed all the clothes she had gotten at the thrift shop into the duffel bag Dante gave her at lunch. Elena was in charge of the toiletries, as she placed what little they were able to carry into the tote. The duffel was heavier than she thought it would be, and she almost fell over when she lifted it from the chair. Elena caught her before she stumbled. "Easy there, Mami." She giggled. "We're not on the boat yet." Sister Margaret Mary appeared out of nowhere with a dolly. Elena and Sylvia looked at each other. Elena mouthed the words "How do they do that?" They remained mystified by the timely and magical arrival of food, clean clothes, and now a dolly. Sylvia shrugged.

The sisters lined up in the hallway to bid them farewell. Lots of bows and handshakes were offered. Sister Margaret Mary and Sister Bernice escorted them out to the parking area. Gabriel was already there waiting, wearing the same but cleaned clothes from when he first arrived. Gabriel heaved the duffel bag into the van, followed by the Disneyland tote. The irony of the cheerful tote bag wasn't lost on anyone.

* * *

Dante looked around his small studio one last time. Earlier, he'd given Sylvia the extra duffel bag, and now he had to decide which of his modest possessions he would bring with him. The things that meant the most were his books, but they would be too heavy and cumbersome. So he settled on four of his favorite novels, which he could read on their way to Mexico: *The Sound and the Fury* by William Faulkner, *East of Eden* by John Steinbeck, *The Accidental Tourist* by Anne Tyler, and his favorite Agatha Christie, *The Murder at the Vicarage*. The title had initially sparked his curiosity. *Who would commit a murder at a church?* All were in English so, if nothing else, the trip would be a linguistic lesson. He took another last look at his collection of books and chuckled to himself. *Moby-Dick* and *The Old Man and the Sea* would not be a good idea. Sister Margaret Mary would find good use for what he left behind.

As he rolled up a pair of slacks, he noticed the ring on his left hand. He was a married man now. This journey and all that followed would test his mettle and how strong of a man he was. He tossed in his toiletries and two photos. One was from the orphanage, the day he left for Cali. The other was of him and Father Bruno with Mother Superior. He sighed. Perhaps, one day, he would return.

Dante strode through the courtyard one last time. He could have cut through the building but wanted to see the landscape of the place where he would often read. He smiled. "*Hasta luego,*" he said to the trees and the glorious flowers.

Dante approached the van where the others were standing. He put his bag in the back and shut the doors.

Gabriel turned to Father Bruno and handed the priest the keys to his truck and Elena's car. "The registrations are in the glove boxes."

Father Bruno hugged Gabriel. "This will help so much with the food drives."

"It's the least we can do," Gabriel replied.

"But you already gave me the deed to the property," Father Bruno reminded him.

"I wanted to move a while ago. This was God or something greater than me, forcing me to do it. You were here to help us." Gabriel sighed. "I can never thank you enough."

Father Bruno reached into his pocket and produced several envelopes. "These are letters asking for asylum. One for each of you." Then he turned to Dante. "And your marriage certificate." Father Bruno said one last prayer before they took their seats. "I also pray Sister Bernice won't put the pedal to the metal too much!"

"We should let the newlyweds sit together," Gabriel teased as Sylvia and Elena scrambled into the back.

Dante turned to him. "If anyone is looking for you, it's best you are in the back. Besides, I'll be able to slam on the brake if Sister Bernice tries to test the speed limit." Everyone buckled themselves in as they began the long journey into the unknown. The group waved and shouted *"Vaya con Dios!"* as Sister Bernice revved the engine.

"Disneyland, here we come!" Elena chortled. "Or not!"

# Chapter Six

# The Voyage/Honeymoon

*Buenaventura to Puerto Vallarta*

**D**ante could understand why Father Bruno had said a prayer for Sister Bernice. She drove like Mario Andretti, whipping around turns like a professional race car driver. Several times, Sylvia clung to Gabriel's shirtsleeve. Lots of eye-rolling and breath-holding was happening in the very long three-hour drive. Sister Bernice finally screeched into a parking spot across from the dock. The pungent smell of fish hit them all in the face as soon as they opened the car doors. It was a precursor of what was to come. And everyone knew it. Sylvia thought she should take the Dramamine at that very moment. The stench was enough to make you woozy. There was a lot of shouting but not in a threatening way. It was fishmongers calling out to sell their load. Air horns clamored, signaling a boat was leaving the harbor. It was an unmelodious sound native to a boating and fishing community.

"Wait here," Sister Bernice instructed.

"You won't get an argument from me," Sylvia replied.

"Me either," Elena echoed.

Gabriel grunted, anticipating the seafaring adventure they were about to embark on. He patted Dante on the shoulder. "Ready for some soup?" he joked.

"I think I'm past that stage." Dante laughed. "But I will take one of those pills if you don't mind." He held out his hand over the back seat.

Gabriel shook the box as if it were filled with candy treats. Sylvia yanked it out of his hands. "I think I should be in charge of those." Gabriel let go without an argument.

Elena had been unusually quiet during the drive. "Are you okay, *mi princesa*?" Dante asked.

"Yes. Just very nervous." Elena grabbed his hand. "This has been a very big day. It's a lot to comprehend. Yesterday I was planning a wedding, then we spent the night in a convent, and today we got married."

"Yes, we did." Dante was smiling from ear to ear. "Although this wasn't the honeymoon I had in mind."

*Honeymoon.* The word hung in the air. The night before, everyone assumed the men would sleep in

one cabin and the women in another. Dante was
the first to speak. "Elena, what do you want to do?"
Elena and Dante had not slept together, and this
would be their first night together. On a fishing
boat, no less. For their honeymoon, Elena and
Dante had originally discussed going to Cartagena
and getting a cabana on the beach. Now they were
going to be sleeping in an old, stinky boat with
equally stinky fishermen hanging about.

"*This* is my honeymoon. I will sleep with my husband. If I get sick, he will have to take care of me.
He promised that today." She broke out in a huge
grin that belied how nervous she was. She wasn't a
virgin, but she wasn't very experienced, either. She
had only bedded down a couple of times with her
ex-boyfriend, and it had been most unpleasant.
She laughed to herself. *It couldn't be much worse.*

Sister Bernice returned with a very scruffy-looking
man who turned out to be the boat's captain. "Salty
Dog" would be an apt description. He wore water-
proof overalls, a checkered shirt, and rubber shoes.
His beard would rival Santa Claus's, and his hair
was like barbwire poking out from under his hat.
He approached the passenger side of the vehicle
and spoke in Spanish. He explained there would
be eighteen deck hands on the ninety-eight-foot
vessel. Sleeping compartments were below deck.
He counted the heads in the van. He went on to
tell them that the four of them would have to
share a compartment with two sets of bunk beds.
Translation: the four of them would be sleeping in
the same very small space. Sylvia thought she was
going to vomit. Captain Gutteria resumed, giving
them the rundown as to what they could expect

over the next four days. The boat would leave the
dock before sunset; the crew would fish all night
and all day. At the end of the catch, they would
weigh the fish and then put them on ice. The
fishermen slept about two to three hours per day
depending on how well the fish were biting.

He continued to tell them at no time were they
to interact with the crew. They were not even to acknowledge them, and the crew would do the same.
Ignore one another. The less everyone knew, the
better. That way, should an issue with the Coast
Guard or other authorities ever arise, the crew could
say they had no information. And that would be
the truth.

Sylvia shuddered at the thought of marine police or the Coast Guard. Gabriel was aware that his
wife was not taking this information well. Granted,
they knew they weren't going on a cruise, but this
was as primitive and rugged as it got. The captain
also instructed them to remain in their cabin except to use the head. Someone would have to be
on the lookout that no one else was in there. Meals
would be delivered to their door.

The more Captain Gutteria explained the details, the dizzier Sylvia became. Everything was in
slow motion. Gabriel put his arm around her. She
was getting clammy. Sister Bernice motioned to
Dante to open a thermos of water. He poured
some on a handkerchief and handed it to Gabriel
along with the thermos. Gabriel placed the handkerchief on Sylvia's forehead and gave her a sip of
water. The boat captain made a face, laughed, and
muttered something only Sister Bernice could

hear. But Gabriel had a rough idea of what he said. He passed the thermos around so everyone could take their Dramamine. It would take about an hour for the effects to kick in. He hoped he'd bought enough. This was going to be the longest four days of their lives.

Dante got out of the van and helped Elena through the sliding doors. Gabriel asked Sylvia if she was alright to stand. She nodded with trepidation. They said their goodbyes to Sister Bernice, grabbed their few pieces of luggage—if that's what you could call it—and followed the old Salty Dog to where the boat was docked.

The gangway was made of wood. Very old wood. It was basically a ramp with rope that served as handrails. Sylvia fought back hysterics. She felt as if she were marching toward death. Gabriel held onto her as tightly as possible as the four of them ducked the beams and nets and sidestepped the large wooden boxes filled with ice and the rest of the rigs. They came to a narrow ladder that led below deck. Sylvia took one last look at the shore. She thought it might be her last.

The passageway to the sleeping quarters was narrow at best. It could only accommodate one person facing forward at a time. Should you come upon another person in the skinny passageway, you had to turn sideways and hope you didn't rub any of your body parts against any of theirs. The captain opened one of the folding doors and nodded for them to enter the space. It wasn't much bigger than a closet. Four pull-down bunk beds faced each other with stowaway compartments above, barely large enough to accommodate their duffel bags. Once the beds were pulled down, there was little room to move about. Four days living like this could possibly drive anyone mad. *No wonder the fishermen only slept two to three hours per day*, thought Sylvia. Claustrophobia was not a condition you would want under those circumstances. Just four walls with a sliver of a window. It could have been a jail cell.

Dante was the first to enter. He pulled down one of the bunk beds farthest from the door, giving Sylvia and Elena a place to sit. If he pulled down the bed on the opposite wall, they wouldn't be able to sit and face each other without smacking into each other's knees. "We should probably leave the middle beds stowed so we have room to turn around."

A hush fell over the tight quarters. "Maybe I can just sleep through this," Sylvia said.

"Me too, Mami," Elena broke in.

Dante was trying his best to keep everyone from having a meltdown. He set his duffel bag down on the floor. "I brought a few books for us. I don't know if you've read any of them, but they are classics, except for the Agatha Christie, although I think it's a classic mystery. I thought it would help pass the time." He laid them out on the cot-like bunk. "I know our worlds have been turned upside down, but we have to keep thinking, hoping, and praying that we are on the road—I mean the sea—to better lives." Dante was pulling out all the stops.

Gabriel had been quietly observing. He knew his wife wouldn't be able to pull it together until they were in Mexico. Elena might be able to steel her way through, provided it was calm waters. One thing he was sure of—Dante was a stand-up guy. A person who didn't falter under pressure. Gabriel was thankful Dante was making the journey with them. If it hadn't been for Dante, Gabriel would have felt the sole burden of keeping his wife and daughter safe.

Sylvia changed the subject abruptly. "How many of those pills can I take?" she asked half-jokingly.

"Uh-uh. I don't want you falling all over me," Gabriel said. "At least not in front of the children!" That got a big laugh.

Elena rested her elbow on her knee and placed her chin on her fist. "What do you think they'll serve us for dinner?" She bit her lip, stifling a grin.

"Fish!" Sylvia and Gabriel answered in unison. More laugher resounded. They were truly on the verge of delirium.

"Oh, look. We have a little window," Elena pointed out.

"It's called a *port*, like porthole," Dante informed her.

"Well, it's a teensy-weensy port." Sylvia was starting to feel the effects of the Dramamine and began to relax. A little. She was trying to resign herself to the situation. There was nothing she could do now except wait out the next few days until they got back on terra firma, where she could start a new nervous breakdown.

A loud knock at the door caused everyone to flinch. "*Comida*," announced a male voice from the other side of the door. They heard a tray rattle and footsteps moving in the opposite direction.

Dante pulled open the bifold door. He peered down the passageway and then to the floor, where a tray sat holding four bowls of some kind of stew. He leaned down, picked up the tray, and brought it in. There was a small pull-down table that could fit two people, just big enough for the tray of food. "It surely doesn't look like *your* cooking, *suegra*." Dante smiled at his first use of "mother-in-law."

Sylvia gave him a sideways look. "Thank you, but I don't think I like that name. Maybe La Ley." Everyone snickered.

"Oh, do not tease me. It means 'the law,' and I am the mother-in-*law*, no?"

"That is for certain," Gabriel answered with a bit of a smirk.

"So it is. La Ley." Dante nodded then turned to Gabriel. "And you, sir?"

"You can call me *suegro*," Gabriel replied.

"And do I have a nickname?" Elena batted her eyes at her husband.

"*Querida*," Dante said warmly.

"Okay. Let's see what we have here." Gabriel shuffled over to the tray. It didn't smell terrible, but it surely didn't smell like home. "Dante, I think you should try it first. Not that we have much of a choice, but at least we will be prepared."

Dante took one of the bowls and a metal spoon and gave the stew a taste. "It isn't terrible."

"Oh, that is quite the endorsement," Elena joked.

"But we were correct. It is fish stew," Dante added as he passed everyone a bowl, a spoon, and a brown paper towel.

Sylvia took a bite. She shrugged and tossed her head from side to side. "And you were also correct, Dante. It is nothing like my cooking. And it's not terrible." She paused with her spoon midair. "As long as I don't know what's in it."

Elena was much slower to touch her lips to the spoon as she eyed everyone's reaction. Gabriel looked at his daughter. "It is fish stew, *mi hija.*"

"I'm certain it's the only thing on the menu," Sylvia added, and everyone agreed heartily, at the same time dreading the next four days.

When they finished, Dante piled the bowls on the tray and left it outside their quarters. No one was in sight in the passageway. By the sound of the noise from above, everyone was on deck, preparing for the trip.

Dante then motioned toward the small porthole window. "The sun is going down. We'll probably be leaving shortly." As predicted, three blasts of a loud horn signaled a boat was about to leave the dock. "This might be a good time to use the head."

Elena was the first to jump up. "Oh, I am so glad. I thought my bladder was going to burst." Elena grabbed the tote bag that contained their toothpaste and toothbrushes. Sylvia was right behind her. "Me as well."

"Do you think there is a shower?" Elena asked innocently. It was the first time it had occurred to her.

"I suppose we are about to find out." Sylvia had seemed to regain her poise. A relaxed poise.

Gabriel decided to wait until his wife and daughter returned. No sense in clogging up the passageway. He heard footsteps coming from the hatch that led to the deck above. He immediately closed the door and hoped his family wouldn't encounter anyone. He listened carefully. The footsteps retreated back from where they came. This was indeed going to be the longest four days of their lives.

# Chapter Seven

# Terra Firma

*Almost There*

The water had been calm. Calmer than expected. The first night, the boat headed west, which allowed for a longer sunset than being on land. It was as if they were following the sun. The family took turns peeping out the small port to get a glimpse of the spectacular colors against the darkening sea.

"At least it's pretty," Sylvia said.

Dante checked his watch. It was almost nine p.m. The noise from the deck was relentless. Probably another reason why the sailors only usually slept two to three hours per day.

The evening hours passed as they talked about what they thought would be waiting for them once they left the boat. Gabriel and Sylvia had traveled to Mexico when they were first married, but once they took over the bakery, there was little time for lengthy vacations. The language was similar and the culture varied, but still familiar. They could assimilate easily enough. But there was the big question of attempting to get into the United States. Would they dare try?

They ruminated over how Father Bruno was able to negotiate their passage with lightning speed. Dante said he was relatively certain the people at the other side of this sojourn would be properly equipped to help find them housing.

Not knowing what was ahead of them, they debated whether it would be a good idea to stay in Puerto Vallarta for a few months instead of hurrying to the US border. They needed to have a solid plan and not rush things. Once they were in Mexico, they were far out of the reach of any two-bit hoodlums from Colombia. Whoever planted the bomb must have been a low-level soldier of the cartels, and even if Gabriel had been an unsuspecting mule, he hadn't been dealing with major hauls of cocaine. Even if the guards had been planting packages in the wheel well of the company van, it could not have been in quantities that would merit an all-out war. It could have been one of the guards doing a little local drug dealing on the side—not any kind of international distribution. Nonetheless, someone was pissed, and they had taken out their anger on the Lozano Bakery.

They continued to plot ideas. First, they would look for a place where the four of them could live on a month-by-month basis. Anything would be better than the accommodations they were in at that moment. Next would be getting jobs. Even though they had enough money to get them through a couple of months, they didn't want to just depend on what they had. Gabriel decided he would look for a job driving a truck. Maybe local deliveries. Sylvia would try to get work at a bakery. It was fortunate all of them spoke English. Elena and Dante were particularly fluent. Puerto Vallarta was a big tourist town that could benefit from Elena's and Dante's bilingual skills. They would check the local hotels once they got the lay of the land. Both could easily work a front desk.

Before they left Cali, Dante had asked Sister Bernice to post a letter for him. It was to his future employer, stating that due to a family emergency, he would have to take a leave of absence. He apologized profusely and said he hoped they would take him back once things were settled. He used the convent as his return address. He knew Father Bruno would keep his mail safe until they settled somewhere. Dante trusted Father Bruno would be in touch using whatever means possible. In the meantime, he would focus on getting a job, making some money, and figuring out what their next move would be. Working at a hotel wouldn't be the worst thing. Certainly not worse than being part of the cargo on a fishing boat.

With such little room to move, and amenities sorely lacking, it was surprising no one had lost their temper or become hysterical. Gabriel credited the Dramamine. But by the third day, everyone was getting a bit stir crazy. Sylvia had spent most of the trip lying prone on the bed, dozing on and off. At first, she tried to read, but focusing was difficult with the boat moving up and down. She tried to get in rhythm with it, but being flat on her back seemed to work the best.

Elena was engrossed in the Anne Tyler novel about a travel writer who becomes withdrawn from life, miserable, and grief-stricken. But ultimately it was a love story that underscored the magic and mystery of life. Elena thought it was a good omen she chose to read that particular book.

Gabriel was working his way through the Faulkner, constantly asking Dante what certain words meant. Dante was almost at the point where he wanted to rip it from Gabriel's hands and read it out loud. But that would be tedious and quickly get on everyone's one last nerve. As much as he had maintained his serenity and dignity, Dante admitted to himself he was losing it. *I should have insisted he read the Agatha Christie*, he thought. He kept telling himself this part of the trek would soon be over. *Please, God.*

On the third day, there came a knock on the door that signaled the arrival of the catch of the day. Included was a note with instructions, which Dante read aloud to everyone. The first sentence ordered them to leave the boat at sunrise. The second was an address.

*The answer to my prayers*, Dante thought. *At least one of them.*

"Sunrise? Tomorrow? You mean we will be there in the morning?" Sylvia's face brightened. She was almost giddy.

"Yes, La Ley." Dante heaved a sigh of relief. He slithered over to Elena, who looked up from her book. "*Querida.* We are almost there." He placed his arm around her, nearly knocking her in the head. The smooth dance teacher lost his balance and tumbled off the small bed. Legs and arms were poking in different directions. It was comical. Everyone laughed in surprise at Dante's awkwardness. And then they laughed with relief. It was a laughter that came from deep down inside themselves.

Gabriel let out a grunt of sorts. "*Dios mío!*"

They finished their last chow down and placed the tray outside. Not that they had a lot to pack, but they were overjoyed to undertake the small ritual. Funny how putting your toothbrush in a tote bag could bring such glee.

Elena looked at her clothes. "Which dirty pair of pants should I wear?" she joked. It wasn't as if she had done anything for the past three days except get creases in them.

Sylvia regained the color in her cheeks. A better color. She went from pale chartreuse to a light blush. Gabriel squeezed through the cabin. "*Mi amor*, I am so happy to see you smile." He held her chin in his hand and kissed her on the tip of her nose.

"Ay. Who are the newlyweds here?" Elena teased. Dante was still crumbled between the beds and grappled his way up to a sitting position next to her. She turned to face him as he planted a big smacker on her lips, making a loud *mwah.*

Part of the cloud that had been hanging over their heads was beginning to part and show signs of a brighter future for them all.

They could barely sleep. The anticipation of

getting off that nasty-smelling vessel and being able to stretch their arms without fear of smacking each other or hitting the wall was coursing through their veins. No one noticed the seas had gotten rougher as they headed northeast. They were riding the waves with delight.

Eventually, everyone nodded off at one point or another, but as soon as a sliver of light came through the tiny port, they were up. Dante peered down the passageway to see if anyone was near the head. He could hear voices coming from the deck above. From what he could make out, the crew was pulling the boat into the pier, preparing to dock. "We should use the facilities, pronto." He waved Elena and Sylvia to follow him.

The three scurried out into the hallway. The women entered the head while Dante stood guard. As soon as they exited, they hurried back toward their minuscule accommodations and sent Gabriel in their place. A few minutes later, both men returned when there was a knock on the door.

"*Apúrate!*" A familiar deep voice commanded them to hurry up.

They grabbed what little belongings they had, darted out the door, down the passageway, up through the hatch, and across a slippery deck, once again carefully sidestepping ropes and gear. Dante must have checked and rechecked his pocket a half dozen times, making sure the paper with the address was still on him. The night before, he had written it down on three other slips of paper and handed a copy to each of them. The conversation went like this:

"Just in case," Dante had said.

"In case of what?" Sylvia asked blankly.

"Better to be prepared. If, for any reason, we get split up, we will know where we are supposed to go," Dante explained.

"Oh, I don't intend to let go of your hand," Elena said.

"I am not going to let go of your belt." Sylvia tugged at Gabriel's waist.

Now, when they reached the gangway, Dante moved down the wooden plank, Elena close behind. Gabriel followed with Sylvia in tow.

As soon as their feet touched the solid surface of the dock, they cheered. Then they stopped abruptly. They didn't want to bring attention to themselves. "Come." Dante nodded toward the street as he hauled two duffel bags. Gabriel had another, Sylvia had her tote, and Elena clung to her Disneyland bag.

The sidewalk was brimming with street merchants and fishmongers. It appeared to be a marketplace for local restaurants and hotels.

Sylvia noted the smell wasn't any better than the boat.

"Mami, I think you have too much fish stink in your nostrils," she hooted.

They walked several blocks before they were able to find a taxi. All of them managed to clean up their act as best they could so they wouldn't look like refugees. Even if they were.

Both Dante and Gabriel had managed to shave most of their facial hair while still on the boat. Elena had pulled her hair into a ponytail, and Sylvia used a few clips to shape her wavy hair into something presentable. With the exception of their odd luggage, they could pass for tourists—a little crumpled, but not completely disheveled. The only other giveaway was their gait. Being on the water for over three days gave them sea legs, as their bodies had adjusted to the constant motion of the ship. Now they had to readjust to solid ground. It didn't take more than a few minutes for Gabriel and Dante, but Sylvia and Elena were staggering a bit longer, causing the two men to snicker. They locked arms and happily moved ahead.

The sounds of the streets reminded them of home. Even at this early hour, people were shouting to each other, car horns were blaring, some street musicians were playing, and a few vendors were selling empanadas, sodas, and street corn. The smells filled the air, bringing Sylvia's olfactory senses back to something more enjoyable. "Ah, this is much better than fish." She smiled and nodded to the young man strumming a guitar. She elbowed Gabriel. "Please do not ask me to make fish ever again."

Dante spotted two taxis sitting at the next corner. One driver was smoking a cigarette and talking to another driver in the car across the street. It was more like shouting but in a friendly way, debating what kind of day was ahead.

Dante approached one of the cabs, wondering if an argument between the drivers would ensue. But here they had rules. Unwritten rules. If a customer flagged you down, another driver would not try to steal your ride. Not like in other cities.

Dante handed the cabbie the slip of paper with the address. The driver nodded for them to get in while he placed their bags in the trunk. They were nervous and excited, thrilled they were off that wreck of a sailing vessel. Tears started rolling down Sylvia's face.

"What is it?" Gabriel turned to face her.

"Everything." She burst into tears.

The driver looked up into the rearview mirror with a bit of alarm. Gabriel gave him an offhand explanation about them relocating without revealing the details. She was homesick.

Elena whispered in her mother's ear, "Better than being seasick."

Sylvia snorted and wiped her face. "You always make me laugh." She patted her daughter's hand.

Elena gave her a peck on the cheek.

# Chapter Eight
# The Refuge

The ride in the taxi took less than fifteen minutes. They pulled in front of a stucco house in a modest middle-class neighborhood. The house had typical Mexican architecture with white walls and a terra-cotta roof. Baskets of ferns hung from the eaves. The front yard was well manicured, with many tropical plants surrounded by a low concrete and stucco wall with a gate. A much taller wall enclosed the rear yard, giving the house ample privacy in an area where neighbors were close together.

Dante paid the driver and helped him retrieve the bags from the trunk. The four of them stood in front of the gate when a woman in her early fifties opened the front door. She had a big smile that matched her broad physique; an apron was tied around her waist.

She shuffled across the patio and the sidewalk, waving them in. *"Bienvenida! Me llamo Yolanda."*

Gabriel introduced everyone as Yolanda ushered them inside. She showed them to a room in the back of the house. It had four twin beds. She apologized and explained she usually got families with children. However, no one cared at this point. Clean sheets, a shower, and solid ground was enough for now.

Elena poked Dante in the ribs. "Our honeymoon suite. Mami? Papá? Where will you be sleeping?" Everyone chuckled. It would be another few days before Elena and Dante would be alone together.

Something coming from the kitchen smelled delicious. Sylvia asked their hostess what she was making. "Birria." *Stew—as long as it's not fish*, Sylvia prayed.

Yolanda showed them where the bathroom was and gave them towels and washcloths. Sylvia could only imagine the stink coming off of them after being stowed away on a fishing boat. Sylvia apologized profusely, and Yolanda just pointed to the shower and grinned.

The women had first dibs on the amenities. Sylvia suggested the men sit on the back patio as to alleviate the aroma. Their clothes were permeated with the smell of fish. Even the clothes in their bags were odoriferous.

Yolanda brought a large plastic laundry bin into the bedroom and instructed everyone to put all of their clothes inside. She handed each of them a well-worn but clean bathrobe. Compared to where they had spent the last few days, it was like being at a spa.

Sylvia was the first in the shower. She cooed with delight as the warm water flowed over her. She shampooed her hair for the first time in almost a week. She could have spent an hour under the faucet but knew there was a finite amount of hot water. She dried herself, wrapped her hair in a towel, donned the robe, and made way for Elena. Elena also uttered sounds of utmost delight as she swayed back and forth, lathering her tired body, not once but twice. She put soap suds on her fingertips and massaged her nostrils, erasing the scent of the sea. She could hear her father making noises through the bathroom window. He was pacing on the back patio, encouraging her to hurry up. It was more of a tease than a command.

Elena and Sylvia sat down on two of the beds while Gabriel took his turn in the shower. "Don't take too long, Papá. Leave some hot water for Dante!" Elena said.

It took less than half an hour for all of them to clean up. Elena pulled a comb through her long hair. She didn't suppose Yolanda would have a blow-dryer, but before she could finish that thought, Yolanda brought one into the bedroom and set it on the dresser, telling them not to run the fan and the blow-dryer at the same time. Elena leaned in closer to her mother and whispered, "Do you suppose she was trained by one of those magical nuns?" Sylvia hooted. It seemed as if someone were watching over them, delivering what they needed, when they needed it. They expressed their gratitude. Again. Yolanda told them their clothes would be ready in a little over an hour. In the meantime, they could have something to eat. Dante and Gabriel were not exactly thrilled to traipse around in bathrobes, but they could not say no to their hostess.

The four meandered into the kitchen, where pots were brimming with delectable food. Sylvia walked over to the stove where the birria was simmering. Yolanda explained it was made with lamb boiled in a spicy sauce with cumin, ginger, oregano, and served with lime and tortillas. She would serve it to her grandson for lunch today and to her husband tomorrow. But now she would make them huevos rancheros, soft tortillas topped with salsa fresca, fried eggs, and served with fried potatoes, avocado, and refried beans. It was a hearty breakfast, indeed. And much more delicious than the powdered eggs they had every morning on the boat. At least that's what they had told themselves they were eating. After the first day on the boat, everything tasted like fish.

Yolanda handed plates, flatware, and napkins to Gabriel and instructed him to set the table on the back patio. It faced a well-kept vegetable garden with a row of herbs. The yard was surrounded by a six-foot-high wall of stucco and terra-cotta. The space was quaint, luscious, and private. Gabriel kept fidgeting with his robe. He was not accustomed to being half-naked in front of anyone other than his wife.

Yolanda could sense his discomfort and disappeared to another section of the house. She returned with two pairs of her husband's pants. One for Gabriel, one for Dante. They could keep the robes on until their shirts were dry.

Again, the magical appearance of something needed. Sylvia and Elena raised their eyebrows. Gabriel looked at both of them. "What is it?"

"Nothing, Papá." Elena didn't want to discuss the mysteries of the universe at that moment. She simply wanted to enjoy it. Elena and Sylvia were less concerned about their clothing at that second. They let Yolanda know they were fine with the massive robes. They were big enough to fit two people at once and were secured with an inner tie and a large belt on the outside. It actually felt good to be in simple fabric.

Gabriel and Dante went into the bedroom and put on the pants. Evidently, the robes were not the only extra-large items in the wardrobe. Gabriel wondered out loud how big Yolanda's husband must be, based on the size of the pants. In just a few minutes, they returned to the back patio, where the women were chatting. The conversation with Yolanda was comfortable and easygoing, as if they had all known each other for years.

Dante let out a silent sigh. He was relieved to see Elena's beautiful smile again. She had been in a catatonic-like state, probably waiting for the other shoe to drop. Dante wondered if there were any shoes left. It was as if God had dumped a truckload on the family. He could see some of the tension in Elena's shoulders relax as she threw her head back in laughter.

Dante listened intently at the variation in their accents, intonation, and pronunciation of certain words. The Colombian accent was more singsong, whereas the Mexican one was a bit more clipped. The differences came from many influences, whether they were European, Caribbean, or from Indigenous people. He commented on how interesting it was that they spoke the same language, yet the different characteristics were noticeable. From there, they started comparing the different use of words. It became a game, each offering up a different phrase or way of saying something.

The food, the sun, and the company were a welcome and wonderful respite. They lingered at the table for over an hour. It was almost noon by the time they cleared their plates. Their fresh clean clothes were coming out of the dryer. It almost felt normal.

Yolanda suggested they get dressed. She had some very important information to discuss. When they returned to the patio, Yolanda had a manila folder in front of her. She explained Father Bruno had sent her a fax the day before, explaining in more detail their circumstances along with their especial talents, ages, and any other information he thought was pertinent.

She smiled at Elena and Dante and joked about this being their honeymoon. She promised a very special dinner celebration for them the next evening. Yolanda opened the file and gave each of them a sheet of paper with a place for possible employment, should they decide to stay in Puerto Vallarta. The list also included names they were to use as references on the applications. She explained that putting those names on their job applications was a code, alerting the employer that they should take special care with these new people and find them appropriate work. Dante's page was for an assistant manager position at an import/export company. Elena's was for a front-desk receptionist at a high-end hotel that accommodated many Americans. Sylvia's was for a pastry kitchen manager at the same hotel as Elena's job, and Gabriel was assigned to a company that needed delivery drivers at the port.

Next were two possible places to rent. One was a two-bedroom apartment within walking distance of the busiest part of town. Another was a small house a little farther out. It was a lot for them to absorb.

Gabriel was the first to speak. "Thank you so much. Yes, we are planning to stay for at least three months until we can figure out our next plan. When should we apply for the jobs?"

In answer, Yolanda went to the phone and made several calls, jotting down information and passing it on to the four of them. With a snap of a finger, their interviews were arranged for the following day. Elena and Sylvia gave each other a sideways look. *Another magical angel at work.*

"What if we don't get the jobs?" Gabriel had to ask.

Yolanda folded her arms across her ample bosom and spoke in English for the first time. "Do I look like I don't know what I am doing?" Sylvia and Elena almost spit out the coffee they were drinking.

"All this time, you spoke English?" Elena asked rhetorically.

"You can never be too careful. Father Bruno

and I have been working together for several years. He was once located here, and he became a dear friend of the family. He was transferred to Colombia several years ago. Ever since Escobar started wiping out entire families, we developed a network of sympathizers to help people get a new start in life."

"You are doing God's work," Sylvia said with reverence.

"We also help women and children who come from abusive situations. What good are we as people if we cannot help each other in a time of need?" Yolanda added. "And dogs, cats, and other animals." She broke into a huge smile. A few minutes later, the sound of a barking dog came from up the front sidewalk.

"Speaking of dogs, that's my grandson Julio and our dog Bruno. We named him after Father Bruno. He is our big protector." The front door opened, and a chubby young boy around the age of nine came barreling in behind a big mastiff. Gabriel bit his lip, thinking everyone in this house was big. Big in size and big in heart. The huge dog galloped toward Gabriel and started licking his face and ears.

"He likes you," Yolanda said. "*Siéntate*," she commanded, and the dog quickly disengaged himself from Gabriel's lap and sat upright next to him. "Julio is home for lunch. His school is a few blocks away."

"Abuela makes the best lunch!" Julio grinned. "I hope my English is okay."

"We speak English whenever we have the opportunity," Yolanda explained. "Puerto Vallarta gets over a million tourists from the north. Americans and Canadians. It's important for Julio's future to be able to converse in both languages."

Elena's eyes brightened. "That's what I was studying to do. Teach English as a second language." Then her face tightened. "I was supposed to start a job at an international securities company."

Dante was the next to speak. "All of us had something to look forward to, but God laughs when we make plans."

Sylvia looked around the room. "We were planning a wedding and met with the florist the morning our van exploded."

The word *exploded* caught Julio's ear. "Wow! Your van blew up?"

"Julio, how many times have I told you to mind your own business?" This time, Yolanda spoke in Spanish, which caused a bit of a chuckle around the room. "Your English is so good, I forgot for a moment." Yolanda blushed, looking at Elena sheepishly.

"Depending on how long we are in Puerto Vallarta, I would be happy to tutor Julio," Elena offered. "It is the least I can do for everything you have done for us."

Julio perked up. He wouldn't mind having a lesson from the very beautiful lady with the long black hair. "Seriously?" He looked at his grandmother.

"Let these nice people get settled, and then we will see." Yolanda patted him on the behind. "Go get your lunch. It's on the stove. Be careful—it's hot." Yolanda was referring to the birria stew Sylvia had commented on earlier. "Warm tamales are in the oven." She turned back to her guests. "He's a good boy. Sometimes a little overenthusiastic."

Elena spoke again. "I am sincerely willing to help him with his English." She paused, realizing she was making a commitment before she had any clue as to what the next day would bring. "That is, once we get settled."

"Speaking of getting settled—after your interviews tomorrow, I want you to go look at the properties. Both locations are on a month-by-month basis."

"Very good." Gabriel nodded. "In three months' time, we should have a plan in place. We need time to think."

Yolanda nodded in agreement. "Yes. These are big decisions; decisions you did not know you would have to make. I think it is a good idea to wait before you go to America. And I believe you will like working for the people I am sending you to. They understand that it is temporary, unless you discover you love Puerto Vallarta and wish to stay." She chuckled, as if she were in on her own personal joke. Everybody loved Puerto Vallarta. It was considered the friendliest city in Mexico.

Yolanda continued. "Now, you must go to the shops and get new clothes. Sylvia, for work, they will give you a uniform so you can wear whatever you want, but I encourage you to get comfortable shoes. Elena, you will need to have at least two white blouses, either black skirts or black pants. The hotel will provide a blazer and an ascot. You should also find a pair of comfortable shoes. Gabriel, you will also have a uniform. You will need a pair of work boots. Dante? Office clothes for you."

"I was fortunate to have been able to bring a few of my own things before we left Colombia. I will sort through them and decide what I need." Dante quickly excused himself and went to the bedroom and opened his duffel bag. Before he left Cali, he was able to pack his one good suit. He hoped he would wear it for whatever celebration they might have in the future.

Back on the patio, Sylvia pulled at her shirt. "We went shopping at a thrift store before we left Colombia."

"Ah. The one at the church?" Yolanda said. It was more of a statement than a question. "Julio will show you the way to the clothing shops after he finishes his lunch." She called into the kitchen and told him to hurry up. Then she shouted toward the bedroom. "You too, Dante!"

"Any place in particular you recommend?" Elena asked.

"Bettina's Boutique is good." Yolanda wrote down the name and address. "Not as expensive as it sounds. Tell her I sent you." She turned to the men. "There is a store a few doors down. Rodrigo's for Men. You should also tell them I sent you."

Elena gave Yolanda a big hug. "You are an angel."

"A magical angel," Sylvia added, glancing at Elena in their mother-daughter silent language.

"I don't think my husband would agree." Yolanda belted out a laugh. "He will be home for dinner. You will meet him later. Now go. It has been a long day for you, and it is only half over."

Sylvia and Elena grabbed their purses, the men pocketed their wallets, and they all followed Julio as he slowly rode his bicycle and the others walked. He pointed out his friend's house, the one where they played *fútbol*, the game known as soccer in most English-speaking countries.

"You a *fútbol* fan, Julio?" Dante asked. "I used to play when I was in college."

Julio stopped his bike. "You still play?"

"No. Now I dance." Dante smiled.

"Dance?" Julio looked perplexed.

"I was a dance instructor before we left Colombia." Dante nodded toward Elena, who had her arm linked through his. "That's how we met."

"Huh." Julio wasn't really interested in romance. Not yet. Maybe in a couple of years. He wanted to know more about Dante's *fútbol* days, and Dante was happy to oblige. He told Julio that when he was growing up, he lived in an orphanage with a few other boys. After their lessons, they were allowed to go out and play in the field. He became very good at it but then went to college and became engrossed in his studies. He had to earn extra money, and salsa was becoming very popular. Because of his athletic agility, dancing came to him easily. At this point of the conversation, Julio was getting bored.

Gabriel sensed the lack of interest and switched the subject back to Julio's interest in the game. He asked him who his favorite player was, his favorite team. Julio was more than happy to engage in that conversation. He and his father would watch games on television on Sunday afternoons. They would hoot and holler so loud, Yolanda would chase them around with a dish towel.

Dante saw the light in Julio's eyes when he was speaking about his father. An intense pang echoed through his psyche. He never had the experience Julio was describing. He never gave it much thought before, but seeing the joy in this young boy's eyes showed him what he had missed. He realized how much one could appreciate that experience.

Within a few blocks, they were on a main street buzzing with people, cars, dogs, and food carts. Julio pointed in the direction they should go, waved, and headed back to school.

The women walked toward Bettina's Boutique, and the men strolled a little farther to a store that featured fine men's clothing. Gabriel leaned in to Dante's ear. "I hope this isn't too expensive. Why do I need fancy clothes to drive a truck?"

Inside the store, a slender, well-groomed man with slicked-back hair greeted them in both Spanish and English. Dante and Gabriel also kept switching back and forth. The man seemed pleasant enough and not interested in selling them high-priced items, especially after they told him Yolanda sent them.

Dante explained he needed several items for an office job. The salesman showed him two jackets, four pairs of trousers, four shirts, two vests, socks, and five ties. He showed Dante how he could rotate different combinations so it wouldn't look like the same pieces of clothing. He could also rotate in some of the clothes he brought from Colombia, as few as they were.

The gentleman showed Gabriel a few pairs of trousers and three shirts for when he wasn't on the job. When they finished their shopping, he pointed out the window to the shoe store across the street. "Tell them Evian sent you." When Evian rang up the items, he said, "You qualify for a family discount," and deducted fifteen percent off the bill. Gabriel and Dante expressed their gratitude and walked to the shoe store.

A young man in his twenties greeted them. Gabriel told him he was looking for a pair of work boots, and Dante was in the market for two pairs of shoes. As soon as Gabriel mentioned Evian, they were brought to the back of the store, where they were shown shoes, boots, and sneakers. Dante opted for a pair of black loafers and a pair of deep burgundy dress shoes. Again, they were offered "the family discount."

Meanwhile, Sylvia and Elena browsed the boutique, deciding what they should buy. Sylvia wanted at least one nice dress. Something to wear to church. The store's owner, Bettina, showed her a two-piece outfit that could be changed up with a different blouse or sweater. Sylvia also eyed a few casual dresses, slacks, and blouses. Enough to get her through the week. Elena's slim figure was easy to fit into a pencil skirt. She bought two, and two pairs of slacks, and three white shirts. Bettina wrapped their items in tissue and placed them in a couple of shopping bags before also offering them a "family discount." The women were elated. They had showered, washed their hair, and had new clothes to wear. It was a good day. Bettina directed them to the shoe store, where they spotted Gabriel and Dante exiting.

Elena dashed across the cobblestone street, shopping bags bouncing in her hands. She had the biggest smile on her face. She threw her arms around Dante and gave him a big kiss on the lips. Then she turned to her father and kissed him on both cheeks. Sylvia was a few feet behind. She was also beaming.

It was the first time in days that their moods were light. Optimistic. Everyone started talking at the same time about how wonderfully they had been treated. Elena explained she and Sylvia had to go into the shoe store and suggested the men go to a café, and they would meet up with them in a few minutes. Gabriel was happy for the suggestion. He was not big on shopping to begin with. Having a little rest from it would be nice. Dante pointed to a small café with outdoor seating. "We will be over there." He took Elena's shopping bags, and Gabriel grabbed Sylvia's.

It didn't take long for the two women to find the shoes they needed. The also decided they would buy a pair of something they wanted. The things on their feet had seen better days. Once again, the "family discount" was applied, and the women expressed their appreciation. They strolled toward the café where Dante and Gabriel were sipping espresso. At that moment, everything seemed normal. The four of them sat and discussed their purchases. Then they moved on to their upcoming interviews. "What if we don't get the jobs?" Elena asked with a frightened tone.

"I suppose it's a formality," Dante mused. "I cannot imagine Yolanda sending us out to buy clothes if she wasn't confident we would be accepted."

"That makes sense." Elena dabbed her lips with a napkin and furrowed her brow. "All of this seems very organized. From the minute we met Father Bruno." Then she gave Dante a wary glance. "Did you know Father Bruno was running this underground operation?" She sat back and waited for his response, which was slower than expected.

He cleared his throat. "To be honest, I had heard rumors. Many. I suspected something was going on. People coming and going at the mission. It wasn't every week, or even every month, but I would say a half dozen times, perhaps."

"Is that why you brought us there?" Gabriel asked.

"At first, all I wanted was to find a safe place for you. It so happened Father Bruno was a conduit for another purpose."

"A higher purpose." Sylvia nodded. "Another magical angel."

"You keep speaking of these magical angels." Gabriel grunted. "What do you mean?"

Sylvia smiled slyly. "Have you not noticed that whenever we needed something, it miraculously appeared?"

Gabriel thought for a moment and tilted his head to one side. "That is an interesting observation. But couldn't he come up with a better miracle than a fishing boat?" He guffawed and looked up at the sky. "I am kidding!"

"And who are you talking to?" Sylvia teased.

"Whoever is watching over us." Gabriel winked.

"We'll make a believer out of you." Dante slapped

his father-in-law on the back, and turning to Sylvia, said, "Right, La Ley?"

Yes, for the first time in days, it felt almost normal.

Dante glanced at the clock tower at the end of the block. "We should get back to Yolanda's. She might think we got lost."

They divided the shopping bags and walked the several blocks back to the house. When they entered, the scent of food permeated the air. *Oohs* and *aahs* echoed in the living room. Yolanda appeared, wearing a different apron than before; her hair was neatly wrapped in a printed scarf that matched the dress under the apron. She even had a hint of lipstick on.

Sylvia was the first to comment. "You look very nice. And something smells delicious. The birria?"

"No, that was for lunch. I am making a mole sauce to serve with chicken, rice, and beans."

"I never had mole before." Elena took another whiff of the fragrant air.

"It is made with over twenty ingredients, including chiles and chocolate." Yolanda grinned. "I think you may like it."

"I like smelling it." Elena laughed.

Yolanda glanced down at the numerous shopping bags they were holding. "I see *mis amigos* were of service?"

"Oh, yes. Bettina was lovely," Sylvia answered.

"And so helpful," Elena added.

Yolanda looked at Gabriel. "And Evian?"

"Extremely helpful," Dante replied.

"They gave us a family discount," Gabriel noted.

"I should hope so!" Yolanda exclaimed. "I send

them lots of business!" She hesitated. "Not everyone in the same situation as you, but visitors, tourists." She waved them toward the bedroom. "Go put your things away. We will have an early dinner tonight, so you can get a good night's sleep. You need to be your best for your interviews."

Elena snapped her head in the direction of Dante.

"You have been so wonderful to us. Can you tell us more about the interviews?" Dante knew Elena needed some reassurance.

"You will have the opportunity to, let's just say, 'rehearse' with your potential employers tonight over dinner."

All the faces turned to Yolanda, looking completely befuddled.

"I'm sorry. Can you explain?" Gabriel chimed in.

"Tonight, during dinner, you will meet the people who are interviewing you." Yolanda thought she had been clear in her previous comment.

Dante took the lead. "Please excuse me if I appear dense. If I am understanding you correctly, the three people we are meeting tomorrow we will be meeting tonight instead?"

"Not instead. In addition." Yolanda smiled and shook her head. "You must go through the process of a customary interview. It is for their files should anyone ask questions. People can be nosy. Especially in this town. You will go to the interview, fill out the paperwork, and be given instructions as to when you can start. Now go get ready. They will be here in an hour. *Vamos!*"

The four hurried into the large bedroom, plopped

their bags on the twin beds, and began to unpack, hang, and fold their new acquisitions.

Dante watched Elena and Sylvia pull out the clothes as they gabbed. Both of them seemed to have reached acceptance of their situation. At least for now. Perhaps it was just that they had no time to really think about anything. It was a matter of going through many motions. Getting from Point A to Point B. The rest of the alphabet would come later.

Gabriel pulled out his new boots. *"Bonito!"*

Sylvia laughed. "I would not call your work boots pretty."

"But they are much prettier than what I was wearing." Gabriel was referring to the scuffed and well-worn work shoes he had removed from his feet at the front door. It was the same pair he had on the day of the explosion. Then there was the boat trip, where they absorbed the odor of tuna and seaweed like a sponge.

Everyone was beginning to feel as if the end of the world wasn't happening. At least not yet. It was important for all of them to keep a positive outlook—and why not? They had been fortunate so far.

Elena picked out one of her new casual skirts and a blouse to wear for dinner. She would save the more formal business attire for her interview. Sylvia and Elena were going to be interviewed by the hotel manager. Gabriel was going to meet the port supervisor of a trucking company, and Dante would be introduced to one of the partners of the import/export company.

"I think it is good we are meeting these people

tonight. It will be more casual. They will get to know us a little better," Gabriel suggested.

"You are right, Papá. I was very nervous about the interview tomorrow. Now it will be less uncomfortable," said Elena.

"Think of it as a rehearsal." Dante hearkened back to the days when they danced competitively, which weren't that long ago. It only *seemed* like a lifetime had passed since then.

"Oh, that is a wonderful suggestion." Elena smiled. "See, Mami, this is why I married him."

"And I thought it was because of my dancing," Dante teased back.

"No. Because of your *fútbol*," Gabriel chimed in.

Everyone took their turn in the bathroom to freshen up and don one of their new outfits. Each of them admitted they felt like new people. "Imagine, it was only yesterday we were on that dreadful boat," Sylvia mused.

"It seems like weeks ago." Elena sighed.

The dog began barking, signaling visitors. Lots of chatter came from the front hallway. Elena looked at her mother. "Do I look okay?"

"You look beautiful," Sylvia reassured her.

"Always," Dante added.

"And what about me?" Gabriel pretended a pout.

"You look beautiful, too." Sylvia straightened the collar of his new shirt.

To see the four of them together, one could never guess the turmoil they recently experienced.

"Shall we?" Gabriel swept his arm in the direction of the door.

Sylvia entered first, followed by Elena, then Gabriel, then Dante. The potential employers were also casually dressed. It was a dinner party. Not an interview.

Yolanda stood in the entry, holding a tray of ceramic goblets filled with her special sangria. The secret to her recipe was a dash of tequila. As each guest arrived, she made introductions.

First was Esteban Bandera, executive manager of La Costa Hotel, a luxury resort on a pristine beach with a spectacular view of the ocean. He was another slicked-back-hair man in his mid-forties, wearing cargo pants, a pinstriped shirt, and an ascot. He was just this close from being *too* slick. But it worked for the hotel's clientele. Next was Adolpho García, more on the rotund side, with thinning black hair and a bushy but well-shaped mustache. He was the owner of the import/export company. A burly, tan-skinned giant of a man stepped forward. His size was imposing, but his smile was charming.

"This is Leandro Ferrara, dock manager at the port," Yolanda declared. Handshakes and wineglasses were exchanged, along with smiles and greetings.

"Rodrigo? Please show our guests to the patio," Yolanda instructed her husband, another giant of a man with a wide smile.

On one side of the patio, a long wooden table was set with colorful plates made by local artisans. Bright red and purple flowers graced several handmade vases placed on a buffet table with trays of empanadas and more pitchers of sangria.

The sunlight filtered through the palm trees as they swayed in the gentle breeze, moving in sync with the music of classical guitar virtuoso Andrés

Segovia playing over the stereo. They could not have asked for a more perfect atmosphere. Elena commented on the beauty of the evening and the extraordinary talent of the guitarist.

"Are you a guitar aficionado?" Bandera asked.

"Me? Oh, no. Not really. But I love music."

"She is a wonderful dancer," Sylvia said with pride.

"Really? Any particular style?" Bandera asked.

"I was doing a lot of salsa dancing before we left." Elena stopped speaking abruptly. She didn't know how much Bandera knew, and she did not want to create a problem.

However, Sylvia had no trouble cutting in. "That's how she met her husband. He was her dance teacher. They won many contests together."

"A champion dancer?" Bandera smiled brightly. "We often have dance nights at the hotel when the ballrooms are available. Perhaps you and Dante would like to join? Or be judges in the contests?"

Elena was grateful for the offer. She was still apprehensive about discussing the hotel and future employment. "I would be happy to officiate. I think Dante would enjoy that, as well. Please keep us in mind." *There. End of that subject*, she thought.

For a few moments, Sylvia and Elena forgot they were conversing with their perspective employers. Esteban made an attempt at humor by pointing to the ascot around his neck. "Bandera, bandana."

Elena giggled. Not because it was particularly funny, but because she could tell he was a little nervous, as well. "How long have you known Yolanda?" Esteban asked innocently.

Elena and Sylvia shot each other a glance. "We

were planning to relocate, and one of the parish priests put us in touch with Yolanda."

Sylvia broke in. "Who had been so generous to host us for a few days." Neither said anything about interviews or jobs.

Esteban nodded. "It is a pleasure to have you in our city. I hope you will find it most accommodating."

Yolanda made her way to the two women and the Bandera-Bandana man. "Please have some empanadas." She turned to Sylvia and winked. "I promise, no fish tonight."

Esteban gave Sylvia a quizzical look. "Are you allergic?"

Sylvia thought perhaps Esteban wasn't aware of their recent travel arrangements, only that they needed employment. *Ask no questions. Tell no lies.* "Not allergic. But I have never been a lover of fish." That much was true, even more so now.

Several feet away, Dante was engrossed in conversation with Adolpho, Leandro, Gabriel, and Rodrigo about *fútbol.* Dante kept far away from the subject of how they had gotten here, what they needed, and why. It was surprisingly simple to avoid when you brought up the topic of *fútbol.* The men were animated, joking and poking fun at one of the local losing teams. It was becoming a party-like atmosphere.

Yolanda excused herself to check on dinner. The mixture of chocolate and a smoky heat drifted through the kitchen window out to where everyone else was standing. For a split second, Sylvia became lightheaded. "Excuse me a moment." She placed her glass on the buffet table.

"Mami? Are you alright?" Elena looked concerned and started following her into the house. She turned to Esteban. "Excuse me for a moment, as well, *por favor*." He nodded in appreciation for a daughter's concern for her mother.

"Oh yes, *mi amor*. I am going to get a glass of water." *And pour it over my head*, Sylvia thought to herself as she scurried into the kitchen. Her face was flushed. "Please, go back outside. We don't want to make a spectacle of ourselves."

Elena gave her mother a steady look and retreated to the patio, where the other guests were still chatting and laughing.

Yolanda grabbed a clean cloth and ran it under cold water. She placed in on the back of Sylvia's neck and motioned her to the sink. "Come. Run your wrists under this."

Sylvia didn't know if she should laugh or cry. "I don't know what is happening to me." She took the wet cloth and dabbed her forehead. "I hardly drank any of the sangria."

"What about the mood swings?" Yolanda had a suspicion of what was going on.

Sylvia bucked her head. "How do you mean?" Surely after the past few days, her moods were swinging like a trapeze.

"Sleeping well?" Yolanda peered at her.

"Not recently." She gave an ironic chuckle. "Could it be that thing I don't want to think about?"

"It is possible. Mild symptoms start in our late forties. We do not notice it until we find ourselves swimming in sweat in the middle of the night or screaming at someone who looked at you the wrong way." Yolanda chortled.

"*Ay caramba!*" Sylvia moaned. "How did you handle it?"

"Herbal teas. Cool baths. Daily walks." Yolanda opened one of the pantry doors and pulled out a bag of loose tea. "It's a mixture of buckthorn, jasmine, sage, and fennel. I grow and dry the leaves myself. It took several different combinations until I discovered one that worked. I'll make some for you after dinner."

"And tell me—how long does it last?" Sylvia look forlorn.

"The flashes? For me, they would come and go. I never knew when I would get hit with one. *Muy caliente!* Mood swings? It is hard to say. I never knew when the roller coaster would take a dive!" She laughed out loud. "Bless Rodrigo. I was not an easy person to live with." She laughed again. "Maybe I am not easy now, either!"

Sylvia chuckled.

"But maybe three to four years. I think the tea is what saved me. And Rodrigo. I wasn't sure who was going to kill who first!" Yolanda laughed again. "Now go back to the guests. And we will keep this conversation between us. Unless you want to share it with Elena."

"Surely not Gabriel!" Sylvia hooted.

"*Vamos!*" Yolanda snapped a kitchen towel at Sylvia's buttocks and called for Rodrigo to come and help her.

Yolanda had the foresight and experience to know that if you wanted to control the room, you needed to be in control. That meant being a gracious and attentive hostess and "manage" conversations, should it become necessary. After jockeying around the overabundant platters, Yolanda called everyone to the dinner table.

There were trays of chicken covered in mole sauce, rice, beans, tortillas, and a pork loin—called *lomo asado*—stretched across the table from one end to the other. It was a magnificent feast. Murmurs of delight added to the lilting music.

Yolanda directed everyone to their appointed places. No one would consider contradicting her, and they gladly took their assigned seats. As expected, everyone clasped the hand of the person next to them, forming a circle. A circle of a fortuitous future together. Gabriel glanced around the room. He was probably the least religious of the group, but he felt an unusual sense of peace. Camaraderie. Perhaps he had also come to a place of acceptance. And it felt good. Rodrigo spoke a few words of blessings and gratitude. Then everyone raised their glass and toasted their host and hostess.

"Salud!"

"Cin-cin!"

And the customary, *"Arriba, abajo, al centro, con un movimiento, el vaso a la boca y todo adentro!"* Up, down, to the center, with a movement, the glass to the mouth, and everything inside!

During dinner, Esteban brought up Elena's dancing once again. "Dante, I understand you and your wife are dancers."

Dante tried not to blush, either from fear or embarrassment. He wasn't sure. "Yes. I was an instructor while I was finishing an apprenticeship. I was fortunate to have a beautiful and talented student." He raised his glass in Elena's direction.

Sylvia was feeling more like herself and joined in the chatter. "We could not be happier to have such a wonderful son-in-law. Am I right, Gabriel?"

Elena was mortified, but she didn't dare criticize her mother. Instead, she made a desperate attempt to kick her under the table, but her aim was too far to the left, and she accidentally kicked Adolpho. He let out a bit of a yelp.

"Is everything alright?" Rodrigo gasped at his guest.

Adolpho knew exactly what had happened. "It's my knee. Sometimes if I don't sit properly, it gives me a twinge." He gave Elena a subtle elbow tap, signaling her secret was safe with him.

Dinner lasted over two hours. Yolanda moved seamlessly among the guests, swapping out used plates with clean ones, filling glasses, and making sure the tortillas were warm and plentiful. Sylvia was particularly impressed by how Yolanda transformed from a doting grandmother that morning into a very capable hostess several hours later.

Dessert plates were brought out next, along with carafes of coffee, hot milk, dark melted chocolate, and the pastries Sylvia bought when they were shopping earlier. They had accomplished a week's worth of errands and meetings in less than one day. Yolanda checked the clock. It was time to get the additional company out the door so her houseguests could get a good night's rest before their interviews.

Given the mood and the conviviality of the group, she was almost certain everything would go as she and Father Bruno had planned. It always had, with the exception of one person. It turned out he was a fugitive of the law posing as a homeless man who had been able to convince Father Bruno his life was in danger because he had witnessed a crime. It just happened to be a crime he committed himself. Yolanda had no problem turning him over to the authorities, although it was a little tricky. Fortunately, Leandro used his connections at the dock, and the pretender unfortunately found himself on a ship headed back to Colombia.

Everyone said their good-nights and went to their rooms. Gabriel nudged Sylvia. He nodded toward two of the beds. Someone had pushed them closer together. While lovemaking wasn't an option, hand holding was acceptable. The young couple had had no time alone for the past couple of days. And it would most likely be a couple more before they did.

The four of them were sound asleep as soon as their heads hit the pillow. Yolanda assured them they would be up in time for breakfast, showers, and their interviews.

As promised, not only was Bruno a good companion, but he was also a good alarm clock. He nudged the bedroom door open and gave a soft woof. No response. Then another woof. Again, nothing. He kept at it, each bark getting a little louder, until Gabriel catapulted out of his bed and resorted to his native language. "*Qué? Qué pasa?*" Then he remembered where he was and smiled at the big dog. At that point, everyone was awake.

"Me first!" Elena shouted, grabbed her robe, and dashed into the bathroom.

*"Yo soy la siguiente!"* Sylvia proclaimed, staking her place in line.

Gabriel nodded at Dante. "This is what you have to look forward to."

"And I am." Dante grinned.

"Let us see if Yolanda will give us some coffee as we wait our turn," Gabriel suggested. He pulled on a pair of pants and wrapped a robe around him. Dante did the same, and they paraded into the kitchen, where Yolanda was fixing a very robust breakfast.

*"Buenos días!"* Yolanda smiled. "Good morning."

*"Buenos días!"* Gabriel and Dante answered the greeting.

They continued to speak, in English now. It was important for all of them to be articulate and fluent.

A half hour later, the two women appeared, dressed for success. Their hair was beautifully groomed and each wore the appropriate amount of makeup. Sylvia was wearing the matching skirt and top, her chin-length hair pulled to one side with a simple comb. She looked stylish, feminine, and put-together. Most importantly, she looked confident; a person of authority, like a manager you would not want to question. Elena had donned black slacks and a white blouse with long, slightly billowing sleeves and a tie-bow. Her hair pulled back in a bun. She looked like the poster girl for the hotel and hospitality business.

*"Qué bien!"* Gabriel exclaimed. The night before, his wife had looked lovely, but nervous. Today she looked bold and self-assured. It was the woman he married.

Dante also commented on Sylvia's commanding aura. He then turned to Elena. "And you? I would sign your guest registry every day of the year." Then he blushed. Everyone hooted at Dante's cheeky comment.

Gabriel rose from the table and thanked Yolanda for the coffee. Dante followed.

"Don't take too long. Breakfast will be on the table in a few minutes," Yolanda shouted after them.

"Where is Rodrigo?" Sylvia asked.

"He had to be at the station early today."

"Station?" Elena asked. It occurred to her that no one had mentioned what Rodrigo did for a living.

"Yes. He works with the government," Yolanda said nonchalantly.

Sylvia blinked several times. She wasn't sure she should ask any more questions.

As if she read her mind, Yolanda explained that Rodrigo worked in a special operations group that monitored people coming in and out of Puerto Vallarta. "We don't want Mexico to become the next haven for the cartels."

Now it was all making sense. It was no wonder Yolanda had a special place in her heart for people who tried to flee from the oppression of narco-terrorists. Unfortunately, little did anyone know that over the next twenty years, Mexico would be rampant with them.

Yolanda began to fry the eggs for the huevos rancheros. It was the same thing she had served the day before: a soft tortilla topped with salsa fresca, fried eggs, fried potatoes, avocado, and refried beans.

Dante and Gabriel entered the kitchen and sat down just as Yolanda began to dish out the fried eggs.

"Do you eat this every morning?" Gabriel asked after he wiped some of the yolk off his chin.

"It depends. If it is going to be a long day, or a busy day, yes. Lunchtime can be a challenge."

"Does Julio come by every day?" Elena asked.

"Most of the time. If I am not here, he knows there is something for him to eat. No respectable *abuela* would do any less." She chuckled.

They finished their meal and were about to help clear the table. Yolanda swatted them out of the kitchen. "I don't want you to get messy. You are lucky you aren't wearing your food, Señor Espinosa," Yolanda teased Gabriel for his robust appetite. He had practically inhaled his breakfast.

Yolanda arranged for a taxi for Gabriel and Dante, as they were going in the same direction, and one for Sylvia and Elena, as they were going to the same hotel. After today, they would have to walk, take a bus, or buy a car. Of course, that would be a matter of where they chose to live.

Yolanda walked them to the door and wished them *"Buena suerte."* She would miss them. In the short time she'd known them, she'd come to like these people. They were gracious, humble, bright, and appreciative. Besides, Father Bruno wouldn't send bad people to her for help. Not ever again. She shooed them out the door and waved them off.

\*   \*   \*

Sylvia's interview was a snap. Señor Bandera spent less than ten minutes with her while Elena waited in the outer office. Elena was a bit startled when the two of them exited so quickly. Bandera swung the main door open and stepped into the room. He was wearing a charcoal gray, hand-tailored double-breasted suit with wide lapels. A white shirt and a gray paisley tie peeked from under his jacket. And the same slicked-back hair. He had a broad smile and said, "I am going to show your mother the kitchen. I'll be a few minutes. Andrea? Please get Señora Castillo a cup of coffee and have her fill out the paperwork. Señora Espinosa can do hers downstairs." Andrea handed a clipboard to Elena and one to Sylvia.

*Señora Castillo.* It was the first time anyone other than Father Bruno had spoken those words. It gave Elena the flutters. She took a deep breath. Andrea smiled as she handed Elena the coffee. "He is a very nice man. A good boss." It was as if Andrea were giving her employer a good recommendation. Not that he needed it, but Elena wasn't going to reveal their meeting the night before. She was learning what to say, and more importantly, what not to say.

"Yes, he seems to be," Elena answered vaguely.

Andrea made small talk. She spoke about when the hotel was busiest, with weddings and parties. "Many people come to the bar in the evening to watch the sunset. It is quite spectacular."

*Much better than peering through a porthole,* Elena thought to herself. "I am sure it is."

"How long have you been in Puerto Vallarta?" Andrea asked.

"We just arrived."

Andrea immediately became animated as she ticked off the many attributes of their small city. "We have an area called Zona Romántica. It is a little south of here. A very big honeymoon destination. There is exceptional nightlife, shops, bars. And of course, the famous church, Nuestra Señora de Guadalupe."

Elena chuckled. "You would make a wonderful tour guide."

"That was one of my first jobs at the hotel. I would put tours together for guests." Andrea gave a bit of a huff. "After a few years, I got a promotion as an executive assistant. They said it was because I was very organized." She grinned. "You use your talents where and when you can."

Elena soaked that in quickly. That was exactly what she was about to do. "Yes. That is very true."

"Where are you from originally? You speak impeccable English."

Elena wasn't sure if she should tell her the truth, but if she lied, it would quickly catch up with her. "We are from Colombia."

"I heard it is a very dangerous country." Andrea's eyes went wide.

Elena nodded. "Yes, it is in many places."

"I hope they can catch that criminal Escobar. I worry they will take over Mexico." Andrea had a horrified look on her face.

"Yes, he is the scourge of Colombia, but there are many more like him." Elena hesitated but decided to reveal a half-truth. "It is the reason why we are here." She sat up tall. "We just got married, and my father and mother did not want us to raise their grandchildren in such a tumultuous place."

"Were you in the hospitality business in Colombia?" Andrea asked innocently.

"My plan was to be a teacher for people who wanted English as their second language. One day, I may finish my training, but for now I can use my talents to assist people communicating when they are in a foreign country."

"You have a lovely lilt to your voice and a beautiful smile. I am sure you will be a great asset to our hotel."

Elena blushed. "I have not been offered a job yet."

Andrea gave her a conspiratorial wink. "Señor Bandera only sees people who have been vetted by other members of the community. Otherwise, he would be interviewing people all day. Who would not want to work in such a beautiful location?"

Elena nodded. It was time for her to shut up.

"I apologize if I kept you waiting too long." Esteban glided back into the room.

Elena rose from her chair. "Oh, not at all. I was having a lovely conversation with Andrea."

He opened the door to the inner office. "Please, come in." He moved behind the desk and motioned for her to sit. "I understand you want to teach English as a second language."

Elena was slightly caught off guard. "Yes. That was the plan."

"And what brought you to our beautiful city?"

The question had not been brought up the night before, so Elena repeated the same story she'd told Andrea. It was believable enough, and it was mostly true. The speed and means of how it happened did not call for conversation. She just hoped her mother had told a similar story, if asked— they should have coordinated this part better.

The interview lasted only a few more minutes. Esteban rose from his desk. "I think you will make a very good concierge. Your English is wonderful. It is important that we can meet the needs of our guests. We do not want anything to get lost in translation, as they say."

Elena put her hand out. "Thank you, Señor Bandera. I wasn't quite expecting that kind of responsibility. Not that I don't think I can do the job properly. I thought since I was new, I would start the front desk."

"After speaking with you, I realized your fluency would be better utilized with more in-depth interaction."

"Thank you very much. I appreciate your confidence in me." They shook hands, never once mentioning the dinner the night before, before stepping back out into the reception area.

"Andrea, please check the schedule and set up a training session for Elena," Esteban said. "We'll get her started as soon as she is available." He turned to Elena. "I hope you enjoy working here." With that, he went back into his office.

Elena was a little flummoxed. Things were happening quickly. *Everything* was happening quickly.

Andrea gave Elena an *I told you so* look. "Come sit." Andrea gestured to the chair across from her desk. "When will you be available?"

Elena and her family had to find a place to live

as soon as possible, but she didn't want to put off starting a new job for too long. "Five days?"

Andrea marked her calendar. "Very good. We will see you in five days. Now I want you to go to the lower level. There is a maintenance office. They will find the right size blazer for you. Everything will be dry-cleaned before you wear it."

"Thank you so much." Elena shook her hand.

"Welcome aboard, as they say."

At Andrea's words, Elena had a seasick flashback to the boat. But she didn't let it show. She took the elevator to the lower level and met up with her mother, who was also being fitted for her uniform. They were almost giddy.

Later that morning, everyone reconvened at Yolanda's and shared their experiences. Gabriel was very excited about working at the port. "Good thing my English is not so bad." He grinned. "I will be working on the schedules once I get accustomed to the maps. Instead of being a delivery man, I will be telling them where to go!" He let out a guffaw.

"But Papá, you don't know anything about Puerto Vallarta!" Elena said.

"Yes, but they gave me maps to study." He pulled out a manila envelope with several maps of the city and the surrounding area. "I have homework!"

Dante's day was pretty cut-and-dried. "I met with Adolpho, and he said my job was to answer the phones and write things down."

"That's it?" Elena asked.

"I have to write them down in the right places, *princesa*."

Everyone laughed and breathed a sigh of relief.

Phase One was complete—or was it Phase Eleven? Or maybe Phase Twelve? But this much they could cross off their long list. They were now all gainfully employed.

Yolanda set down a plate of enchiladas. "No fish." She grinned. "You have appointments this afternoon to see the apartment and the cottage."

Gabriel gave a nod in her direction. "This lady is bossy." They all howled, including Yolanda.

"I will drive you. Let's have lunch, and then we shall go," Yolanda said.

After washing up, they all reconvened on the patio, ate their lunch, and discussed the residences they were about to see.

Yolanda explained the cottage was a little farther out but still within walking distance of the market area, but far enough that they would all need transportation to their places of employment. The buses were reliable enough, so they wouldn't have to buy or rent a car until they made a decision as to the next phase. The apartment was a few blocks away and was slightly more convenient, but it was also smaller and didn't offer much privacy. The cottage had two bedrooms separated by a bathroom. "At least a little privacy," Yolanda said, and then chuckled at Elena and Dante. Both properties were modestly furnished but required a deposit for the utilities and a phone. Three months' rent in advance was also required.

The plate of enchiladas quickly disappeared. "I didn't realize I was so hungry." Elena patted her lips with her napkin. "That was delicious. Would you share your recipe?"

"Only when Sylvia shows me how to make her famous bread," Yolanda stated.

Sylvia was delighted to accommodate her gracious hostess. "As soon as we get settled."

They rose from the table, cleared their plates, washed and dried them in the kitchen, and followed Yolanda to her car, which was parked in the alley.

The first stop was the cottage. The living room faced the rear of the house, where there was a small patio. A small kitchen was to one side and the two bedrooms on the other, separated by a bathroom, as Yolanda had said. It was a little tight for four people, but there was room enough for everyone to be able to have a bit of privacy either in the living room, the patio, or one of the bedrooms. True, the furnishings were sparse, but there was also seating in the small area outside. After their seafaring adventure, they could make the space work for them, especially if it was temporary.

They then drove to the apartment, which was much smaller. It would have been perfect for one couple. A young couple who wanted to be closer to the bars and restaurants. The cottage was the easy choice. Another thing to check off their to-do list.

Gabriel counted out the money for the first three months' rent and handed it to Yolanda, who would give it to the landlord. Unbeknownst to the others, the properties were owned by Yolanda and Rodrigo, but they preferred to keep that confidential. "*Bueno*," Yolanda said. "I will take care of the utility deposits for you, too."

Things were falling into place for the Castillo-

Espinosa family. Sylvia felt as if she could breathe again. "When can we move in?" she asked Yolanda.

"Tomorrow, if you desire."

They all looked at each other and nodded. It wasn't as if they had much to pack. The only thing they would need was groceries. Yolanda offered to drive them from the market to the cottage the next day. She also gave them several bus schedules.

While they were packing, Elena suggested they take Yolanda and Rodrigo out to dinner as a thank-you, and everyone agreed. When they made the invitation, Yolanda was tickled pink. Not that she and Rodrigo couldn't afford it, but there was always so much to do, and leisure time was a rare commodity. Plus, none of the others she helped had ever offered. She always shrugged it off, figuring they were still too traumatized by their experiences to think of niceties. Everyone who came through her doors for assistance had suffered major upheaval. A dinner at a restaurant was not on their radar. Yolanda phoned Rodrigo to let him know about the kind invitation and that he should get home directly after work. He, too, was delighted they would all share another meal together.

Just after six p.m., the six of them walked down the cobblestone street to the major market area. Most of the spots had outdoor seating, but Yolanda chose a quieter place at the end of the shopping plaza. Once again, they sat for hours, talking, laughing, drinking, and eating. It was the most normal Sylvia, Elena, Dante, and Gabriel had felt in almost a week. A week that seemed like an eternity.

\* \* \*

The following day, Sylvia and Elena walked to the market and picked up enough groceries to last for a few days. Dante and Gabriel were shuffling through the local newspaper, looking for a used car. When the women returned, they packed what little they had, and Yolanda drove them all to the cottage. She showed Sylvia the contents of the cupboards and utility closets. "You know you can rent this place for as long as you need." Yolanda hoped her newly found friends would make this place their home. Or at least stay in Puerto Vallarta. Yolanda sensed an instant bond with Sylvia, and the feeling was mutual. Sylvia was eternally grateful to the woman's kindness, support, and advice.

Yolanda gave Sylvia a hug. "You call me if you need anything."

"Thank you. I will be sure to make you pan de queso!" Sylvia said warmly.

"Good. You can make it in my kitchen and teach me."

"I would be most happy to do that." Sylvia waved as Yolanda stepped outside. *"Hasta luego, mi amiga!"*

It didn't take long for everyone to unpack their clothes and put the groceries away. The four of them then sat at the dining room table in stillness. It lasted for several minutes. Dante was the first to speak. "We are here, and we are safe."

Tears streamed down Elena's face. She was overcome by the gravity of what the family had recently endured. "It all seems like a dream."

"We must focus on the positive things," Sylvia reminded them. "I was sure we were going to die on that ship."

There was a bit of a guffaw from Gabriel. "I thought you were going to kill me." He laughed.

"The vows say, 'in sickness and in health.' Not 'aboard a stinky ship.'" Sylvia folded her arms and gave him a look.

Gabriel put up his hands in a surrender pose. "Yes. You are correct. But we are here now. No more ships."

Sylvia could not resist replying with, "And no more fish!"

The four of them decided to take a walk around the neighborhood before they had lunch. They would walk the few blocks to the bus stop to see how long it took. There were several small specialty markets, and Sylvia made a beeline for the cheese shop. It was then that she realized the cheese in Mexico was different than the cheese in Colombia. She was going to have to experiment to find the right one for her trademark bread.

That evening during dinner, it dawned on Elena that she and Dante would be sleeping in the same bed for the first time without her parents within inches of them. She was getting butterflies. Her face started to flush. Dante took her hand, as if he knew what she was thinking. Her blush turned red as the heat rose to her face.

While they were doing dishes, Sylvia whispered to Elena, "Do not worry. I will be sure to turn on the radio in the bedroom." Elena's legs began to tremble as she speculated what her first night with Dante would be like.

Later that evening, Elena donned a pretty night-gown and brushed her hair, letting it flow down her shoulders. Dante was waiting for her in bed.

The room was lit with a few candles. She smiled at the romantic gesture as he pulled open the bed covers to let her in. He pulled her on top of him and kissed her softly, increasing in intensity with each caress. He pulled off her nightgown, and she threw her head back as he stroked her breasts, her legs splayed across his hips. The rhythm of their lovemaking was as eloquent and expressive as their dancing. They were as powerful in bed as they were on the dance floor. The pent-up anticipation came to a fulfilling climax for both of them. They laid next to each other, their bodies glistening in the candlelight. They were spent. Elena tucked herself next to him as he placed his arms around her, both of them falling into a deep, contented sleep.

The next morning, Elena shuffled to the kitchen and made a pot of dark roasted coffee. She poured a cup for herself and one for her husband. Yes, her husband. For the first time since she said the words "I do," she finally felt officially married.

The coming months would prove to be fruitful for the Espinosa-Castillo family. Gabriel was happily surprised at how he enjoyed not having to worry about running a business. Sylvia was equally relieved at the prospect of sleeping until the sun came up and not *before* it came up. Her duties at work were simple compared to running the bakery. She made schedules, kept an inventory, and ordered supplies. It was almost too easy, so she started teaching some of the pastry chefs to make pan de queso.

Dante and Elena were satisfied with their jobs for the time being. Elena was still certain she would be a teacher, and Dante was determined to continue his training as a project manager. He did not want to waste his engineering education sitting behind a desk shuffling papers. He could do that later in life. Now he wanted to be involved in creating systems that would benefit many. He secretly hoped he would eventually hear from his previous employer but reserved his thoughts to himself. They had been through enough changes, and wanted Elena to feel stable. Uprooting would be a lot to ask.

But the ask came. About two months into their residency in Puerto Vallarta, Dante received a phone call from Yolanda. Father Bruno had a letter that was addressed to Dante. It was from the Bravo Oil Corporation.

"Can you ask him to fax it to you?" Dante said to Yolanda. "I don't know how personal it could be, but it's not as if we have secrets from each other." Not that it was an invitation for everyone to read the letter, but it was inevitable, if not unavoidable. Yolanda was happy to oblige and suggested Dante stop by after work. Yolanda couldn't help but also read the letter as the page slowly moved from the machine. It looked very official on the Bravo Oil Corporation letterhead:

Dear Mr. Castillo,
I hope this letter finds you well and that your family issues have been resolved to your liking.
We are in the process of opening a new

field office in Corpus Christi, Texas. Because of your stellar record, your skills and fluency in both English and Spanish, it could be a great opportunity for you and our company.

I would like to discuss the prospect of you resuming your apprenticeship. Upon completion you would be elevated to project manager for our company. Of course we would pay for your moving expenses and assist you with finding suitable housing.

As you know, the oil business is in a constant state of growth and we would like to share that growth with you.

Kindly call me to let me know if this is of interest to you.

Yours truly,
George Lassiter
V.P. Field Operations
BRAVO OIL CORPORATION

Yolanda knew this was something Dante had wanted but thought the opportunity had passed him by. Through their burgeoning friendship, Sylvia had shared many things with Yolanda, including the guilt she felt about uprooting Elena and Dante. Yolanda reassured her that Elena and Dante were adults, and they could have chosen to stay in Colombia. This job offer could be a spectacular break for the young couple—but the question was whether they could leave Elena's parents behind? Or would Sylvia and Gabriel want to join them in America? It was about an eighteen-hour drive from Puerto Vallarta to Corpus Christi, so they would not be *too* far away. Would Gabriel and Sylvia want to uproot again and start over again? Yolanda drummed her fingers across the letter. In her heart of hearts, Yolanda knew Dante could not refuse the job. She also knew she would miss them, but even more so, her new friend Sylvia. Gabriel and Rodrigo enjoyed watching *fútbol* together with some of the men from the port. It appeared Sylvia and Gabriel had fallen into a nice pace. They seemed happy in spite of having their world turned upside down. They bounced back well. Being positive and grateful was the formula.

On the other hand, Dante and Elena seemed restless. And why wouldn't they be? They were young. They had a whole life ahead of them. They had plans. Plans that could still be accomplished. Yolanda sighed. She folded the letter, placed it on the counter, and waited.

Just after five p.m., Dante knocked on Yolanda's door. She invited him in and told him to have a seat on the patio while she retrieved the letter. As she approached him, she confessed she had read it. It was almost impossible not to. He said he understood and began to scan the paper, the expression on his face turning from inquisitive to elated. He stood and looked at Yolanda. He knew what he had to do, as did she. Yolanda gave him a big bear hug as a tear rolled down her face.

In 1989, only big businesses could afford developing internet access, and mobile phones were available to the rich and powerful, but for now, most people still relied on landlines and the postal systems for communications, and long-distance calls were still a luxury. Dante would have to phone Mr. Lassiter. He could not depend on the mail to get a letter to him in a timely manner. He hurried to the cottage to tell the family the good news, but then he stopped short amid his jubilation. How should he break the news to the family? He must speak to Elena first. He hoped she would come home alone.

A half hour passed, and Dante's palms were sweating. He wanted to get the discussion over with as soon as possible. After his conversation with Elena, there would be another one with Gabriel and Sylvia. That was the one he was most anxious about. Maybe. His mind was bouncing back and forth like a ping-pong ball. Elena would never suggest he refuse the job. Neither would Sylvia and Gabriel. But how would they feel about Elena leaving for America without them? Would they even want to go? He must have checked his watch a dozen times in the last twenty minutes. He began pacing when he heard Elena's and Sylvia's voices coming up the sidewalk. He drew in a deep breath. He had to be patient and wait for the right moment to discuss his news with Elena. That also meant extracting her from her conversation with her mother. He decided to try something different.

"I bought a bottle of a new red wine," Dante said as Elena and Sylvia walked through the door. "I'll open it and let it sit until Gabriel gets home. Meanwhile, Elena, would you like to take a walk?"

It wasn't unusual for them to take walks in the

evening, but it was usually after their evening meal. "What about dinner?" Elena asked.

Sylvia jumped in. "I have some of Yolanda's birria that I will heat up, and I'll fry some plantains. You go. I'll keep an eye on the wine." She winked.

Elena changed out of her work clothes and put on a pair of jeans, a light sweater, and a pair of sneakers. She had finally gotten rid of the pair she wore to and from dance class and had opted for the newest style. She was almost sad the day she threw them in the trash bin. They had carried her feet through many situations. Good and bad. She came bouncing into the living area. "Ready!"

Dante was still in his suit. He had been so wound up, it hadn't occurred to him to change. "I'll just be a moment." He slipped the letter into his jacket pocket. He rehearsed the words over and over in his head: *Elena, I received a letter today. It's a job offer.* Let that sink in. Then: *It's in Texas.* His stomach was turning. He laughed at himself. Getting the family out of Cali and to Mexico seemed like a walk in the park compared to what he was now facing. He stripped off his jacket, tie, and trousers. The shirt was going into the wash later, so no sense in changing it now. He opted for a casual pair of pants and his everyday loafers. He tied the arms of his sweater around his neck. He pulled the letter from his suit jacket and put it in his back pocket. He stood tall and proceeded to remind himself that Elena loved him, and they would work this out.

He thought about having a glass of wine first, but that would seem a little suspicious. Even though it would help him relax a bit, he needed to have all of his wits about him. This was a big deal. No, it was a *huge* deal.

Just as the two of them were about to leave, Gabriel walked in. "Where are you going?"

"Just a short walk. Dante opened a bottle of wine and wants it to breathe." Elena knew her father enjoyed a good bottle of wine, so no further explanation was necessary.

*"Bueno!"* Gabriel gave Sylvia a kiss on the cheek and washed his hands in the kitchen sink.

Elena and Dante began their stroll down the sidewalk, holding hands. He wanted to be sure they were not in earshot of Sylvia and Gabriel. They walked the two blocks to a small courtyard with benches. It was surrounded by a few markets and a place that served alcoholic beverages. It was a favorite hangout for people coming home from work. Instead of going to a bar, they would purchase a cocktail and sit in the courtyard. Life in Puerto Vallarta was about enjoyment. All day long, if possible.

Dante reached into his rear pocket and pulled out the letter. He began. "Elena, you know I love you more than anything in the world."

Elena's heart immediately started to pound. "What?" She gasped. "What is it?"

"Oh, Elena. It is nothing bad." He brushed the side of her face. "I got a letter today. Mr. Lassiter from Bravo Oil. They are offering me a job. To finish my apprenticeship and become a manager."

Elena's eyes lit up. "Oh, that is wonderful." She paused. "But?"

"But it's in Texas. Corpus Christi." He let it sink in.

"When?" Elena's mind was racing.

"I haven't called him yet. I wanted to speak to you first."

"Wait. How did they know where to find you?" Elena's brows furrowed.

"They sent the letter to the mission. Father Bruno got in touch with Yolanda. Yolanda called me at work and asked what I would like to do. I had Father Bruno fax it to her. I was concerned the postal system here is slow."

"So Yolanda knows about this?" Elena was now worried about her mother finding out before they had a chance to discuss it with them.

"Well, yes. But she promised she would not say a word to anyone. And we know she is the kind of person who keeps very good secrets."

"Like the fact she is really our landlady?" Elena chuckled.

"She is surely the big cheese in this town." Dante was relieved Elena hadn't freaked out.

Getting back to the subject at hand, Elena asked, "So what do we do now?"

"We speak to your parents," Dante replied. "You are okay with this?" His eyes were almost pleading.

"Of course!" She threw her arms around him. "This is what you wanted, and it will help us get into the US." Elena was grinning. "Don't you see? This is another blessing."

Dante thought he was going to cry. "And this is why I love you." He felt as if an anvil had been lifted from his shoulders.

Elena jumped up. "Come. Let's have that wine."

"But what do we tell your parents?"

"We tell them you have a job offer in America!" Elena assumed it was a foregone conclusion.

"But how?" Now Dante's eyes were pleading.

"We shall pour the wine and sit at the table. I will say, 'Papá, Mami, Dante has good news. It is a little complicated, but he will explain.'"

"Ah. An introduction." Dante grinned. "I don't want to sound repetitive, but this is why I love you."

They hurried back to the cottage and blew through the front door. Elena grabbed the tray of glasses, and Dante carried the wine to the patio.

Dante poured a small amount into a glass and handed it to Gabriel, who swirled it around and inhaled the notes and nuances before taking a sip.

"*Bueno.* Very good." Dante tipped the bottle and filled the other glasses. "So to what do we owe this occasion?" Gabriel asked. Not that it was totally out of the ordinary for them to share a bottle of wine, but it was the middle of the week. Those occasions were generally saved for the weekends.

Dante raised his glass. "To the most wonderful family I have known." Everyone responded with their favorite toast and began to drink.

Elena broke the silence. "Mami, Papá, Dante received a letter today." Then she nodded in his direction.

Dante took another sip of courage and then gave a big sigh. He began to explain this new job offer. He said he would not give his answer until they had this family meeting. Gabriel and Sylvia were pleased Dante was showing them a high level of respect, even though they knew Dante would take the offer. They were delighted their son-in-law was getting his career on track, but they were also deflated. Even though Dante explained the four of them could move to Texas, Sylvia and Gabriel knew they would be separated from them. Uprooting themselves again would take its toll. They had fallen into a comfortable rhythm with much less stress. After the first month in Mexico, they had accepted their new life and became acclimated to their new surroundings, jobs, friends, and neighbors.

Sylvia started to cry. "Oh, Mami! Please don't!" Elena moved close to her mother and squatted in front of her. "Please. We will visit. You can visit. This will work out okay. I promise." Dante's words were indelible in her mind. *This will work out okay. I promise.*

Sylvia took Elena's hand. "I know it will. This is a wonderful chance for Dante. And you. You will bloom in America." They hugged, and so did Gabriel and Dante.

Gabriel whispered in Dante's ear, "I would not trust anyone else with my daughter. I know you will take loving care of her."

The conversation went much easier than either Elena or Dante expected. In truth, Sylvia and Gabriel knew the young couple had many goals, and now there was an opportunity to achieve them.

Dante made the call to Lassiter and accepted the offer. He could be in Corpus Christi in less than four weeks. He wanted to give his and Elena's employers ample notice. It was the right thing to do.

When he finished his phone call, he told Sylvia that Yolanda knew because she was the one who had first received the fax.

"What did you tell her?" Sylvia asked.

"Nothing."

"Ah. Yolanda. She knows what to say and when to say it. And she knows what not to say and when not to say it." Sylvia chuckled. "I should call her and tell her Gabriel and I are not moving away." Then she looked at Gabriel. "We are not, correct?" It was more of a statement than a question.

"I feel we have made a home here. So you are correct. We are not leaving." Gabriel hugged his wife. He knew she was really the boss. Whatever Sylvia wanted, Gabriel would oblige. Happily so.

The following few weeks were a flurry of preparations for Elena and Dante's move. Not that they had many personal belongings, but they wanted to have a decent wardrobe for their new city and corporate lifestyle. This was the big world of Texas oil. Then there was the situation of passports. Neither had one. They had been either destroyed or left behind during the car blast. Rodrigo brought them to his office and made special arrangements for them. The letters from Father Bruno made the process go smoothly. It seemed as if everyone in Mexico reviled Escobar and all the families he destroyed. Families all over the world. His reach was global, and narco-terrorism was making its way up through Latin America. Mexican authorities, at least those associated with Rodrigo and Yolanda, were steadfast in preserving their community. They were committed to helping people, especially those who had fallen victim to the curse of Escobar.

The week before Elena and Dante were scheduled to leave, Yolanda threw them a festive party. Included on the guest list were Esteban Bandera, Adolpho García, and Leandro Ferrara, the three men the family had met early in their stay in Puerto Vallarta. Now they were saying goodbye. Yolanda preferred *hasta que nos volvamos a encontrar.* Until we meet again.

The day Elena and Dante left, Sylvia gave Elena a small spiral notebook. "I was trying to remember all the family recipes. I wrote down as many as I could."

"And I promise I will make every one of them." Elena gave her mother the biggest hug. Then her father. It was an emotional sendoff, but also an optimistic one.

# Chapter Nine

# The Next Chapter

*Monterrey*
*Nuevo León, Mexico*
*US Department of Immigration and Naturalization*

It was going to take Elena and Dante almost the entire day to drive from Puerto Vallarta to the town of Monterrey, right on the US border. They wanted to be sure they got to the US Customs and Immigration office in time for their appointment. Dante's new employer had arranged for them to apply for work visas. The letter from Father Bruno would help in expediting the process.

Elena kept checking and rechecking her bag for their documents.

"Elena, if you look inside that bag one more

time, I am going to take it away from you," Dante teased.

Elena sighed. "I am so very nervous."

"*Mi amor*, you spent a night in a convent, three nights as a stowaway on a fishing boat, two nights at a total stranger's house, started a new job, and moved into a cottage with me and your parents. I think you will be fine." He reached over and patted her on the knee.

Elena squeezed his hand. "Did you ever wonder what life would be like if we stayed in Colombia?"

Dante thought for a minute. "It depends on what would have happened after the explosion. Would your parents have rebuilt the business? Or would they have moved away like your father wanted?"

"No—I mean, what if *we* stayed."

He shot her a startled look. "You mean if your parents left and we stayed behind?"

Elena had a sheepish look on her face. "I know it wasn't really Papá's fault, but it does not seem fair that our lives had to be disrupted, too."

"Elena Espinosa Castillo! I am so surprised to hear you say that!" Dante was truly shocked.

"And I feel guilty saying it. But I do wonder. I wonder what kind of wedding we would have had. Where we would have lived. When we could have started a family of our own." She stared blankly out the window. "All of those things."

Dante became pensive. The last two months had been a whirlwind. They had settled into a routine with Sylvia and Gabriel, each of them conscious of everyone's need for space, especially in such a small place. It took communication and cooperation. Now, he had a job offer to return to the company he had been with in Cali, but they needed him in their Corpus Christi facility. He was completely distracted by the excitement of another chance at being a project manager for a major oil company. So much so, his only focus was getting there. His life was getting back on track. Or so he hoped. He suddenly felt ashamed he hadn't thought about Elena's dreams and goals. Elena had not finished her studies and would have to look for a new job again. But this time, there was no Yolanda to pave the way.

"I'm sorry if I have been selfish. You have given up so much to be with me." He kissed the back of her hand.

"We will be fine. You will get the job, and I will find one, as well." Elena continued to look out the window. "But I will miss the ocean."

"But we will have the Gulf of Mexico!" Dante smiled at her. He could only imagine all the other thoughts going through her head now. Now that she had reminded him that she had a few dreams of her own. "I promise we will have a good life."

"Yes. I know." She leaned over to peck him on the cheek, but the seat belt prevented her from getting too close, so she blew him a kiss instead.

They went over their itinerary again. The first night, they would stay at a motel in Monterrey. Depending on how long it would take at immigration, they would either stay another night or drive the five hours to Corpus Christi. Dante's new employer had arranged for them to stay in one of the company's apartments until they found something on their own. He wasn't going to make a huge salary at first, as he still had to finish one of the training programs. As soon as he qualified, he would get an increase in pay. At the same time, Elena would look for translation jobs until Dante got his raise, and then she, too, would finish her studies and become a certified translator. Not that certification was mandatory, but then you could charge more per hour. And with the influx of Latin Americans in management, Elena's skills would be welcomed by many of the housewives who only knew Spanish. But for now, they had to go through the nail-biting, nerve-wracking process of an interview with someone from the United States Department of Immigration. They had to pass that hurdle before anything else could happen.

They pulled into the parking lot of a small motel a few miles away from the immigration office, checked in, and went to their room. It wasn't quite the luxury hotel where Elena had once worked, but it was also very different from the cabin in the boat.

Elena immediately pulled the chenille bedspread off the bed and tossed it in the corner. "You don't want to know what people do on top of these things." She made a sour face. "Hand me the brown suitcase, please." Dante lugged it onto the flimsy rack that was supposed to support a suitcase. Elena imagined most people who stayed there did not have luggage. She had learned a lot about the hotel business in a short time. It didn't matter how much money you had or didn't have or the size or type of accommodations—hotels would always attract at least some unsavory clientele. At least they had high-priced hookers at her hotel. And they were very discreet. Elena unzipped the bag and pulled out a set of sheets and pillowcases.

Dante stopped in his tracks. "You brought bed linens?"

Elena raised an eyebrow. "You didn't expect me to sleep on something where who-knows-who was doing who knows-what, to who-knows-whom." Then she muttered something in Spanish. Dante hung the garment bag on the hook behind the door.

Once they were settled—as much as they could be—Elena suggested they go for something to eat. At least the restaurant down the street didn't look too unappetizing.

When they returned to the motel, they put their sheets on the bed and switched on the small TV. The local newscaster was talking about human trafficking. There was a ring promising safe passage to the US, but it was a ruse to sell young women to international billionaires if they were pretty. If not, they became street prostitutes who usually became addicted to heroin or cocaine. The men who ran the operation took every measure to keep the women under their control. Even if it meant turning them into addicts.

It was after midnight when Elena woke with a start to a commotion outside. "Dante!" she whispered in his ear. "Something is going on outside."

"So it is better if we stay inside." He rolled over and went back to sleep.

Elena crept out of bed and peered through the crooked blinds. Four young women in their late teens or early twenties were being ushered into the back of a van. One was crying, *"Mi bebé, mi hijo!"* A man abruptly shoved her into the vehicle, and then it screeched out of the parking lot. Elena was unnerved. *There is something wrong here.* She shook Dante awake. "I think some women may have just been kidnapped!"

"What are you talking about?" Dante rubbed his face.

Elena described what she witnessed.

"They could have been prostitutes," Dante said cautiously.

Elena tilted her head. "True. A room like this could be one of their hospitality suites. But what about the baby?"

"Maybe you misheard what she said? She could have been talking about anyone or anything."

"She seemed very distressed." Elena moved away from the window. Dante pulled her close.

"These last few months have been incredibly challenging. I know you are on your one last nerve." He lowered her to the pillow and stroked her hair. "Please try to relax." He held her close. "We are starting a new life. It will be a good life." He kissed her on her forehead.

Elena sighed. "But we will be so far away from my family." Tears welled up in her eyes.

"It is not very far by plane, *princesa.*" Dante continued to stroke her hair. "They seem happy in their new surroundings. La Ley is solid friends with Yolanda now and is baking bread for some of the local restaurants. Your papá is also happy with his job as a dispatcher. He no longer has to worry about maintaining the business, and he has made many new friends. They both have. *Mi amor*, please try not to worry."

Elena settled back against the pillow and dozed off. It was around six o'clock in the morning when she woke with a start. "Did you hear that?"

"What?" Dante asked with a yawn.

"Listen . . ."

"It's probably a cat."

Elena threw the covers off. "No. I don't think so."

"Elena!" Dante called out to her more sternly than he ever had before. His nerves were also on edge. "What are you doing?"

Elena swung the door open and leaned outside. She cocked her head in the direction of the sound. It was coming from two doors down from theirs. She peered farther as Dante jumped out of bed and began to pull her back inside. Elena wrestled her wrist free from his hand. "I definitely heard something, and it was not a cat." She pulled her nightgown close to her body and slowly walked in the direction of the sound. Dante was hot on her heels. He grabbed her by the shoulder and spun her around.

"Elena, listen to me. This is none of our business." Dante was losing his patience. "And it could be dangerous. Let's go." He tugged on her arm, but she resisted. He had no choice but to follow her.

The noise got louder. It was coming from a door that was cracked open. "Elena! Stop!" Dante demanded in a harsh whisper.

Elena softly knocked on the door. There was more crying, but no one came to answer. Elena stared inside. A baby, about six months old, was in a makeshift carrier. Elena spoke softly, "*Hola? Alguien aquí?*" Elena scanned the room as Dante looked over her shoulder. The place was a mess. Junk food wrappers were strewn on the floor. Empty soda cans cluttered the distressed dresser. Dirty diapers were sloppily tossed in the trash can. A small bag with a baby bottle, pacifier, and two clean disposable diapers was tossed on the bed. Something that looked like milk was in a plastic container. Elena spun around and looked directly at Dante. "I told you something happened here! We need to call the police."

Dante grabbed her by both shoulders. "Let's not do that yet. If something foul happened here, we could be detained and miss our appointment. Let's bring the baby with us to immigration and turn him over to the authorities when we get there. This way, we won't be late, and the police can take over."

Elena picked up the now wailing child. She wiped his face with the bottom of her nightgown and rocked him back and forth. "Check that container and see if it is milk or something the baby can drink."

Dante opened the plastic container and winced. "It smells disgusting."

"Come on." Elena gathered up whatever appeared to belong to the baby. "Let's bring him back to our room. I will clean him up. You go to the coffee shop and get some milk and see if they have applesauce."

Dante always knew Elena was a take-charge woman, but she was in overdrive at the moment. He pulled on a pair of pants, shirt, and shoes and headed toward the coffee shop a few hundred yards from the motel. Elena took the baby into the bathroom and began to give him a bath in the sink. She was surprised how quiet he had become. She wiped his face and gave him a kiss on his rosy cheeks. She swaddled him in a towel and rocked him back and forth as she softly sang a nursery rhyme to him in Spanish.

When Dante returned, he was surprised at what he saw. Elena's maternal instincts had immediately kicked in. He smiled at his wife as she cradled the little boy. Dante washed out the baby bottle and warmed the milk in the sink. Elena sat the baby up and brought the bottle to his face. He gladly took it with his tiny hands. Dante peeled the plastic wrap off the apple pie. He saw the questioning look on Elena's face. "They didn't have apple-sauce. I thought he might eat some of the apple filling instead."

"It's filled with sugar," Elena said.

"I'll rinse off the chunks. And eat the crust. No sense in it going to waste."

Elena gave him an ironic smile.

Dante dug through the worn-out baby bag one more time and pulled out a clean onesie for the baby. "At least he'll look respectable." Dante brushed the child's face with his finger. "He's a handsome young man."

Elena put the child down on the bed and surrounded him with pillows so he would be safe in one place. She and Dante got dressed and packed their bags. Even if the day ran long, they were not going to spend another night in that fleabag motel. Unfortunately, it had been the only room available on such short notice, but they decided they would drive until they found something more suitable.

Dante put their bags in the car, and Elena wrapped the baby in one of her sweaters. They drove to the field office and parked the car. When they entered, they showed the guard their identification and their letters from the Bravo Oil Corporation and Father Bruno. The guard pointed to a waiting area outside of a private office. About half an hour later, a man wearing a tactical-looking uniform opened the door and invited them in.

"Please, have a seat. I'm Inspector Gannon. You speak English, I assume?"

"Yes, we both are fluent," Dante replied.

The officer squinted at the paperwork. "It says nothing about a baby here." He shuffled the papers around.

"This is not . . ." Dante's sentence was cut off abruptly by another officer barging into the room.

"Sorry, sir. We have an emergency."

Gannon looked up from his desk. "There is always an emergency, Cartwright. What is it this time?"

Cartwright hesitated to speak in front of civilians.

"What?" Gannon shouted.

"There's been an accident."

"And?"

"It was a van carrying four women and two men. It went off the bridge. They were trying to cross the border and were being pursued by law enforcement."

"And?" Gannon was growing even more impatient.

"And, before she died, one of the women said something about a baby. At the motel. The same place that gets raided every month."

Elena started to shake. Dante put his hand on her leg.

Gannon got up from his chair and walked toward Cartwright. The two men stood in the doorway. "Did anyone check it out?" Gannon asked.

"Yes. We sent someone over. There was no baby at the motel. Just a bunch of junk food wrappers."

"That's a relief. I'd hate to have to fill out more paperwork and turn it over to social services. You know what a pain in the ass they are."

Dante froze. He looked at the baby in Elena's arms. She was cooing at the child, who was gurgling and smiling in return. Dante leaned over and whispered, "This is going to be our child."

"What?" Elena tried not to shout. "What do you mean?"

"Elena, this is not a coincidence." He lowered his voice. "I feel as if there has been divine intervention. Remember, I was raised in an orphanage. I never knew my parents. I never had a real childhood. A real family. This is my chance to change that for someone. Please." He pleaded with her. "You must trust me."

As absurd as it sounded, Elena knew instinctively that Dante was right. The poor child would end up who knows where, and Mexico was becoming a hotbed of corruption—something they had fled from just a few short months ago.

Gannon returned to his seat. "Sorry. Things like this happen a lot around here. Abandoned kids. It's really a shame. And Mexican babies are not high on the adoption lists." He picked up the paperwork again. "Now, where were we? Oh. Right. The paperwork doesn't say anything about a child. But never mind. I'll issue a visa for him, too. It'll just take a little longer to get you folks outta here." Gannon started writing on the forms. "Name?"

Without flinching, Elena said, "Mateo." Her eyes welled up. The name Mateo meant *God's gift.*

Gannon fiddled around with more papers, pulled out a stamp, and handed them visas for the United States of America. "I'll get Mateo's visa. Sit tight. I'll be back in about fifteen minutes."

Elena's palms were sweating. "What if they ask for a birth certificate?"

"Then we show him Father Bruno's letters about asylum."

"But won't Father Bruno's letter just confuse everything?" Elena tried to maintain her composure, which was no easy task, sitting in this official government office, with official government plaques, and official government posters bearing warnings about illegal aliens. Their future was hanging on the line. She thought she was going to throw up. Dante took the child from her and began walking him around the room. Elena watched with scrutiny. The way Dante looked and spoke to the little boy was kind and gentle. She had to admit, Dante looked like a natural with Mateo.

Inspector Gannon returned with three visas. "Here you go." They all shook hands. "Good luck. Take care of that handsome kid."

"We will." Elena smiled, wiping a tear of joy from her face.

They hurried out of the offices and bolted toward the car. Dante resisted the temptation to peel the wheels out of the parking lot. They couldn't get out of there fast enough.

Once they were about half a mile away, both Elena and Dante started speaking at the same time. Dante blurted out, "It was as if he gave us permission."

"We have no birth certificate!" Elena bellowed.

"We'll get him baptized. That will be good enough for the time being. Once we get settled, we can go to someone, I don't know who, but we'll figure out how to get him the documents we need. We have time, *mi amor*." He looked at the child, smiling up at Elena. "No one would question that you are his mother."

Elena was shaking, holding the baby close to her. "Can we really do this?"

"We have come this far. Yes, we can." Dante was gripping the steering wheel tightly. "Elena, it was meant to be. Think about it. The only room we could get was in that dreadful place. A woman is abducted, dies, and leaves a baby behind. He would have ended up in some horrible place. His future was bleak at best. He would end up being one of those kids who begs for food or money. I was lucky. Whoever found me took me to a convent. I will never know who my parents were. It has left a big hole in my heart. Now I can fill that space by giving a child something I did not have. A mother. A father. A family. A home."

Elena looked down at the baby in her arms. "What are we going to tell Mami and Papá?"

"We can tell them you are pregnant, and they can come visit after the baby is born."

"So we have to pretend for almost a year and a half? He must be around six months old. And how did I give birth to a six-month-old?"

Dante chuckled. "Or we can tell them the truth."

Elena sighed. "I never lied to my parents." She was contemplative. "But as we have learned, people can only tell what they know if they are forced to answer."

"The less they know the better, *mi amor*." Dante looked ahead at the bridge that would take them to the United States of America.

When they reached the checkpoint at the bridge, they showed their brand-new visas to the guard. He simply nodded and waved them through.

Elena started shaking again, having second thoughts. "Dante, I don't know if this is right. We are kidnappers!"

Dante looked straight ahead. Their new life was unfolding. True, it was a bit different than he expected or imagined, but he was sure they were doing the right thing. He was positive.

As they crossed the Rio Grande, Elena burst into tears. It had been a tumultuous time, and now they were an instant family, moving to a new city in a new country. It was overwhelming.

Dante also started to get misty-eyed. They had come a long way in a very short period of time. Colombia seemed like a lifetime ago.

"Elena, I know this may seem wrong at the moment, but you must believe we are truly doing the right thing by this child."

Elena was overwrought, and then the baby started crying, as if he felt her soul. "Shh . . ." She began to rock him back and forth. As soon as she calmed herself, the little boy responded in kind.

"See? He already knows you." Dante wiped his nose on his sleeve.

"Dante! Don't do that! You are going to teach this child unpleasant habits." She was half-joking. Dante had never done anything unbecoming before. At least not in front of her. She groped around for a tissue and handed it to him. "I think we should stop at the nearest store, where we can buy some things for him. We need diapers and clothes."

Dante got off at the next exit and found a shopping mall with a Big-Mart. The three of them parked and entered the store. It occurred to Elena they needed more than diapers and clothes. A diaper bag. A baby seat. Bibs. Bottles. Pacifiers. Blankets. Baby food. Crib. By the time they were finished shopping, the bill was several hundred dollars.

"We'll get a stroller, changing table, and a playpen tomorrow, and the other furniture when we move into our own place." Dante was on a mission. He was determined they would have everything under control soon.

They finally arrived at the building where the corporate apartment was located. It was a new high-rise building with a circular driveway. A man stood at the entrance. Elena rolled down her window, and Dante leaned over. "Good evening. We are the Castillos. We are staying at the Bravo apartment."

The man opened Elena's door. "Welcome. I'm Bennett. That's my first name." He was a brawny fellow in his early twenties with a wide, toothy grin. "We have been expecting you." He held out his hand and realized Elena had a small child in her arms. "Oh, we weren't aware you had a baby."

"My apologies." Dante spoke with authority. "Everything happened so quickly. I hope it isn't a problem."

"No. Not at all. It's just that we don't have the apartment set up with a crib or any of the amenities for a baby."

Elena stayed silent, convinced Dante would manage the situation skillfully.

Dante continued in his confident tone. "We have a crib in the trunk. We can get whatever else we need tomorrow. I trust there are stores nearby?"

"Yes, of course," the valet said. "There are several. I will make a list for you."

Dante popped the trunk and wrestled out a box containing the parts for a crib and the shopping bags filled with baby items. The car was small, and the makings for a crib wouldn't fit with the luggage, so Dante had juggled their limited belongings and put some in the back seat.

The valet pulled the dolly around to the rear passenger door of the car and began to remove the suitcases. He looked down at the worn piece of luggage, one with a very faded rendering of the Disneyland logo. Elena had not wanted to part with it. It represented what they had endured and served as a reminder to be grateful for the kindness and support they were given in their time of need. Elena finally spoke. "Sentimental value." Bennett smiled and nodded. She was relieved he didn't ask any other questions, like which ride had she liked the most. Or who was her favorite Disney character?

Bennett led the way to the reception desk of a very modern, sleek lobby. It reminded Elena of La Costa. Not in style, but the same level affluence with its highly polished floors, marble walls with mirrors, and floor-to-ceiling panels of lighting. Bennett introduced them to Alice, a stout woman with a military haircut. "This is Mr. and Mrs. Castillo, and their baby . . ." His voice drifted off.

"Mateo," Dante said clearly.

"Nice to meet you," Alice said stiffly, and then gave them a harsh look. "We weren't expecting a baby."

Dante didn't flinch. Neither did Elena. "Yes. My apologies. When Mr. Lassiter summoned me, it was a bit of a shuffle to get here on time."

Alice scribbled something down on her pad. Dante continued, his voice steady. "Is this going to present a problem?"

The stern woman looked up from her paper. Her expression softened just a bit. "Oh, no, sir. I was making a note for security purposes. A lot of people come and go, and we try to take every safety precaution for our guests."

Dante nodded. "We appreciate that."

Alice gave each of them a laminated security pass and two keys. "You will have to show this pass to whoever is at the desk when you come and go.

We keep a log." In 1985, Corpus Christi had become an international port, bringing more people, trade—and potential criminals. It was still considered a very safe city, and the local government and businesses intended to keep it that way.

Elena finally spoke. "Is there a place nearby where we can have dinner?" Then she realized she was holding a baby. "I mean, where we can pick something up?"

"There are a few take-out places that deliver." Alice craned her head to peek at the dolly laden with their belongings. "You're gonna probably need a screwdriver or two." She pulled out a three-ring binder. "Here are some menus. They're all pretty good. I'll call maintenance and see if they can loan you some tools." She picked up the phone and waved them off.

"Follow me," Bennett chimed in.

Elena made sure to wave good night to Alice. She could be a good resource, and Elena was going to need all the help she could get. She had no clue about mothering. Not that Alice seemed the maternal type, but she seemed capable of handling things.

Bennett motioned for them to get in the elevator first and then followed with the cart. "Alice's bark is worse than her bite," he joked, and pushed the button for the fourteenth floor.

Once they disembarked, Bennett wheeled the cart down a long hallway. "Here we are."

Dante put the key in the lock when he paused. "Excuse me. But there is something I have to do." He flung the door wide open and scooped Elena and Mateo both up into his arms and carried them across the threshold.

Elena gave out a "Whoop!"

Dante looked over his shoulder at a bewildered Bennett. "We do this every time we move!" he said with a big grin.

Bennett smiled and rubbed his chin. "That's kinda sweet." He followed the couple into the apartment, pushing the cart.

Dante set Elena down gently as Bennett began to unload the big box with the crib. Within a few minutes, a man wearing a uniform appeared in the doorway. "Someone needs a screwdriver?"

Bennett jerked his thumb. "This is Gerry. Head of maintenance."

"Yep. I'm the guy you call if you need anything fixed." The man had a distinct Texas drawl.

Elena gave the box containing the crib a sideways glance. Dante was a man of many talents, but she was doubtful when it came to putting something together with his hands. Not that she had any real experience watching him, but her instincts told her he was much more cerebral than mechanical.

"I'm Dante Castillo, and this is my wife Elena and our son Mateo." The words slid off his lips as if he had been saying them much longer than ten hours.

"You gonna need a hand with this?" Gerry gave the box a light kick.

Dante glanced at Elena, who was giving him a look that said *Yes, please!*

"That would be a big help," Dante acquiesced.

"But we were about to order something for dinner."

"I get off work in about an hour. Why don't I come by then?" Gerry offered.

"Much appreciated. Of course, I will pay you for your time."

"Mister, you are in Texas. We are bighearted people. It wouldn't be kindly of me to welcome you by taking your money."

Bennett rolled his eyes and broke in. "Where would you like me to put the rest of these?" Bennett was originally from the Midwest and was still getting used to the boldness of Texas hospitality.

"Suitcases can go in the bedroom; shopping bags in the kitchen, please." Elena was beginning to feel more comfortable.

Gerry tipped his invisible hat. "Catch y'all later. Oh, and order from that pizzeria place. They make great spaghetti and meatballs."

"Thanks!" Dante said as he walked Gerry out to the hallway. "Seriously, I greatly appreciate your help."

Bennett was finished unloading everything and started toward the door. Dante reached in his pocket to give him a tip, but Bennett turned and said in a half-mocking tone, "Mister, you are in Texas. We are bighearted people. It wouldn't be kindly of me to welcome you by taking your money."

Dante laughed and patted him on the back. "Bennett, you're a good man."

"Thank you, sir. Oh, and, if you want *really good* Italian food, order from Nanna's. They are a little pricey but worth it."

"Thanks, Bennett. Good night."

Elena pulled a blanket out of the closet and placed it on the floor. She set Mateo down amid a cluster of pillows. She stared at the helpless child and then started to weep.

"*Mi amor*—what is it?" Dante exclaimed.

"All of it, Dante. All of it." And to think, it had been just a year ago when she stomped her feet at her mother, exclaiming, "Something! Anything!" because she had been bored. *Be careful what you wish for!*

He gently pulled her close to him. "We will be fine. You will be fine. We will raise this child together, Elena. I promise you."

She let out a huge sigh. "For better or worse."

"That's my girl—the love of my life." He kissed her softly on the lips.

They ordered from Nanna's and wolfed it down as if they hadn't eaten in days. The baby seemed fine with the strained jars of muck they had purchased. Elena thought there had to be better food for a growing child. As promised, Gerry returned and put the crib together in what seemed like five minutes. Elena feigned wiping her forehead. "Whew! That could have been an ugly scene."

Dante insisted Gerry take a twenty-dollar bill. "Please. Buy yourself a drink. Bring flowers to your wife."

Gerry let out a guffaw. "Now that, sir, would make her think I was up to something." Dante chuckled and walked Gerry to the door once more.

After Dante heard the elevator doors close, he leaned his back against the door and slid down to the floor. Mateo gave a shriek of glee. The three of them settled in, wondering what kind of night it would be. A crying baby every two hours? Every three hours? In their haste and naivete, they hadn't thought about the minute-to-minute details required to raise a kid.

Maybe it was due to all the commotion Mateo had experienced, but he slept for almost six hours before waking up. He uttered a soft cry, as if he didn't want to disturb his new parents. Dante got out of bed and warmed up a bottle of milk, which Mateo took gladly. After a few minutes, Dante remembered something about burping a baby, so he took his best shot. Aside from spittle dripping out of the baby's mouth and all over Dante's pajama top, it went reasonably well. Dante sat down on the sofa with the little boy on his chest. The two drifted off for the few hours left before they would start a new day. A new life.

Elena shuffled into the living room and halted when she saw Dante and Mateo comfortably dozing together. Again, she thought, *He's a natural at this.* She got dressed and took the baby from Dante so he could get ready for work. She fed the baby one more time, changed his diaper, and put him in a fresh set of clothes. The three then headed out the door, down the elevator, and past Alice. Once they reached their car, Elena strapped the baby into the car seat.

"You look like a pro!" Dante said encouragingly.

"I read the pamphlet a dozen times," Elena replied.

Dante pulled out the map once again and marked the route to his new job. It was less than ten minutes away. When they got there, he quickly realized he could have walked. That would be a big help during the day so Elena could have the car. Once she dropped Dante off at his new office, Elena drove to the Big-Mart store and perused the many aisles of baby goods. She wasn't even sure if Mateo was five months or six months. And whom could she ask?

Sure enough, the dreaded question came when a shopper next to her stopped and said, "He's adorable! How old?"

Elena decided it was time to lie. Sort of. "We just adopted him. They said he's six months old."

"Adoption? Well, bless your heart," the woman declared. "There are so many orphans right across the border. Last week, some smugglers tossed an infant over the bridge. It's just terrible what's going on."

Elena was horrified. "That is terrible. We are lucky to have such a sweet boy."

"Well, by the looks of him, he's pretty lucky, too. Latino?"

Elena was taken aback by the woman's boldness. "Yes. I'm originally from Colombia." Elena looked exotic, but it was hard for others to pinpoint her ethnicity or cultural background, especially with her fluency in English.

Then the woman gave her a dubious look. "Huh. That's an awful place, I hear." The woman shook her head. "A bunch of criminals."

Elena gave her a wry smile. "Yes. That's why we left."

"And what does your husband do for a living?"

Elena resisted the temptation to say, "We're

drug runners for Pablo Escobar. We smuggle them in the baby's diapers. He can easily manage a pound of cocaine." But she didn't. Instead, she said, "He works for Bravo Oil." Elena decided she had had enough conversation with this total stranger and didn't want it to get to the point where the rude woman would require the response, "None of your business." Elena faked looking at her watch. "I must finish my shopping. Enjoy the rest of your day." For a moment, Elena thought the woman was never going to move, but "Attention, Big-Mart shoppers" came over the PA system, and the woman immediately charged toward the blinking light announcing an instant sale.

Elena continued to move up and down the aisles when she spotted another woman with a child that looked around the same age as Mateo. She could tell it was a girl, because the mother had put a band with a bow around her head. Elena smiled at her. "Good morning. Lovely little girl. How old is she?"

"Going on six months," the woman replied. "And yours?"

"The same," Elena answered.

"They say the next few months will be a nightmare, what with teething and all."

Elena hadn't thought about that. She hadn't thought about much of anything as far as raising a baby. She hadn't been given enough time. "Oh, I am not looking forward to that." She figured this might be a good opportunity to get some helpful information.

"He's my first," Elena admitted. At least that

wasn't a lie. "My mother is in Mexico, and it's expensive to call every time there is an issue."

The woman chuckled. "And there is an issue every single day."

Elena rolled her eyes. "That is very true." That, too, wasn't a lie. "Have you discovered any helpful information about teething?" Elena was always quick on her feet. "And anything else you could recommend?" Elena then decided to tell the half-lie again. "He's adopted, and the agency wasn't very forthcoming with helpful suggestions. I think they wanted to get the paperwork done and get their money."

"I'd be happy to help," the young mother said with a knowing smile.

"I appreciate it very much. My name is Elena."

"I'm Sally. Nice to meet you." She extended her hand. "Follow me." She led the way down several aisles, pointing to things. "Do you have one of these? Those?" And so on. Elena was surprised at all the things she hadn't thought of—but then again, why would she?

It had been close to an hour when the women had fully stocked their carts and moved toward the cash registers. Sally opened her purse and pulled out a small pad and pen. She wrote her name and phone number down and handed it to Elena. "It's a local call." She smiled. "Feel free to ring me up if you need anything."

Elena was pleased that not every shopper was a busybody. As Sally began to exit, she called back to Elena, "Maybe we can have a playdate sometime."

"That would be nice. Thank you again for your help."

Elena knew what Sally was really offering—companionship, a sympathetic ear, and a shoulder to lean on. Yes, a playdate for Elena would be welcome. The kids were still a bit too young. That much she knew.

The corporate apartment was only temporary, and so the family found a small house to rent within a few weeks. Dante's future seemed secure as long as he went wherever the company sent him. That meant being transferred every five years, or whenever a project was completed.

Elena fell into a good routine with Mateo once she got used to his patterns. She stockpiled books about raising kids and devoured every one of them. Her goal was to stay one step ahead of Mateo's development. From what she read, that first year was a doozy. Not that the rest were easy-peasy, but changes came swiftly.

Mateo had no problem accepting Elena and Dante into his world. Not that he was aware of the exact circumstances. He was alert enough to know that he did not like being left alone in a baby seat for hours in wet diapers. He didn't cry often. He instinctively knew it garnered no response. Now there were two people giving him love, attention, food, and dry pants. He was comfortable, and he felt safe.

Elena phoned her parents once a week to keep them up-to-date, but still avoided the Mateo situation. "I can't keep this from them much longer," she reminded Dante. "We have been here for six months. He's almost a year old now."

"Then let's tell them we adopted a baby. We can tell them just part of the story. The mother was killed in a car accident, and Mateo was going into foster care. That much is true."

"And how did we come across all this information?" Elena was standing with her arms akimbo.

"Your friend Sally." Dante smiled, kissed her, and headed toward the door. "I gotta run. Early meeting."

"But . . ." Elena looked down at Mateo. "Okay, kiddo, but you will never know the real story. I will make sure Mami and Papá swear to secrecy. Or at least swear to the lie I am about to tell them." She didn't want to wait any longer and dialed their number.

Sylvia answered with a worried tone. "Elena? Is everything alright?"

"Yes, Mami. I have some big news for you. Dante and I have been talking about a family, but it has been hard for me to get pregnant." That part wasn't necessarily a lie, but for all the sex they had over the past six months, something should have happened by now. Elena would deal with that at a later date. For now, she had to come clean and stop the smokescreen.

"*Dios mío!*" Sylvia exclaimed over the phone. "Are you going to be okay? Have you seen a doctor?"

"I have a friend who is recommending someone to me. But Mami, Dante and I decided to adopt a little boy."

"Adopt?" Sylvia was stunned. "But don't you want to have your own children?"

"Mami, it's not about chromosomes. It's about love." She took in a deep breath. "We heard about a little boy whose mother was killed in a car accident. There is no family, so they were going to place him in social services. When we saw the little boy on television, it broke our hearts to think what a sad life he might have."

Sylvia caught on right away. "And Dante was an orphan, so he felt some kind of bond?"

That much was certainly true. "Yes, Mami."

"Did you meet the child yet?" Sylvia asked.

"Yes. He is very sweet." Elena looked down at the sleeping child, who was taking a nap.

"If that is what you want, then I am happy for you." Sylvia got choked up. "I am going to be an abuela!"

Tears stung Elena's eyes. She could hear the joy in her mother's voice, and the sense of relief from within. Another issue was resolved.

*Four years later*

Dante was doing well at work and was on the fast track for upper management. Elena took care of Mateo while continuously reading and practicing her English. At one point, Dante commented that she had no accent left at all, just a lilt in her voice that hinted her native tongue was a romance language. For four years, their lives were typical of those of a young family, with no major incidents or upheaval, until they had to enroll Mateo in school—which required a birth certificate.

"We knew this day would come. Now what do we do?" Elena paced the kitchen.

"Maybe we should hire a private detective to check all the local hospitals near Monterrey. There can't be that many," Dante suggested.

"And then what?" Elena asked curtly.

"And then we get a copy of his birth certificate."

"But we don't know who his parents were. Or if he was even born in a hospital! How do we do find all that information?"

"We ask the private investigator to follow the trail. That is what they get paid to do."

"How much to you think it will cost?" Elena asked.

"I have no idea, but I will find out." Dante snapped his fingers. "You know who would know?" Before he let her answer, he continued, "Yolanda and Rodrigo."

Elena squinted as she ran that through her head. "They do seem to be fixers. They surely fixed things for us, before and during our sojourn."

"I will call Rodrigo and explain everything to him."

"You mean about how we kidnapped a baby?" Elena resumed her pacing.

"Well, not exactly. I'll figure it out." Dante had a faraway look in his eyes. Elena could see the wheels in his head turning.

Later that evening, Dante phoned Rodrigo and asked if he could recommend a good private investigator near the US border.

"Ah, there are many, but a good one? I think I know one or two." Rodrigo waited for Dante to respond. He wasn't going to get up in Dante's business.

"That would be much appreciated. And Rodrigo? Please let's keep this conversation between us, please?"

"Of course. Man-to-man. I understand." Rodrigo was naturally curious, but as long as he could give Dante the information he needed, he'd be satisfied.

It took about two weeks before Elena and Dante received a report from the PI they'd hired based on Rodrigo's recommendation. They'd supplied the investigator with the little information they already knew, such as the city and approximate date of Mateo's birth. The report revealed that Mateo had been delivered by a midwife who registered the child as Muchacho Bebé Domenica Lopez. *Padre desconocido.* Father unknown. The investigator confirmed Mateo's mother had been killed in a van accident and had no immediate living relatives. He was able to secure a copy of Mateo's birth certificate, though of course, neither Dante's nor Elena's names were on it. Which left them with another problem to solve—but it was a start.

Again, Dante enlisted Rodrigo and Yolanda's aid. They suggested the name of a lawyer who was experienced in cases that were slightly outside the parameters of legal documentation.

Dante phoned the lawyer, who assured him that he could produce a birth certificate and papers transferring legal parental rights to Dante and Elena. Dante asked no other questions. He had to put his faith in Rodrigo's recommendation. They had no choice. One month later, a registered letter arrived at their home. What had been promised was inside, along with a bill for ten thousand dollars. Apparently, that was the going rate to adopt children on the black market. Elena and Dante breathed a bit easier, knowing they finally had the needed documentation to enroll Mateo in school and be legally recognized as his parents.

It was coming up on the five-year anniversary of Dante's employment. He had proven himself an invaluable member of the team and was promoted to upper-level management. It came with a significant raise and benefits, but they would have to relocate to Tennessee. It would mean a little more upheaval, but the pros outweighed the cons, and they packed up the furniture they had accumulated, the toys, and other valuables and moved to Nashville, where Bravo Oil had their executive offices for the Mid-South. Elena wasn't a big fan of country music, even though that's pretty much all they heard their entire stay in Texas. She still preferred Latino and classical music. But she was resolute. She would adapt. Again.

When they moved to Nashville, they enrolled Mateo in school, and Elena got a job substitute teaching. At night, she would study so she could finish her college degree. She always made a point to cook one of her mother's recipes on Sunday, to keep them connected to their roots. Dante would take Mateo outside, where he taught him how to play soccer. As much as Mateo enjoyed the game and spending time with his dad, he was always more fascinated by what his mother was doing in the kitchen. He would hurry home after school to watch his mother move about the kitchen, mixing this with that, frying that in there, chopping, grating, kneading, and baking. By the time Mateo was eight, Elena had earned her degree and applied for a full-time teaching position at Mateo's school. She promised she wouldn't fawn over him or do anything to cause embarrassment.

"It's okay, Mamita." Mateo only called her that when they were at home. "Maybe you can work in the kitchen, too. The food is pretty crummy." Elena laughed at that—not realizing that the school cafeteria would be just one stop on a much greater culinary journey to come.

# Part III

## Secrets Revealed

# Chapter Ten

# The Mystery

*Present Day*
*New York City*

Doctors, patients, and visitors swept up and down the hallways and in and out of the rooms of the always bustling NYU Langone Tisch Hospital. Among them were Dr. Adrian Ardell, who entered Mateo Castillo's room alongside one of her colleagues.

"This is Dr. Vieiro," Dr. Ardell said by way of introduction. "He will be administering an IV sedative. The procedure itself should take approximately twenty minutes, and then several minutes for you to come around. We will be taking the sample from the top ridge of the back of the hipbone. The posterior iliac crest. You may experience some soreness from the site, but it should be tolerable with acetaminophen. I will personally be administering the procedure as well as performing the tests in the lab."

Dr. Vieiro smiled at Mateo. "You are in excellent hands with Dr. Ardell."

"Yours too, I trust." Mateo smiled and extended the arm that wasn't hooked up to a piece of equipment.

Dr. Ardell checked her watch when it beeped. "Alright, Mr. Castillo. Time to say good night."

Mateo gave a slight wave. "*Hasta luego.*"


Elena was frantic. She must have left three messages in the last hour for Dante to call her. She paced the floor of her classroom. At least school was over for the day. She could have retired several years before, but she still enjoyed her work. She taught English to Spanish-speaking students, and Spanish to English-speaking students. Elena loved the cultural diversity of living near New York City.

Twenty years earlier, they had become US citizens. Eventually, Dante got his second promotion, and they relocated to Upper Montclair, New Jersey. At that point, Mateo was a freshman in high school and had no trouble making new friends, although he would have rather been in a kitchen than on a soccer field.

Dante worked his way up as a high-level executive at Bravo Oil Corporation. It afforded the family the opportunity to enjoy fine dining, Broadway plays, and family vacations. Elena and Dante would occasionally go salsa dancing in clubs in New York.

They didn't live an overly opulent life, but a nice, comfortable one.

An hour after she left her third message, the phone rang. Elena jumped as she caught her breath and answered the phone.

"Elena? What is it?" Dante sounded almost as frantic as she was. Elena wasn't the type to panic. This had to be urgent. He was gripping the corner of his desk.

"It's Mateo." Elena's voice was shaking.

"Is he alright?" Dante shot out of his chair.

"He's in the hospital. They are doing a bone marrow biopsy. Something about him fainting, and blood transfusions."

"Do they know why, or what?" Dante tried to keep his voice even.

"He has high levels of mercury in his blood. This is his second trip to the hospital in three weeks."

"Second trip? Why didn't he tell us?" Dante was also pacing now.

"I don't know." There was a great deal of frustration in Elena's voice. *Why hadn't their son come to them?*

"Perhaps he thought it wasn't a big deal. We will get to the bottom of this."

"Dante, they want samples of our blood. To see if we're matches for a potential transfusion."

It took several seconds for this to sink in. "Blood tests," Dante finally said flatly. It wasn't a question.

"Yes. What if we don't match?" Elena's voice was almost shrill.

Again, it took a few seconds for Dante to realize that was a possible outcome. It never occurred to him that one day they might have to match blood types.

"If it doesn't match, then he will know he was adopted." Elena paused. "And technically, legally, he wasn't even adopted." Elena was getting light-headed. "He was stolen."

"Elena, please don't talk like that. He was rescued. The government would have done nothing to protect him."

"And now? How can we protect him?" Elena was choking back tears.

"Elena, listen to me, please. We gave Mateo so much love. No one could have done a better job than you as his mother. And I will take credit for being a good father. Look how far he has come. And on his own. We taught him values. Responsibility. Gratitude. Compassion. Kindness. Loyalty. Integrity."

"Ah. But what about *our* integrity?" Elena stopped him in his tracks. "We have lied to him his entire life."

"Elena, we never lied to him. Not outright."

"That's only because he never asked. Imagine the conversation—'Mamita, Pappy, was I ever abandoned in a dumpy motel, and did my birth mother die in an accident because she was a prostitute?'" Dante couldn't help but smile at his wife's attempt at humor during this scary moment. Elena was beginning to calm down a bit.

"Technically, we never lied to him," Dante said slowly. "That's my point, *mi amor.*"

"Are you saying a lie of omission is not a lie?" Elena was trying to wrap her head around the ethical conundrum of that question.

"Elena, let's not quarrel. We will tell him he was adopted if the situation requires it. One of us could very well be a match anyway, and then the problem is no longer a problem. And until it becomes a problem, then it isn't one."

Elena smiled. Dante always knew what to say. "You are correct. We will wait until it becomes a problem." Even though Dante was right, she was worried about the legal ramifications. They could be exposed as kidnappers if someone decided to follow the paper trail. She prayed that would not happen, but there had been a campaign against immigrants, legal or not, regardless of where they were from.

Mateo was an emerging star in the arena of fine cuisine. It was an industry of driven, creative people. Many weren't very nice, and jealousy was no stranger to the business. With the competition in the forefront, anyone could become a formidable rival, on or off the line. Social media could destroy someone's reputation without there being any basis for it. The internet was a blessing and a curse. Elena had been ecstatic when she and her mother first got email accounts. Then the social media thing happened. It had been good at first—before every crackpot had access to it. She worried more about those types of online attacks than Mateo getting mugged on the subway. At least he could look over his shoulder when he was standing on a subway platform. Social media was filled with invisible enemies.

Mateo was not only a brilliant and creative chef, but he also had a charming and generous personality. Even as a child, he would share whatever was in his possession, whether it was a box of crayons or a muffuletta made by his own hands. She'd always thought he was an easy target but refrained from being too motherly or suffocating as many mothers could be.

Over the past two years, Mateo had appeared on many of the weekend morning shows doing cooking demonstrations. He was also lauded for reviving one of New York's iconic restaurants after it had suffered a downturn during the pandemic. He was surely one of the city's most eligible and well-liked bachelors but had experienced a string of disappointing relationships. If you could even call them relationships. He was invited to many high-profile parties and events. Any social climber would want to be on the arm of the tall, dark, and handsome chef. Elena had been happy when he swore off girlfriends for the time being. His work required his undivided attention.

Focusing back on the task at hand, Elena phoned their primary care physician and explained that she and Dante needed to schedule blood tests, particularly for compatibility typing. Elena knew the doctor was bound by HIPAA confidentiality rules, so she felt free to explain the reason for the tests. She left out the "stolen baby" part. Then she silently admonished herself for thinking of Mateo's adoption that way.

The next day, Dante and Elena went to the lab and had their blood drawn. The results of the tests would be sent immediately to Dr. Ardell, who would then compare them to Mateo's.

Elena was a nervous wreck. Their lives could be dramatically changed in a short amount of time.

Not that she hadn't been through that before, but now, in her mid-fifties, she didn't think she had the wherewithal for that kind of upheaval.

Mateo recognized the fluorescent lights as they moved quickly overhead. Dr. Ardell was looking down at him as the gurney rolled down the corridor. "How do you feel?" she asked.

As much of a fog as he was in, Mateo could not resist squeezing out the words, "Like I have a bloody hangover, no pun intended."

Dr. Ardell broke into a wide smile. "I am glad we didn't remove any of your sense of humor."

Mateo gave her a thumbs-up and floated back through the clouds.

"Get some rest. They will be serving dinner in about an hour. I am sure you are awaiting that in great anticipation." Dr. Ardell was testing her repartee.

"Indeed I am." Mateo motioned with one finger for her to come closer. He whispered, "Grilled cheese, please?"

Dr. Ardell placed her hand on his arm. "I think you earned it." She turned and walked out of the room. Just like that.

*These abrupt exits must be a thing with her,* Mateo thought to himself.

Perky Becky appeared next to the curtain dividing Mateo's room. "Welcome back. It's just you and me now." She jerked her thumb toward the side of the room where Mr. Obnoxious had been staying. "His daddy put him in a private room, with a private nurse. La-di-da. As if I wasn't takin' good care of him." The twentysomething nurse's aide pouted.

"He was a bit of a jerk. He didn't deserve you." Mateo had regained all of his faculties at that point.

Becky gave a little giggle. "Aw. You're sweet."

"I am sure there are a lot of people who would disagree with you." If anything, Mateo was humble.

Just before the mystery meal was brought in, another aide carried in a tray with two grilled cheese sandwiches, a carton of milk, an apple, and a piece of iceberg lettuce with a sad looking slice of tomato on top. *Well, they tried.* Mateo laughed to himself. It was still better than whatever else they could present. He reminded himself of what he said to Mr. Jock about having to serve hundreds of people, and then he gave thanks.

Mateo was relieved he didn't have to listen to any more of Coleman's effusive, phony friends. He actually welcomed the solitude, as much as one could have in a busy hospital. But he was alone with his thoughts. That was something he wasn't accustomed to. When he was actually alone, he was usually sleeping or getting ready for work. His life was filled with hustle and bustle. He resigned himself to his situation. He had no option. He picked up the TV remote and started scanning shows and came upon *The Price is Right.* For the longest time, he thought the show was silly, until he realized it was probably the happiest day of the contestants' lives. *Isn't it nice to know there are people out there who are enjoying themselves to the fullest?* And what about him? Was he really enjoying his life? Parts of it? Certainly when it came to work. His past failed romances flipped through his head. Was it him? Was he not involved enough? Did he put too much emphasis on work? Career? Financial success? His mother would often say the exact words he had said to Becky earlier: "They didn't deserve you." True, the women he had dated were shallow. But wasn't he, as well? His mind was swinging all over the place. Maybe being alone wasn't such a good thing—whether in the hospital, or in life in general.

Just after noon, Elena received a phone call from Dr. Ardell. "Is everything alright?" Elena held her breath.

"I'm not sure." Dr. Ardell hesitated. How did you ask the question: *Are you Mateo's birth parents?* She knew there was only one way to say it and so broached the subject head-on.

Elena remained quiet after the question was asked.

"Mrs. Castillo? This is very important." Dr. Ardell tried to imagine what was going through the other woman's mind.

"Yes, I am here." After a moment, Elena held her head up high and replied. "Dr. Ardell, Mateo was adopted, but he is not aware of it. His mother died in a car accident, and there is no record of his birth father. Dante and I discussed this situation many, many times. Then we decided it would not matter if we decided not to tell him. There was no way for him to search for his birth father, and why would he?" She almost answered her own question.

"For reasons such as this. His health."

Elena kept her calm. "If he is put in the National Transplant Registry, how will that affect him?"

"What do you mean?" Dr. Ardell was puzzled.

"Will people find out he's adopted?" Elena knew the answer to her question was *no*, but with technology today and the dark, deep web, hackers were everywhere. No information was truly protected. Look what they'd done to international financial institutions. The US Government. Power grids. Oil pipelines. The scams and spams. It was endless. And even though Mateo was a very small potato in the big messy salad of life, people could be cruel. Then there was the real threat of legal ramifications. Could all three of them be deported? Could she and Dante be arrested for kidnapping? Her skin began to crawl up the back of her neck.

Dr. Ardell broke Elena's panic. "It's highly unlikely," she said, but as if reading her mind, she added, "But anything is possible, Mrs. Castillo."

"What should we tell Mateo?" Elena asked in earnest.

"We can tell him that you are type AB negative, and Mr. Castillo is B negative. Mateo is O positive. We could have him draw his own conclusions—if he knows that an AB and a B do not bear children with type O, he can easily figure things out. But I believe you should be direct and tell him the truth. We haven't come to the final conclusion that he will actually need a bone marrow transplant; we want to be ready just in case."

"So he could be alright?" Elena had hope in her voice.

"We are doing a series of chelation and transfusion procedures. If his mercury levels are significantly lower as a result, than we can monitor him for six weeks to be sure the situation hasn't recurred or worsened."

"Thank you, Doctor. I will keep praying for a miracle." Elena meant that with all her heart.

"As much I am a scientist, I like to think miracles can happen. I hope my research can prove that for someone someday." Dr. Ardell thought about her brother and her dream of finding as many cures for blood disorders as she could. "I will be in touch, but I will leave it to you to discuss Mateo's lineage with him."

"Thank you again, Dr. Ardell." Elena hung up the phone and immediately called Dante. She was breathless. "Our blood does not match." She heaved her words into the phone.

"I didn't expect it to, but I was still hopeful," Dante said with resignation. "What does that mean for Mateo?" He drummed his fingers on his desk.

"For now, they are going to continue the two therapies, chelation and transfusion. Then they will check him again in six weeks. Thankfully, the restaurant is closed for two weeks, so he can get some rest."

"Should we encourage him to come home?" Dante furrowed his brow. Many men at Mateo's age were still either living in their parents' basements or their childhood bedrooms, but Mateo was different. He wanted to strike out on his own. Granted, Dante had paid for Mateo's culinary school training, but Mateo was diligently paying his father a regular sum each week.

"I will call him and ask, but I am not going to pressure him," Elena said.

"Good idea. Let me know what he says. Meanwhile, I will call and see how he's doing. I won't mention the blood work until you and I speak again later today. How does that sound?"

"But what if we get caught?"

"Caught?" Dante asked.

"We could be deported. Arrested." Elena was trying not to shriek into the phone.

Dante reassured her that no matter what happened, they would work through it. Together. "Just like we always have." Dante was confident and supportive as usual, but secretly, he too was concerned about what kind of blowback any of this might create.

Before she phoned Mateo, Elena checked the time. Puerto Vallarta was only one time zone away. Aside from ongoing emails, she would contact her parents every Sunday via Skype. It was one of the technologies she truly appreciated. She decided to video chat with her parents now.

"Hi, Mami," Elena greeted her mother in a little girl tone as Sylvia appeared on the computer screen.

"Elena? Are you alright? You look very upset." Sylvia was now in her late seventies, but she was still beautiful, with wisps of gray running through her hair, which she wore in a wavy chin-length style.

Elena sighed. "Is Papá around?"

"Yes. What is it?" Sylvia knew when something was seriously troubling her daughter.

"Please go get him. I have something I must tell you."

"*Dios mío!*" Sylvia exclaimed. "Are you sick? Is it Dante? Mateo?"

"Mateo has a blood disorder," Elena said.

"Gabriel! Come here!" Sylvia shouted over her shoulder. He rushed to where Sylvia was sitting in front of her computer.

"What's wrong?" Gabriel looked truly troubled.

"Mateo has something wrong with his blood," Sylvia said breathlessly.

Everyone started talking at once, half in Spanish, half in English.

"Please." Elena tried to calm them. "He is doing alright. They are giving him transfusions."

"But why?" Sylvia asked.

Elena explained the best she could with what little information anyone had. "But there is more."

"What could be more?" Gabriel was leaning over Sylvia's shoulder, facing into the camera.

Elena hung her head. "I've lied to you and Mami."

"When? Why?" Sylvia was startled by this news. They had always had an open and honest rapport with their only daughter.

Elena recounted every incident, from the motel, the meeting at immigration, the news about Mateo's birth mother, his missing father, the birth certificate, and the false documents. The entire big adoption lie. However, she didn't tell them about Yolanda's and Rodrigo's involvement. She didn't want to violate their trust or ruin their friendship. Then she broke down in tears.

Sylvia put her hand on the monitor screen, wanting to hug her daughter. "*Hija*. Does Mateo know?"

"Not yet. We didn't think there was any reason to tell him. There was no one he could trace."

"Is he in some kind of trouble?" Gabriel asked.

"Only his health. But he has a very good doctor, who told me she was on a mission."

"So what is the problem?" Gabriel said. "As long as there are no legal issues . . ." His voice trailed off.

"Not yet." Elena was sniffling and blowing her nose. "Sorry."

"What can we do to help?" Sylvia asked.

"Nothing. If this treatment doesn't work, he may need a bone marrow transplant. Dante and I had blood work done, and we are not a match."

"And this is why you need to tell him the truth." Sylvia stated the obvious.

"Yes, Mami."

"You have been wonderful parents. He is a wonderful young man. I cannot imagine he would be upset."

"Maybe because we have lied to him all these years? And to you," Elena reminded her.

"You were protecting him." Gabriel was the voice of reason. Sylvia murmured her agreement.

"That is only part of it," Elena continued. "If he goes into the bone marrow registry, someone may find out he was, how do I say this . . . inappropriately adopted?"

Gabriel was the first to answer. "Let's not think about that now. It's not a problem until it becomes a problem."

Elena's face froze, and then she smiled. "Dante said the same thing to me only a few minutes ago."

"See? That is a sign," Sylvia said.

"Mami, you always know what to say." Elena wiped the tears from her face.

"Do you want us to come to New Jersey?" Sylvia asked. They had made the trip many times over the years, entering the US with visitor visas.

"No. Not yet. Dante and I are going to try to talk Mateo into coming here for a few days to rest."

"That is a very good idea." Gabriel nodded.

Elena was relieved the secret she had been carrying for almost thirty-five years was finally out in the open.

"*Hija*, everything will be alright," Gabriel added. "Remember, good things can come from bad situations. Look what happened with us! One day our world was torn apart, but now we can say we have had a very happy life. Moving to Puerto Vallarta was the best thing that happened to us. We had less stress, made many friends. Do not worry. Mateo is a good man. He knows how much you and Dante love him. That is all that matters."

"Thank you, Mami. Thank you, Papá. I am sorry I never told you. We never thought much of it once Mateo went to school. He could not be more of a son to us."

"And he is our grandson," Gabriel said with certainty.

After saying goodbye to her parents, Elena next

called Mateo's cell phone. He had been drifting in and out of sleep. The salsa music ringtone startled him awake once more.

"Mamita?" There was grogginess in his voice.

"Mateo. How are you feeling?"

"Not terrible. I'm just a little tired. I don't know why. I've been laying around for two days."

"Your body is telling you to rest." Elena's voice was soothing.

"You are probably right." Mateo was getting used to the idea he wasn't as robust as he once thought. That was the case for many Latin men in their mid-thirties. There was a certain type of machismo that was part of their culture, regardless of age. It also had nothing to do with their opinion of women. They loved and respected women, especially their mothers, if the man had been raised properly, as Mateo had been. Women secretly knew they were stronger than men, but they let the men believe the opposite. It was an innate understanding women had with each other. "Let them think they are boss!" would always bring howls of delight.

"Mamita?" Mateo noticed his mother was quiet on the other end of the call.

"Would you want to come and stay with us for a few days?"

"Let's see what the doctor says later. I think I am going to be a hostage here for another day or so. She mentioned doing this blood therapy thing one or two more times before she lets me out of here." It was a tempting invitation, but Mateo didn't want to stray too far from Dr. Ardell, and he doubted she made house calls to New Jersey. "Did you get the blood test results?"

Elena froze. Then she lied. Sort of. "Yes, but I didn't quite understand them. Too many letters and pluses and minuses." She was still quick on her feet.

Mateo chuckled. "I think Papá will be able to explain it."

"Yes, I am sure." Elena was relieved that she had put an end to the inquisition quickly. "Do you want us to visit you? I can bring you some *good* food." She emphasized the word *good*.

"I don't want you to have to come into the city. Let's wait a few days, and then we can decide what to do. Maybe you can come to my apartment after I leave here."

"Oh, that would be nice. Then we can have dinner together instead of looking for a microwave oven in the hospital."

Mateo heard the sound of footsteps getting closer to his door. Nurse Stenhouse was back to poke him. At least it was through the port in his hand and, as promised, she didn't have to put another hole in him. "Mamita, I have to go. Nurse Stenhouse is here to torture me again."

"Okay, son. I will talk to you later. *Te amo hijo mio.*" Elena clicked off the phone with a sigh.

For Mateo, the day seemed endless. It was just like the day before. The sterile smell, the very unflattering and not very relaxing lighting, the bells, the flashing lights, and the occasional moans from other patients being wheeled past his room. He wondered how many more grilled cheese sandwiches he could wrangle from his doctor. She didn't appear to be concerned about his cholesterol. He smiled at that thought. At least he had something different for breakfast that morning. He wasn't sure what it was, but it had resembled French toast. There was a side of melon along with orange juice and milk. Either it was an improvement, or he was just getting used to the bland, unappetizing gastronomy.

He flipped through the weekday morning shows. They were vastly different from the weekend shows he had appeared on, which were much more instructional and informational. They had lesser-known hosts who seemed genuinely interested in the subjects they were covering that day. They seemed to have more empathy. More connection. But these mega-morning shows, with the same fake faces smiling into the camera and the shameless celebrity self-promoters, were almost depressing. What irked him was the nonchalant way they spoke about their trips to London or a weekend in the Hamptons while they were clothed in designer wear. Did these talking heads really think their audience could relate to what they were discussing? They were all a bunch of Marie Antoinettes. When the queen was told the people had no bread, she had allegedly replied, "Let them eat cake." No wonder they took off her head. Not that Mateo wanted the TV hosts to be victims of a mad massacre, but maybe a few days working at a soup kitchen when there weren't cameras rolling might give them a reality check. How could anyone sitting at a desk wearing a 5,000-dollar suit, 1,000-dollar shoes, a 300-dollar tie, and a 500-dollar shirt relate to someone who had to hold down two jobs to feed their family?

Mateo recalled an afternoon TV host complaining she had to cancel her trip to Italy because Russia had invaded Ukraine. *Boo-hoo*, he thought. *Your private jet is just going to have to wait on the tarmac.* People were out of touch. Unfortunately, social media made it seem quite the opposite. The hype was all that mattered, and people's empathy was being challenged. Mateo ruminated a little more. He believed that most people were good. The key was accessing that inner particle of empathy and expanding it to care about others instead of how many followers you had. He let out a loud, "Ugh."

He wondered why he was suddenly in a sour mood. Maybe it *was* the TV. It had a way of preying on your conscious and subconscious mind. Time to turn it off. He decided to ask Becky to get him a book. A murder mystery. Dr. Ardell had used the word *mystery* a few times, and it had lodged in his brain. Maybe it would create another opportunity for a little small talk.

That afternoon, Dante phoned to check on his son. "How are you feeling?" he asked.

"I'm okay, Papá. Just a little down about all of this."

"Yes, tell me. What has happened?" Dante didn't want to start on the defensive with *Why didn't you tell us you were in the hospital?*

Mateo talked his father through the series of events over the past three weeks, ending with, "I can't explain it. I felt fine one day, and the next thing I knew, I was being rushed to the hospital.

They said it was from ingesting too much mercury. So I stopped eating seafood for over two weeks, and then, *boom!* It happened again, but this time, they said there was even *more* mercury in my system than before. At first, they thought it was too much seafood."

Dante did a double take at the phone. Fish? The bane of La Ley's existence. She had never eaten it again once they got off that ship. Dante snapped himself back to the present conversation. "That does seem odd. And suspicious, no?" Dante couldn't understand how something like this could come on so quickly.

"I wouldn't call it suspicious, but surely mysterious," Mateo said.

"Yes. That's what I meant." Dante was keenly aware his own behavior could be considered fishy if people knew their family history. He surely had a few things to hide, including knowingly accepting false documents.

"Did your mother talk to you about coming home for a few days? You'll need someone to cook for you."

Mateo chuckled. "Ironic, isn't it? Someone has to cook for *me*."

"I am sure your mother would be overjoyed to have you back in her kitchen." Dante's voice did not give any hint of concern. He and Elena would tell Mateo the truth. But not yet. Not until it was necessary. Even if they weren't forced to, they would tell him eventually. He deserved to know. What he would do with the information was surely up to him, but he couldn't condemn his parents

for his upbringing. They were loving and supportive. *Mateo has no cause for complaints*, Dante thought
to himself.

"Maybe for a day or so." Mateo didn't want to
hurt his parents' feelings by refusing their generous offer to care for him, but he didn't want Dr.
Ardell to get away from him, either. He was convinced she was unattached. He could tell by the
way she touched his arm the day before and told
him he earned a grilled cheese. She wasn't the
warm and fuzzy type, so Mateo took it as a signal.
Maybe a subliminal move on her part. Or so he
hoped.

After the call with his father, the hours dragged
on once more for Mateo. He clicked the television
on again. Maybe there would be a movie or an old
TV show. He came across an episode of *Seinfeld*.
He took it as a sign. He would be a little more
forthcoming with his interest in his doctor. Then
he thought she probably had a rule about not dating patients. All the more reason for him to get
better, so she would no longer be his doctor!

That afternoon, Dr. Ardell paid Mateo a visit.
She didn't know if his parents had spoken to him,
and she was not about to ask. If they told him
about his past, that was none of her business; it
only mattered to the extent of finding a bone marrow donor. But they weren't quite there just yet. If
she could only find the source of his mercury
levels.

"How are you feeling?" Her hair was loose
around her neck, and she was wearing lipstick.

"Much, much better." Mateo couldn't resist saying, "You look very nice. Do you have a date tonight?" Then he feigned embarrassment. "My apologies. It's none of my business."

She was quite happy he asked. It gave her the opportunity to say, "No, I do not, but thank you." She averted her eyes from his. "This place can be very drab. I thought I would add a little color. If not on the walls, at least on my face," she said casually.

"Well, you certainly brightened up my room." Mateo was going full-out now.

Dr. Ardell maintained her cool. "Good. I want my patients to be cheered."

"So, what's the latest?"

"Did you speak to your parents?"

"Yes. My mother wants me to spend a few days at their house. She wants to cook for me, but I'll be honest—I think she wants me to cook for her!" He was exuding charm.

"That might be a good idea."

*Boom.* He was deflated once more.

Dr. Ardell continued. "I have a seminar this weekend, so there will be no one around to look after you should you fall down somewhere." She noted something in the tablet she was holding.

"I'm really not *that* uncoordinated," Mateo bantered.

"You may be extremely coordinated, but you have landed in my care twice because something caused you to fall." She leaned against the end of the bed. "Having someone around would be of great importance."

"Okay. So I'll stay at my parents' the weekend

you are away. Then I come back to . . . where? Here? My apartment?"

"How about this: you come back next Tuesday for routine blood work. That will give us an entire week to see if this protocol is helping. If not, we will take other measures. How does that sound?"

"That works for me."

"And if you are well enough, maybe you can show me 'the line,' as you call it. It might help me to unravel this mystery of yours." Mateo's condition was idiopathic. Maybe there was a clue to be found in the restaurant kitchen. Or perhaps his apartment. She would cross that bridge after more results were in.

"You've got a deal." Mateo hadn't felt this good in several days. Maybe months.

Dr. Ardell said good night after telling Mateo he would be released the next day. After the doctor left, Mateo phoned his mother and accepted her offer. "But just through the weekend, Mamita."

Elena was overjoyed. "Your father and I will pick you up at the hospital tomorrow."

"Mamita? Can you do me a favor, please?"

"Whatever you want. Pan de queso?" She laughed nervously.

"Ha, yes, but also something else. The nurses and the aides have been very kind to me. Could you pick up a basket of soaps or candles? Just a little something to show my appreciation?"

*And here he's thinking about other people while he's the one whose life is on the line,* Elena thought. "Of course! How many soaps do you need?"

"Fifteen?" He wasn't quite sure.

"I will bring twenty!" Elena said with enthusiasm. She then phoned Dante and apprised him of the situation. They both agreed that the two of them would decide how to break the news to Mateo. It could go fine, or it could go sideways. She prayed for fine.

Back at the hospital, Mateo phoned his friend Roger and asked if he could continue to feed Newman and also bring him some clothes. "And maybe one of those caprese sandwiches from Mangia?" He could already taste the fresh mozzarella, fresh tomato, basil, and a drizzle of balsamic glaze, served on a ciabatta roll. "Tell them to add some prosciutto, please," he instructed.

The next day, Elena and Dante went to the hospital. Elena carried a wicker basket filled with a variety of special soaps, including some with a more masculine fragrance for the male orderlies. When they arrived at the hospital, Mateo was waiting for them in a wheelchair.

"*Dios mío!* Can you not walk?" She tried to contain herself and not smother her son with kisses. Elena didn't realize they had to wheel every patient out when they were discharged.

Dante smiled to himself. He knew exactly how she felt. Mateo was surely a blessing in their life. Not only was he smart, ambitious, and kind, he was their only son. Their only child. After they moved to Corpus Christi, despite many months of lovemaking, Elena never got pregnant. She finally went to the OB-GYN her friend Sally recommended, and they discovered why. Elena suffered from severe ovarian cysts that rendered her incapable of a successful pregnancy. Yes, Mateo was truly "God's gift" to them.

Becky rolled Mateo to the sidewalk. He climbed into the back seat of his father's SUV. The aroma of freshly baked pan de queso filled the car.

"Mamita!" Mateo ripped off the paper wrapper and pulled pieces from the warm bread. "This is much better than any medicine they could give me!" He was savoring the delicious, salty taste, breadcrumbs falling all over his shirt.

Elena resisted the temptation to point it out. She was busy enjoying her son enjoying himself. "I am so happy you decided to come and stay with us for the weekend."

Licking his lips, Mateo mumbled, "Me, too."

The drive to Upper Montclair from the city normally took under an hour without traffic. Mateo settled into his seat. It was the first time he felt comfortable in some time. His life had been on the crazy train for a couple of years. It was exciting, but also exhausting. Physically, mentally, and spiritually. He thought about how easy it was to get caught up in the glamour and the accolades. The attention. It was a funny thing, but Mateo never looked for notoriety. He simply loved food and loved to cook. He especially enjoyed sharing meals with friends and family. But ever since he took over as executive chef at Le Mer, there was little time for that. With his schedule, it was almost impossible. It left a nagging feeling inside. But when he saw the bread in the back seat, it brought him to another place. A place he remembered. A place he wanted to be. Not necessarily a building, but a place of companionship. Camaraderie. A time and place to enjoy friendship. Family.

Soon they pulled into the driveway of the two-story colonial. Dante took Mateo's duffel bag up to what was now the guest room. Gone were the soccer posters and the Texas Rangers pennant. No more Nashville neon guitars. The only thing that remained were the ribbons Mateo had won for cooking contests, including the gold banner for his chili cook-off victory. He had learned a lot from his mother about using herbs and spices, and it paid off with a 500-dollar prize. He was only fourteen at the time but had used the money to take his family to a four-star restaurant in New York. For a teenager, he had a great deal of sophistication and poise. Perhaps it came from adapting to new locations while he was growing up, and the influence of his parents' education and cultural talents.

Mateo was feeling good. He had almost all of his strength back and had a clear head. Things were looking up. Elena put some music on, and they went into the kitchen. He helped his mother prepare a French onion soup with a Mexican twist. It was all about the cheese. Lots of it. In the soup. On the toasted bread. A hint of cardamom. The main course would be roasted lamb chops with a creamy parsnip emulsion, covered with crumbled crispy prosciutto. Fennel confit would dress the plate.

Dante came into the kitchen with the biggest smile on his face. "Are you sure you don't want to move back here?"

"I love you, Pop, but I don't want you to get fat." Mateo grinned, then asked, "How about a nice glass of wine?"

"For now or dinner?" Dante asked.

Elena furrowed her brow. "Are you sure you should be drinking?"

"Mamita, they say red wine is very good for the blood," Mateo reassured her.

"Yes, but what does your doctor say?"

Mateo pursed his lips. "Huh. She didn't say anything except no green leafy vegetables, no garlic, no cinnamon."

"Are you sure?" Elena gave him a sideways look.

Mateo blushed. "Honestly? I can't remember."

"Should you call her?" Elena asked.

Mateo balked at the idea of phoning Dr. Ardell to get permission to have a glass of wine. "She's at a seminar. I can't bother her over a glass of wine."

"Alright. But only one. I am not a nurse. I am a teacher."

Dante broke in, "And I am an executive. I don't know how to do anything!" Everyone laughed.

"I know you don't know how to put a crib together." Elena remembered their first night in Corpus Christi, which reminded her of the elephant in the room. She and Dante had agreed they would have the conversation with Mateo over dinner.

"What do you mean?" Mateo was checking on the slow-cooking fennel.

"The first night we arrived in Corpus Christi, your father thought he could put your crib together, but I encouraged him to let the maintenance man do it." Elena sounded very calm, considering the big talk was imminent.

An hour later, they were enjoying their meal together, something they hadn't done in many months.

Dante swirled the wine in his glass. "Mateo, we have something to tell you."

Panic spread across Mateo's face. "Is everyone alright? Mamita? Pop?"

"Yes, we are fine. It is you we are concerned about." Elena placed her hand on Mateo's.

"I'm doing much better. See? No IV lines in my veins." He pulled up his sleeves to accentuate what he was saying.

The room fell silent. Dante looked at Elena and then back at Mateo. "There is something we never told you."

Mateo looked confused. They had always been open with each other. Except for this.

"Before we left Mexico . . ." Dante didn't know how much of the story should be told. He and Elena had agreed they would say it was a simple adoption. Dante continued. "Before we left Mexico, there was a terrible car accident."

Mateo looked even more confused.

"A woman was killed. She had a son, about six months old. They were going to send him to children's services, but we knew the baby would most likely never get adopted." He paused.

Mateo leaned back in his chair. "And that little boy was me." It was a statement. Not a question.

"Yes, Mateo." Elena folded her hands on her lap.

Silence fell across the table. Then Mateo asked the obvious question. "You never told me. Why?"

"Because when we tried to locate your birth father, he was not listed on your birth certificate," Dante replied.

"And my birth mother was dead." Mateo reiterated what he was just told.

"Correct. We never thought there would be a reason to have to tell you," Dante explained. "We never wanted you to think you had been abandoned by someone." Dante cleared his throat. "Abandoned like I was."

Mateo did a double take. "What do you mean?"

"I was left at an orphanage. I never knew who my parents were."

"But you said you went to a Catholic school and that your parents passed away after you and Mamita got married."

"Part of that is true." Dante fiddled with his wineglass, waiting for an emotional outburst. But one never came. "I did grow up in a Catholic environment. I was raised by nuns."

Mateo smirked. "Better than being raised by wolves."

Elena almost choked on her wine, and Dante burst into laughter. "You are taking this very well." Dante was wiping the tears from his eyes.

"I have a confession." Mateo had a bit of a mischievous grin on his face. "You heard about that test you can take for DNA?"

"Yes, of course," Elena replied.

"Well, one of the line chefs got all of us to do it. It was kind of a joke about whose culture was more inclined to be a chef, but also who might be more vulnerable to COVID. I know it sounds stupid now."

"Wait. You took that test?" Dante was incredulous.

"Yes, about a year ago," Mateo admitted. "Mine came back with results saying my ancestry was Mexican and Dutch. Not an iota of Colombian. I shrugged it off as a colossal mistake. It didn't matter to me. Not then. And not now." He chuckled. "I occasionally wondered why I had blue eyes. I figured you both had recessive genes. That's one mystery solved." He stretched his arms. "Coffee, anyone?"

Elena watched Mateo get up and walk to the coffee maker. She didn't know how to react. She looked at Dante, who simply shrugged.

"So, you are not upset with us for keeping this from you?" Dante asked.

"Not really. I never had occasion to wonder if you were my birth parents. Maybe the blue eyes, but according to my seventh-grade science teacher, it was possible. End of story." He pressed the espresso button on the large coffee machine and then began to steam the milk. "As far as I'm concerned, you are my parents. My mamita and papá. And whatever you did to keep me safe and loved, well, that is all that matters to me." He placed the cappuccino in front of his mother, put his arms around her shoulders, and gave her a big, loud smooch on the cheek. He then turned to his father and did the same.

Dante and Elena were gobsmacked. They had expected some kind of reaction. Anger? Disappointment? Resentment? They got none of it. Instead, all they received was appreciation from their son. Yes, *their* son was a man of true loyalty and character.

# Chapter Eleven

# Dinner, Danger, Discovery

*New York City*

Mateo was well rested after a weekend with his family. Yes, *his* family. Finding out he was adopted was not as devastating as it could have been for most people. He felt lucky, especially when he thought about the alternatives. Foster care? That would have been a nightmare all by itself. Then waiting, hoping for a family? No, he was grateful Elena and Dante Castillo had rescued him from a fate he did not want to consider any further.

He checked in at the outpatient desk at the hospital for his latest round of blood work. Nurse

Stenhouse greeted him in the lab. "Ah, my favorite pincushion," she joked.

"They took the port out a few days ago. I didn't want it to be dangling off the back of my hand all weekend."

"No worries. I will be very gentle. Now roll up your sleeve." Terry Stenhouse wrapped the rubber hose around his bicep. "Make a fist."

"Yes, boss." Mateo smiled up at her. "How many gallons are you going to drain from me today?"

"Only five vials."

"Are you sure you don't have some vampire DNA floating through your veins?" he teased.

She cackled. "Oh, darlin', if I did, I would be in pig heaven right now!"

"Ouch!" Mateo's laughter caused the needle to slip a tad.

"Sit still. You know the drill. No more funny talk from either of us." She gave him a wink and continued to pull the blood from his arm. A few minutes later, she put a piece of gauze and tape on the inside of his arm. "There you go, Chef."

Mateo gave her a slight bow. "And I will get you that onion soup recipe. I made it this weekend for my parents." He said the word *parents* with a newfound perspective. Yes, they were truly his parents. No doubt about it.

"And did they like it?" The nurse was disposing of the needles in the hazmat container.

"Very much. I wouldn't give you a recipe if it wasn't good. I might have to come back here someday, and I wouldn't want you to hurt me." He smiled.

"No offense, but I hope I don't see you again after this." She folded her arms. "Except for on television, where you show me how to cook."

"I try to make things easy, delicious, and beautiful. Food is art and needs to be shared. Imagine if Degas or Botticelli never showed their paintings to anyone?"

Nurse Stenhouse had a thoughtful look on her face. "I never really thought about it that way. You're pretty astute for a whippersnapper."

"I'm in my mid-thirties!"

"Honey, compared to me, you are a whippersnapper."

Mateo laughed. "I don't think anyone has ever called me a whippersnapper before."

"First time for everything. Now go sit in the waiting room. Dr. Ardell will be here within the hour. I should have these ready for her."

Mateo took a seat in the waiting area. He pulled out the book Becky had gotten him: *The Adventures of Sherlock Holmes.* It was a short-story collection, so it didn't require a major commitment, although he was thoroughly enjoying it. Soon Mateo heard his name being called. Dr. Ardell was standing in the doorway with her tablet.

"Nice to see you," she said. She was wearing a warm smile on her face. Lipstick included.

"Nice to see you, as well. How was your seminar?" Mateo asked.

"Lots of interesting hypotheses. Sometimes I wonder why I go to them. Lots of schmoozing."

Dante chuckled at her pronunciation of *schmoozing*, with her slight accent.

"What?" She looked at him squarely in the face. "You don't like the way I say *schmooze*?" She knew exactly what she was saying. And it was fun.

Mateo stifled a laugh. "I think it's charming."

She showed him to the chair across from her desk. "Please sit."

"And?" Mateo pointed to the table.

"And your blood work showed all normal levels."

"Could that be right?" Mateo was thrilled but uncertain. It had been only a week since he thought he was at death's door.

"I usually am." She smiled.

Mateo was stunned. "Wow. This is great news!"

"But we have to keep monitoring you for the next several weeks to be sure whatever it was is no longer a threat to you."

"Whatever you say, Doctor." Mateo was over the moon with the prognosis. "Heck, I'll see you once a week if necessary." He was half-serious. Not about blood tests, but about seeing her.

"That won't be necessary." She folded her hands on top of the tablet. "Do you have any questions?"

This was it—the opening he'd been waiting for. "Yes." He waited a beat. "How would you like to have a tour of the kitchen? See the line?"

"Yes. That would be very interesting." She looked more serious than excited.

"The restaurant is closed for the rest of the week, so it would be a good time to go."

"Does that mean I won't get a meal?" She was being bold again, and she was rather liking it.

Mateo tried to keep a straight face. "I'll throw something together."

"I like that idea. How is Wednesday?" She wasn't wasting any time, either.

"Perfect. What time do you want to meet?"

"Six o'clock?"

"Great. Send me a text when you get to the front door."

"I shall. I am looking forward to seeing how *you* operate." Dr. Ardell made another attempt at humor.

"Oh, I get it. Operate." Mateo grinned. He stood and extended his hand for a shake.

"Oh, you are too clever for me." She smiled the biggest smile he had ever seen on her face. It looked good on her.

And she thought it felt good, too.


On Wednesday, Mateo got to the restaurant around five o'clock. He wanted to be sure the place wasn't too much of a mess and that the kitchen was clean. It should be, but since they were closed and contractors were coming in and out, anything was possible.

He walked over to the locker where he kept his personal set of knives. He planned to do a demonstration for the doctor. Most people thought they needed a stockpile of various knives, but there were only three essentials: chef's knife, serrated, and paring.

When he reached his locker, the door was open. He never would have left it that way; he always locked his knives up. In addition to safety reasons, it was too easy for someone to misplace or walk off with a knife, so most chefs kept theirs wrapped and tucked away somewhere. At 350-dollars-plus per knife, it could get expensive to replace them. The only time Mateo's knives were not within his reach or in his locker was when they were out for sharpening. Maybe that was it. Maybe Nora had them sent out. He shrugged and pulled out the knife roll and brought it to the large stainless-steel table. He checked the refrigerators for any signs of something edible that wasn't fish or shellfish. Nothing. He would simply have to take Dr. Ardell out to dinner. There. Problem solved, although he still planned on showing her his paring skills and so grabbed a few onions, a potato, and a sad-looking tomato.

At exactly six o'clock, his phone pinged. Dr. Ardell was at the front door. Mateo picked his way through the stacked chairs and tables and let her in. "Hi! Welcome to Le Mer."

He swept his arm out in front of her.

"Thank you, Chef. Is that what I am supposed to call you?" Dr. Ardell was in a fine mood.

"Mateo is fine." He guided her through the chaos.

He couldn't help but notice she was wearing makeup, and her hair fell in golden waves around her shoulders. He was dazed by her beauty and bumped into a table. She stifled a giggle. "I am off duty. If you hurt yourself, you are on your own." She bit her lip as he regained his balance.

Mateo was grateful the embarrassment on his face didn't show in the shadows. "Follow me." He led her to the kitchen. "Oh, we do have one problem, however."

"What is that?"

He pointed to the onions, potato, and the sorry-looking tomato. "This is all we have on hand. I'm afraid I am going to have to take you to dinner somewhere else."

"Whatever you say, Chef. You are in charge tonight. As I said, I am off duty." She couldn't remember the last time she was out on what could be considered a date. She was surprised at how relaxed she felt around him. The kitchen was rather nippy, so she opted to leave her trench coat on, but unbuttoned the front and let it hang loosely.

"Are you alright? I know it gets a bit chilly in here," Mateo commented.

"I'll be fine. I don't suppose we will be spending too much time here."

Mateo rolled his knife roll open. "Nope. Just a quick demo."

Mateo explained the differences between the knives and what they were used for, as he demonstrated the proper way to handle each one. He handed her the paring knife, and she put her thumb on the shaft as instructed. He gave her the onion to slice. "You're a natural," Mateo said as he watched her.

"In medical school, we had to cut up a few things."

Mateo knew cadavers were on that list. "Ew."

"Ew?" she mocked. "Don't you have to cut up a few things, too?"

"Yes, but I usually wait until someone else has done all the prep work."

"Sissy," she teased. She picked up another knife and made quick work out of the potato. Then she impaled the tomato with the serrated knife. She truly was quite good at wielding sharp objects.

Within the hour, Mateo suggested they go to Gramercy Tavern. It was one of the finest restaurants in New York, with an exceptional menu. He cleaned the knives, rolled them back up, and placed them in his locker. This time, he was sure to check the padlock. Mateo then phoned the Gramercy Tavern and told them he was bringing a guest and they hoped to arrive within the next twenty minutes. They were more than happy to accommodate him.

When they arrived at the restaurant, Dr. Ardell removed her coat and revealed a black knit sheath dress that accentuated her figure. Mateo thought he might faint. The maître d' showed Mateo and his stunning date to a large round table in the corner.

"Enjoy your dinner," the gentleman said as he handed them menus.

A few minutes after they were seated, several of Mateo's restaurant chums came by to say hello. After Mateo's colleague left, Dr. Ardell was very impressed. "You are very popular."

"Nah. They just think I'll do something for them."

"What do you mean?"

"Not everyone is in this business simply for the love of food. It's another avenue for becoming a celebrity." Mateo kept talking while he scanned the wine list. "At one time, there were only a handful of well-known chefs, like Julia Child. People didn't have much access to cooking. Then TV brought some faces into people's homes, like Emeril and Bobby Flay, and then the networks blew up with cooking shows."

"Is that what you want? Your own cooking show?"

Mateo gave her an odd look. "No. Not really. I enjoy teaching people how to prepare meals, but more importantly, I enjoy sharing meals." He paused, thinking about his recent weekend with his parents. "That's what I miss the most now."

She glanced at the wine menu. "May I?"

Mateo was taken aback. Normally, he was the one who always ordered the wine. "Of . . . of course. My apologies."

She smiled. "Let's see if we pick out the same one."

"Okay! What are you in the mood for?"

"Since we are doing the tasting menu, let's start with a white to go with the fish, and then a red for the sirloin," she suggested.

"I would have suggested the same."

"Ah, but now we will see which white and which red."

Mateo pulled out his cell phone.

"Are you expecting a call?" She tried not to sound annoyed.

"Oh, no. Not at all." He showed her the stylus. "I'm going to scribble my choices down so as not to cheat." He grinned and turned his phone face-down on the table.

"How about the Louis Latour Corton-Charlemagne 2017 for the white?" Dr. Ardell suggested.

Mateo nodded. "Excellent choice. And for the red?"

"I've been wanting to try the Orin Swift Cabernet."

Mateo grinned. He flipped his phone over so she could see his choices. They were very similar in vintage, though not the exact same bottles. "You have excellent taste." He summoned the sommelier and placed the order for the two wines and when he wanted them served.

Dr. Ardell fidgeted with her water glass. "Tell me more about your foodie journey. That is what they call it, no?"

Mateo grinned again. "You may call it whatever you'd like." The sommelier brought over the white and poured a tasting for Mateo. It was bright, crisp, and cold. "Perfect."

He waited for both glasses to be filled before he continued. Then he raised his and made a toast: "Here's to good blood!"

She smiled and clinked her glass against his. "Yes. Good blood." It occurred to her he had not mentioned anything about his blood or his family's tests so far that evening. He hadn't said anything during their appointment a few days before, either. She wondered if his parents had told him about his lineage.

Mateo leaned back in his chair. "When I was in junior high school, my mother was a language teacher in the same school. One day, there was a mix-up in the delivery for the cafeteria, and there wasn't going to be anything to eat if you hadn't brought your lunch from home. My mother rounded up a couple of other teachers, drove to the grocery store, and bought a bunch of chopped meat, seasoning, and a crate of taco shells. She began to work her magic in the kitchen, and the students were going bonkers over the tacos. We started running out, and the line got longer. One of the kitchen ladies drove back to the grocery store and cleaned out the chopped meat section. I pitched in to help."

"And that is where you got your start in this business?"

"I guess you could say that." Mateo took another sip of his wine. "When I was in high school, I got a job as a line cook at a national restaurant chain, then moved on to working a food truck. My senior year, I started working at a country club and began experimenting with plating food so it looked like something special. A little garnish here, a little dollop there. I continued to work there while I went to junior college, because I wasn't sure what I wanted to do with my life."

Dr. Ardell was listening attentively.

"Then one evening, one of the club members asked if I would cater a private dinner party for them, and I said yes."

Mateo continued his narrative. He knew back then that he had a lot to learn. His parents were accustomed to fine dining, and they suggested he try culinary school.

"So they encouraged you to get into this business?"

"I don't know if it was about getting into the business. I think it was more about encouraging me to follow my creative instincts."

"You're very close with your parents." It was more of an observation than a question.

"Yes." He took another sip. "I could not have asked for a better upbringing or better people to do the job." He, too, didn't know how much she knew about his ancestry, but with the blood test results, she should have had a major clue.

"After finishing up at CIA—not the government agency." He chuckled. "I worked as a stagiaire, a 'staahj.' That's when you work as an unpaid kitchen intern. It can be for a day, a week, or months. An opportunity to see if you are a good fit with the restaurant."

"And how long did you stay?" Her eyes were locked on his.

"I did a few stints around the city. I was working at a small place in Soho that had an open window to the kitchen, and I suggested we try a chef's table. It's usually a large table that can accommodate about eight people. The chef prepares what he or she wants and spends time discussing the menu with the patrons."

"That sounds very intimate."

"It is, in a way. That's what I enjoy the most. Sharing." He sounded almost melancholy.

"And you feel you've lost some of that now?" She stuck her fork into the pear salad that had been placed before them.

"You catch on very fast," Mateo said. "It only dawned on me this past weekend. No, actually, it started creeping into my head while I was being held prisoner in the hospital."

"Hospitals can do that to a person. Make them contemplate, especially if they have a serious illness."

"Yes, I was contemplating alright. Then when I

spent the weekend with my parents, it really shed light on what I was doing, and where I thought I was going."

"Aren't you preparing for some big contest? On television?"

"I was. Now I'm not sure."

She looked surprised. "Seriously? After all this time and energy?"

"Don't misunderstand me. I thoroughly enjoy doing demos, because afterwards you get to share the food with the people you are working with. In the restaurant, you rarely get to do that. Enjoy the meal, that is. It's quite different than this when you work there." He gestured to the food on the table. "Running a kitchen requires many hours of planning, ordering, evaluating, adjusting product mix, invoices, managing staff. It's not all dazzling, and that part of the business is not what I was after. My career morphed. Believe me, I'm not complaining. I'm just at a point where I need to think about where I want to go and what I want to do. I simply go with the flow, as they say, especially now. After this health scare. Like I said, being in the hospital gave me a new perspective. I have to take more of a conscious role and not let other people push me into what they want from me."

Dr. Ardell looked at him and asked, "So if you were to choose anything in the culinary world, what would it be?"

Mateo scratched his chin. "You know who I admire the most? José Andrés."

"The man who started the World Central Kitchen?" she asked.

"Yes. What he does in the wake of disasters is inspiring. And necessary. I heard him say once that 'the power of a plate of food can be life-changing.' " Mateo had an expression of awe on his face. "Imagine what an impact he has made? I was very disappointed he didn't win the Nobel Prize in 2019."

"There's still time. I'm sure the world will see many more disasters."

"Now there's a not-so-cheery thought," Mateo said wryly.

"It's inevitable. And the world is lucky to have someone like him who is willing to do the work."

Mateo raised his glass. "To the altruistic people who give willingly and without expectation of reward, except knowing they helped humanity."

Adrian raised her glass and clinked his again. "You are a very interesting man." She leaned in closer. Was it a new comfort level, or was it the wine? Perhaps both? But she didn't care. She could not remember the last time she enjoyed a meal with a fascinating and handsome man. Any man, for that matter.

"Now that you know everything about me, let's hear about you." Mateo was about to stick his fork in the smoked arctic char. "Is it okay if I eat this?"

"Char is not known for high levels of mercury, but I would not tempt fate right now." She took a bite of hers and watched his face turn into a sad puppy expression. "Don't worry. It will not go to waste." She plucked the fish from his plate and put it on hers.

"But . . . but . . ." Mateo feigned a protest. "At least I asked them to skip the clams with the broccoli rabe." He was referring to the next course of lumache pasta, also known as large-shell pasta. He propped his elbow on the table and rested his chin on his fist. "Continue, please."

Adrian told him the story about her father and her little brother and how they fled with the help of a humanitarian organization.

"Ah. So that's why you became a doctor. A hematologist, correct?"

"That is correct, Captain Obvious."

Mateo almost fell off his chair in hysterics. He sat up and straightened his sleeves. "You have a very dry sense of humor."

"It's surprising I have one at all," she replied with a twinkle in her eyes.

He sat up and folded his arms. "You realize we have somewhat similar backgrounds."

"Do tell." She polished off the char, emitting sounds of delight. She pointed to the food with her fork. "Fantastic."

"Glad you are enjoying my portion." He pouted again. Then he sprung back and began to explain his parents' journey. At least what he knew of it.

He told her about the family's harrowing journey on the fishing boat. When he was through, Adrian could not help but comment, "Did it ever strike you as ironic that you work in a kitchen that primarily serves seafood?"

"Yes, quite. But I'm a generation removed. It's my abuela who can't stand the sight of it." He went on about Father Bruno and his food pantry. "My family cannot go back to Colombia, so we host a Colombian food festival once a year at a local park and send the money to the mission."

"Hmm." She twirled her glass. "That is very altruistic of you and your family."

Mateo squished up his face. "I never looked at it that way. It's just something we do to help the people who helped our family, so they can continue their good work."

Adrian's expression became softer. "I'm very glad I met you, Mateo. Not necessarily under these circumstances. But your family sounds a lot like mine. We've survived through many challenges."

"I didn't suffer through anything." He shrugged. "Maybe adolescence." They both laughed. "I have my parents to thank. They were brave. Unshakable. The trek from Colombia to Mexico came long before me." He stopped. Was this the time to tell her? Did it even matter? It hadn't made a difference in all his thirty-five years, so why should it now? "Actually, I wasn't born in Colombia. I was born in Mexico, while my parents were deciding whether or not to try to come to America. Then my father got a job offer with a former employer, and they moved to Texas. You know the rest of the story." He ate his pasta and broccoli rabe with gusto. "Who needs clams?" It was a disappointing question that did not require an answer.

By the time dessert was served, Mateo noticed they were the only two remaining in the restaurant. "God, I hate people like us." He grinned.

"What do you mean?" She dreamily licked the dark chocolate mousse from her spoon. "Mmm. This reminds me of when I was younger. My mother would make this wonderful chocolate pudding for holidays. She would always save an extra cup for me." She continued to lick the spoon. Mateo thought he would have a heart attack. *At least there's a doctor in the house.* He chuckled to himself.

"People who linger long after the kitchen has closed. There have been times when we had to drag out the vacuum cleaner."

She hooted. "Well, I surely do not want to be one of *those* people." She emphasized the word *those.*

"Heaven forbid." Mateo took the last sip of the port they served with the mousse. He motioned for someone to bring the check. "Sorry about that," he apologized to the server. "I hate it when we have to flick the lights on and off for people to get the hint it's time to leave." He grinned.

"No worries, sir. It's always a pleasure to see you." The server nodded and took the leather check folder.

"This was a most illuminating and delicious dinner." Adrian dabbed her lips with the linen napkin.

"Thank you for indulging me." Mateo smiled.

"What do you mean?" Adrian was perplexed.

"Allowing me to take you to dinner," Mateo replied.

"The pleasure was all mine." She paused. "I am very happy you are feeling better."

"I am. Thanks to you." Mateo's grin widened. He still wasn't sure if this was even an official date. "Perhaps we can do this again?"

She hesitated, and he got a sinking feeling. Then she replied, "That would be very nice."

"I wasn't sure if you had a rule about dating patients."

"Let us hope you will no longer be my patient." She smiled.

Mateo helped Adrian on with her coat. He was sorry to see her lovely figure covered up with the trench. It wasn't a lecherous thought. He wondered what it would be like to hold her in his arms. Yes, thanks to the doctor, he felt like he had gotten his groove back. He tried to remember the last time he felt like this. Maybe never.

Before they left the restaurant, Mateo called a car service to take Dr. Adrian Ardell home. He would walk the few blocks back to his apartment. There was a crispness in the air, and he was light on his feet. He would have broken into song if he didn't think people were around. But it was New York. There were always people around all the time, so he decided to whistle instead.

Adrian arrived at her apartment building on the Upper East Side. The doorman greeted her with a tip of his cap. She smiled back at him and said, "Have a good night."

As she was turning the key in the lock, she became flush and dizzy. She quickly entered her apartment as a wave of nausea fell over her. She dropped her coat on the floor, hurried to the bathroom, and splashed cold water on her face. It was a very odd feeling. Could she have eaten something that didn't agree with her? Not at the Gramercy Tavern. Maybe she was getting the flu. She peeled off her clothes, pulled a bucket from the broom closet, and placed it next to the bed. Just in case. She checked her temperature. Normal. She peered into the bathroom mirror. "Get some rest," she ordered herself. Adrian wrung out a cold wet washcloth, brought it with her to bed, and placed it on her forehead. Perhaps it was all the excitement of the evening. She thought about how much wine she drank. Two glasses. She skipped the port, so she wasn't drunk. At least, she didn't feel drunk. No, it was probably a stomach bug. If she didn't feel better in the morning, she'd have the lab run a few tests.

Adrian wondered how Mateo might be feeling. She thought about phoning him, but it was almost midnight, and it seemed like an odd thing to do. She would check on him in the morning. He appeared fine when they shook hands good night. She had wanted to kiss him on the cheek but thought better of it. Next time. It had been a very good night. Even if nothing came from it, she had a lovely evening. *Live in the moment. Enjoy life. It's important,* she kept telling herself. *All work and no play makes Adrian dull and uninspired.*

When Adrian woke up the next morning, she had a raging headache. She took a quick shower, pulled on a pair of slacks, a sweater, and walking boots, and tucked her hair into a beret. She moved slowly out the door. Normally, she would walk the ten blocks to work, but she was a little too wobbly, so she took a cab.

Adrian felt like she was in slow motion with a bulldozer crushing her head. She pulled out the magnetic ID card and let herself into the lab. "Hello, Kenneth. Do you have a minute?" she said to one of the phlebotomists.

"Sure, Doc. What's up?"

"I need you to do some blood work."

"Absolutely. Which patient?"

"Me." She rolled up her sleeve and took a seat in one of the procedure chairs used for drawing blood.

"You okay?" he asked. "Sorry. None of my business."

"No, it's okay. I went to dinner last night, and a few hours later, I felt quite ill. Shivers. Nausea. Clammy."

"Fever?"

"No."

"Could it have been something you ate?"

"Possibly, but I would hate to think it was from the restaurant where I had dinner."

"Really? Where?"

"I'd rather not say. Let's see what the test results bring before I have a conniption with the manager."

"Fair enough." The technician wrapped the rubber hose around her bicep, drew three vials, labeled them, and placed them in a small rack for Dr. Ardell to take into the processing lab. "I assume you are going to do this yourself?"

She looked at him and frowned. "I suppose I should give it to a neutral party, but I need to get this done as soon as possible."

"Roger that." He handed her the rack. "If you need anything else, just give me a shout."

"Thanks, Kenneth. I appreciate your discretion." She gave him a knowing look. He nodded in response and made a zipper gesture over his lips.

Adrian walked back to her research lab, turned

on the lights, and fired up the centrifuge. She was starting to feel better after drinking a liter of water. She waited twenty minutes for the blood to clot and then placed the vials into the machine, turned it up to 3,000 rpms, and waited another fifteen minutes before the test was ready to be analyzed.

She checked the sample twice. It showed a high level of mercury. How was that possible? Unless the char she ate was tainted, there was no way she ingested enough mercury to cause this kind of level and reaction. She phoned Mateo immediately.

"Good morning." Her voice was even. "Thank you for a wonderful dinner and fascinating conversation." Before Mateo could respond, she said, "How are you feeling today?"

"Just a little tired, but fine otherwise. Thank you for asking."

"Can you come up here for a quick blood test?"

Mateo was taken aback. "Uh, sure. Why? What's going on?"

"I will explain when you get here. Don't be alarmed. I simply want to check for something." Her voice was even and calm.

"Okay. You're the doc. But does that mean you won't have dinner with me again? I mean, if you're my doctor and all." Mateo was trying to keep the conversation light and direct at the same time.

Adrian couldn't help but smile. "Let's not worry about rules for now. Please come as soon as you can."

Mateo sat on his sofa, staring at the phone in his hand. He pursed his lips. *What could this be about?*

*No time to waste, bro. Get busy.* He slipped on a pair of loafers, grabbed his navy-blue peacoat, and trotted out to the sidewalk. It was just past rush hour, so there were plenty of cabs. He waved his arm at one, hopped in, and gave the driver the address of the hospital.

When Mateo arrived, he went to the outpatient desk. An elderly woman with blue hair greeted him. "Mr. Castillo. I thought we saw the last of you."

"Hi, Mildred. Yes, I thought it was the last of me, too."

"By the way, that was a very nice thing your mother did for us. I love herbal soaps. Most patients never think about the desk help."

"Without you, we wouldn't know where to go or who to see." Mateo flashed his winning smile at the woman.

"You are a darlin'." For a moment, Mateo thought the woman was going to get out of her seat and pinch his cheek. "Dr. Ardell is waiting for you. I believe you know the way."

"Yes, thank you, Mildred. You enjoy your day." Mateo made a quick beeline to Dr. Ardell's lab. "Good morning," he said as he entered. "What's up?"

Dr. Ardell pointed to the procedure chair. "As they say, you know the drill." She motioned for him to roll up his sleeve.

"I thought my levels were okay."

"They were."

"Sooo . . ." He drew the word out.

"I hate to be a Donna Downer, but I had an odd reaction last night after I got home."

"Wait." Mateo interrupted her. "It's 'Debbie Downer,' but continue. What kind of reaction?"

She snorted at her pop-culture-reference faux pas. "Similar to what you had, but I didn't faint."

"Well, that's not good. Do you think it was the food?"

"At first I thought it might be. Then I thought it could be the flu, so I ran some tests on myself this morning, and they came back with elevated mercury levels."

"Seriously?" Mateo was stupefied. "But how?"

"Exactly what I'm wondering. How?" She finished drawing his blood, labeled the vials, and set them aside. "It's going to be at least forty-five minutes before we know anything."

"Want to grab a coffee?" Mateo asked, but then thought the doctor may not want to be seen fraternizing with a patient.

"Coffee would be nice, but I want to wait here. Would you mind going to the cafeteria and bringing it here?"

"You want me to bring you cafeteria coffee?" Mateo gave her an *I don't think so* look.

"My apologies. I didn't mean for you to be my private valet."

"Don't be ridiculous," Mateo balked. "I meant I wouldn't think of bringing you sludge. There is a nice coffee bar around the corner. What would you like? A cappuccino? Latte? Half-caf?"

"They all sound good compared to, as you call it, the sludge. I know they try their best, but it's not easy to make gourmet coffee for hundreds of people."

"I couldn't agree with you more, and I am willing to brave the elements to get you something worthy of your work."

Adrian stifled a giggle. "It's a beautiful day out there."

"I was kidding. Well, not really kidding. Let's just say if it was raining or snowing, I would still be willing to get you a coffee."

"I accept." She gave him a sly smile. "And perhaps a croissant? I'm starting to feel like I can put something in my stomach."

"Glad you are feeling better." Mateo rolled down his sleeve and got up to leave. He felt like kissing her. Not necessarily in a romantic, sensual way, but in an affectionate way. *Maybe later.* In spite of the alarming news about mercury levels, Mateo felt optimistic. Maybe it was an anomaly. Adrian had only two small tastings of char. Unless the food was contaminated, there was no other way she could have been exposed.

Fifteen minutes later, he returned with a cappuccino and a croissant for Adrian, and a scone for himself. His smile dropped from his face when he looked at Adrian. She was not smiling. She almost looked angry.

"What is it?" Mateo set the bag of breakfast pastries and coffee on a counter.

"Your level is up, too. Slightly. Not as much as mine." She pursed her lips. "And you did not have any char."

"So what should we do?"

"We don't need chelation or transfusions, but let's get a lot of fluid into our systems and test again in a few hours."

Mateo was pensive. "I cannot imagine Gramercy Tavern serving bad food. Bad as in spoiled, not as in unappetizing. I know they are extremely careful about refrigeration, sanitation, and contamination. One bad dinner could ruin them."

"Maybe it wasn't the food," Adrian suggested.

"Then what could it be?"

"I'm not sure, but if you didn't have symptoms but still had a slightly elevated mercury reading, perhaps it was something else."

"The wine?"

"Doubtful." She squinted in thought. "Could we go back to Le Mer?"

"Like now?"

"If that's okay with you. I want to retrace our steps."

"Now you are sounding like a detective."

"Yes. I told you I'm a very good one." She checked her appointment schedule. "I'm free for the next two hours."

"Then let's go!" He held out her hand to assist her off the stool she was sitting on.

On their way out, Dr. Ardell told Mildred they would be back in about an hour. Mildred gave them a wink. She liked Dr. Ardell and thought she worked too hard and needed a personal life. Maybe Mateo would be the one to coax her into a more social existence.

When they arrived at the restaurant, Mateo and Adrian started from the front of the house and worked their way back to the kitchen, retracing their movements from the night before. "You never took off your coat," Mateo pointed out.

"You were wearing a sweater and an apron. Where is the apron?"

Mateo went to the laundry bin and pulled it out. "Here."

She looked at it for any kind of substance. Nothing.

"Then you showed me how to use the knives." She walked over to the stainless-steel table and cutting board. "Can you get them?"

"Sure." Mateo went in the back, where the lockers were. The padlock on his locker was open again. He looked inside, and his knife apron was gone, along with all of the knives. He returned to the kitchen and pulled out his cell phone and dialed Nora's number.

"Hey, Nora. It's Mateo. Yeah. I'm doing alright. I'm actually at the restaurant. I'm showing a friend around. Listen, did you send my knives out for sharpening?" He nodded. "You must have gotten here early. Okay. Just wanted to be sure no one stole them." He ended the call and turned to Adrian. "That's strange."

"What?"

"We usually send out our knives once, maybe twice a month. It seems like Nora has been sending mine out weekly, and I haven't even been here."

"Maybe you should speak to Nora about it."

"I will. She has a master key for the lockers in case someone forgets their key."

"Does she always send your knives out without telling you?"

Mateo thought about it. "No. Not that I know of." Something was bothering him. Something didn't feel quite right. He called the place where the knives were sharpened.

"Hey, Henry. It's Mateo Castillo. How are you? The family? Good to hear it. Nora said she sent my knives over there this morning. Any chance I can get them back this afternoon?" His brow furrowed. "She didn't bring them in to you today?" There was a pause, and he repeated what Henry said. "She hasn't brought them in for several weeks?" Another pause. "No, no, Henry. We haven't gone elsewhere. You take care of them like they are my babies." Mateo listened for a few more moments and then signed off. He looked at Adrian. "Something isn't right."

He called Nora again. "Hey, Nora, I just spoke to Henry. He said you didn't drop my knives off this morning." He listened. "What do you mean you took them somewhere else? I never authorized a change. You really should have discussed it with me first." He was peeved. "I know you run the front of the house, but I run the back, and those are my tools." His voice was getting rougher. "I need you to get them and bring them to the restaurant, pronto. I'll wait." He ended the call. "I can't believe she did that."

"So she is not authorized to make those decisions?"

"Absolutely not, especially with *my* property." Mateo was heated.

"Do we wait?" Adrian asked.

"You don't have to wait with me. I know you have patients. I'll wait for Nora. Do you want me to come by the hospital when I'm finished here?"

"No. I want to do our own reenactment." Adrian was dead serious.

"You're the boss."

"And so are you." She patted his cheek. "I should be finished by four o'clock. Can we meet back here then?"

"I thought you'd never ask." Mateo was truly feeling much better. His face lit up as a thought occurred to him. "Hey, could you test fish for mercury?"

"Of course." Adrian saw where he was going with this. "You want me to test the char from the restaurant."

"Correct. More than likely, it's the same batch. I am going to call GT and ask them to give you a piece of raw char." Before she could respond, he hit the speed-dial button. "Hey, Charles. Is anyone in the kitchen right now?" He waited a second for a response. "Great. Could you ask them to wrap a small piece of char, preferably from the same lot that was on the menu last night?" He grinned as he listened. "Yes, I know it's a goofy request, but it would be very helpful for an experiment I am doing." He raised his eyebrows at Adrian. "No, nothing unsavory. No pun intended." He chuckled. "A colleague of mine will stop by and pick it up. Please make sure it's wrapped well so she doesn't get chased by cats!" He snickered. "Thanks. She'll be there in about fifteen minutes."

"Brilliant." Adrian was impressed at Mateo's plan. "Process of elimination."

"So which one of us is Sherlock Holmes again?"

"It depends on who can solve the case first." She spun on her heel and left the room. *It was definitely a thing with her*, Mateo decided.

\* \* \*

Adrian hopped in a taxi and then asked the cabbie to wait as she ran into the restaurant to fetch the possible culprit. Then she returned to the hospital. Something was nagging at her. Regardless of what they ate the night before, nothing should have caused her mercury levels to rise that dramatically, and Mateo had less of an elevation. Once back at her lab, she reran their blood samples, yielding the same results. She had a few ideas, but it was like trying to find a needle in a haystack. She didn't think it was a coincidence that three weeks after his system was clear, he would have another toxic episode. It was as if he were being poisoned gradually. The mercury was being introduced into Mateo's system over the course of time. But how? And why weren't his levels as high as hers from the night before?

She used forceps to pick at the pieces of fish and in order to run a simple test. She pulled out a blue bottle and placed a few drops on the fleshy meat of the char. As she suspected, the test results showed no signs of mercury.

So then what was it?

Mateo was pacing in the kitchen when Nora arrived. She had a very innocent and embarrassed expression on her face. Before he had a chance to speak, she began to immediately apologize. "I'm very sorry, Mateo. I knew you were working on a new dish and probably needed to have your knives sharpened more frequently. I wanted them to be ready for you when you came back to work, and Henry was too busy. I didn't think you would be here during the renovation." She handed over a plastic shopping bag with the knife apron inside.

Mateo took the bag and glanced at the contents. "Thanks, Nora, but next time, check with me, okay?"

Nora placed her hand on his upper arm in an affectionate gesture. "Of course. I am so sorry if I upset you."

"No problem. Thanks for bringing them back." He slowly pulled himself away from her.

"Sure thing. So what are you doing here today?" she said coyly. Clearly, she didn't want to be in his bad graces. Too much was on the line. She had ambitions.

Mateo surely wasn't going to tell her why. He looked around the kitchen. "I missed the place."

"Oh, you chefs. Can't get enough, huh?" She shrugged.

"Speaking of chefs—how is your new boyfriend doing?" Mateo pretended to be interested. She seemed surprised at the question.

"Great. He's been working some private chef stuff with a few celebs."

"Anyone I might know?" Mateo knew it took no talent to be a celebrity chef in today's culture. All you had to do was call yourself one and pretend you had a talent until people realized you had none and they moved on to the next celeb du jour. "I've been out of the loop."

"It's one of the Real Housewives," Nora said with pride.

Mateo thought he was going to puke. Not from mercury but from the other thing that was eating at him, toxic self-obsession. And it was almost impossible to escape. He tried not to snort, but his response was an involuntary reflex. "Ah. A *real* celebrity."

"Jealous?" Nora sneered.

"Busted! You got me." Mateo wasn't sure if she caught the sarcasm.

"Well, if any of the other wives are looking for someone, I'll tell Neil to recommend you."

Mateo was about to bust a gut. He bit his lip. "Yes, please. You do that. Thanks." He grabbed his jacket and the shopping bag and bolted out the door. "See you next week."

He groaned at the thought of working one of those private parties. It was more like a few rounds with the World Federation of Wrestling in Versace jumpsuits. *Poor Gianni. He must be rolling in his grave. He had so much style and grace.* Mateo shook his head and blinked several times, trying to shake the thought of those women screaming and throwing wine in each other's faces. He had to wonder, who married those women? He shivered at the thought.

Mateo stood at the corner and wondered what he should do next. He had a few hours before he was supposed to meet up with Adrian. He decided to walk to his apartment and drop off his knives. He checked his mail. The renewal for his Met membership was in it, and it dawned on him that he hadn't visited the museum in almost a year. He thought some reflective time in the company of the masters could be good for his soul, so he walked uptown to the Metropolitan Museum of Art.

The first exhibit he hit up was Monet. No matter how many times he looked at the paintings on display, he was awed by how Monet could paint such massive works. And that was only a small part of the 250 paintings in the series that he'd worked on over the course of thirty years. Many critics said Monet's best works were his in plein air paintings, all done outdoors. Mateo was even more captivated when he discovered Monet planted the water lilies before he painted them. He organized his property in Giverny as if it were a three-dimensional painting. *Plant the idea and watch it grow.*

Mateo continued to absorb the inspiring mood as he stood among the art. He tried to imagine what was going through Monet's head as he was painting his subject. Talk about a virtual experience—and you didn't even need special glasses to experience it. The man was a genius. No wonder they called him the "Father of Impressionism."

From there, Mateo wandered to the polar opposite of emotions: David Alfaro Siqueiros's *Collective Suicide.* Siqueiros was a Mexican artist who fought in the Mexican Revolution from 1910 to 1920. His art pursuits were constantly being interrupted by political activism as he fought against fascist forces during the Spanish Civil War. Finally, in 1936, he founded the Siqueiros Experimental Workshop, where Jackson Pollock was greatly influenced.

Mateo grew thoughtful. How unique and personal each painting was. In some instances, the inspiration was obvious. Yet not so obvious in others. He recalled the famous Oscar Wilde quote, "Life imitates art far more than art imitates life." Mateo felt like he was hit by lightning. It was an epiphany. He knew at that moment what he wanted to do with his talent. He just had to figure out the details.

Mateo checked his watch. He had been there for over an hour. His stomach was grumbling. He thought of calling Adrian and asking if she wanted him to bring her lunch. He decided not to come on too strong, even though they were collaborating on solving their mystery. Mateo was elated that Dr. Adrian Ardell had taken a personal interest in him. Once she shed the white doctor's jacket, she became a different person. The stony, no-nonsense exterior of Dr. Ardell became a charming, witty, and intriguing Adrian. He liked it. A lot.

He jumped when his cell phone vibrated in his pocket. He had meant to turn the ringer back on once he left the museum. It was Adrian. "Hey. What's up?"

"The char is clean."

"Can we assume it had an alibi?"

Adrian let out a guffaw. "Are you not taking this seriously?" She put on her stern voice.

"Oh, yes, ma'am. Very, actually. I'm just in a good frame of mind today."

"Glad to hear it. But until we find the source, we need to take this seriously. Remember, your life is—"

"On the line." Mateo finished her sentence. "What do we do now?" Mateo asked with more concern in his voice.

"I am getting off in an hour. One patient and one meeting were canceled."

"Is that a good thing or a bad thing?"

"Good about the meeting. I find it hard to focus

when some of my colleagues drone on and on. The patient? I cannot say. She did not give a reason when she spoke to Mildred."

"Do you want to go out to eat now?" Mateo asked.

"If you are available, yes. Where are you?"

"I just left the Met. I needed some brain space."

"That is one of my favorite places. Most museums, actually."

Mateo tucked that tidbit away in his memory bank. *Sunday brunch and maybe the Whitney.* "I have to stop back at my apartment and pick up the knives. Shall we meet at Le Mer in, say, thirty minutes?"

"Perfect." Adrian immediately ended the call.

Mateo looked at his phone. *Yep. It's a thing.*

He hustled back to his apartment and picked up the shopping bag. Mateo hadn't been paying attention earlier when Nora gave it to him. He was too busy trying not to blow his top. When he looked inside, there was a sales receipt for a women's clothing store. It was dated the day before. Odd. Or maybe not. He decided to call Nora using the ruse she may need the receipt for something. "Hey, Nora. It's Mateo. Listen, I found a receipt in the shopping bag you gave me. It's from Putumayo. Do you need it?"

Nora's voice sounded a bit nervous. "Uh, no. It's on my credit card statement."

"Just wanted to be sure before I chucked it," Mateo said. "By the way, where did you get the knives sharpened?" He paused. "Just in case we need to use them again."

"A place in my neighborhood. I figured it was more convenient."

"What's the guy's name?" Mateo asked.

"Rupert. He's a friend."

"I understand wanting to help out our friends, but you really need to talk to me first before you start making these types of decisions." Mateo was being very patient.

"You're right. Sorry. It won't happen again," Nora said with relief.

"Okay. See you next week." Mateo had already ended the call when he realized Nora hadn't given him Rupert's last name. Whatever. He figured Nora wasn't going to pull any more of her stunts.

Mateo wasn't too keen on Nora. She was annoyingly effusive, with her loud nasal voice when she greeted the customers. Some of the customers. The significantly rich customers. She always bought a round of drinks for the people who could well afford to buy the entire restaurant drinks. Of course, she never paid the tab at the end of the night. The owner always wrote it off. Mateo also thought her attire was a bit on the tacky side, with her boobs practically falling out of her dress, way too many cheap baubles, fishnet stockings, and stilettos. It was a bit tawdry and over-the-top for a high-class restaurant. Maybe that's why the owner had hired her. Mateo always suspected there was something going on between them, but Nora was also shrewd. She could manipulate a man into thinking he would eventually get some honey from the Queen Bee.

Mateo wondered how long she would last. It

had been two months so far, but the owner was away in the Caribbean for a few weeks. It had been easy for her to sashay around, playing up to the highly fashionable guests and putting their drinks on the house.

Normally, Nora wasn't Mateo's headache. They didn't spend a lot of time interacting at work. Things were hectic, and everyone had a job to do and do it fast. But that morning, she had managed to thoroughly annoy him. He probably would have agreed to give her friend some business, anyway. It was that she didn't ask him about it first. He shrugged and shook off the irritation, trying to return to the heady mood he was in when he left the museum with all its talent and passion. He realized he'd better get a move on. A special person was waiting for him.

Adrian was already in front of the restaurant when Mateo came jogging down the block. "Sorry I'm late. I had a little chat on the phone with Nora, the hostess."

"She really rattled your ire, didn't she?" Adrian said, half-teasing.

"I know this sounds ridiculous, but my knives . . . well, they are almost an appendage to me. Without them, I cannot wield my craft."

"Are they magic knives?" Adrian was genuinely interested in his attachment to the sharp metal objects, despite her teasing tone.

"Kind of. First of all, they are very personal. Like an artist's brush. As I showed you, there are different knives for different purposes. Second, they are very expensive. The three knives we used last night cost over three hundred and fifty dollars each.

Third, she shouldn't have touched them, and fourth, which really should be first, it's sentimental. They are a symbol of my success as a chef."

"I thought Michelin was a symbol of success."

"That's true as far as the industry is concerned. But for me? It's a symbol that I earned them."

She looked pensive. "You are not what I imagined."

Mateo raised one eyebrow. "What do you mean?"

"When you were admitted to the hospital, there were a few whispers about this chef who was the latest big deal."

Mateo blushed. "Believe me, I am not a big deal."

Adrian smiled. "That is what I am talking about. You are quite humble for a rising star. I was expecting someone more like Gordon Ramsay." She chuckled. "Yelling, screaming, using expletives."

"No, that's not my style. I sulk." Mateo gave her a wicked grin. "By the way, did you know Gordon Ramsay was once an aspiring soccer player?"

"I did not."

"He was injured and had to quit. The sports world's loss, the culinary world's gain."

"Life is full of twists and turns, isn't it? Come on—let's try to solve this mystery for once and for all."

Mateo led the way through the disheveled dining room. "I hope they can finish by next week. It doesn't seem like anything is getting done."

"It's New York. Everything takes twice as long because of the unions." She looked at him. "And yes, we have unions at the hospital, too."

Mateo nodded. "I guess we are all at the mercy of one giant bureaucracy."

"It's everywhere." Adrian positioned herself in the same spot where she had been standing the night before. Mateo grabbed an onion, a potato, and a tomato.

"You came around here." She pointed to the area next to her. "Then you unrolled the knife apron."

"Then I gave you a demonstration." Mateo pulled out the knives and showed her how to slice and dice. He handed her the knives, and she repeated the same procedure.

Adrian peered around the kitchen. There was nothing that looked odd to her, but she wouldn't even know what to look for, so she asked, "Is there anything different about the kitchen?"

"What do you mean?"

"HVAC system? Fans? Air flow?"

"No. We replace the filters frequently, but none of the appliances have been touched."

Adrian looked disappointed. "I really thought we'd find an answer."

"Maybe it was some kind of anomaly."

"We call it idiopathic." Adrian was straining her brain. "And you feel alright today?"

"Yes."

"Any new bruises? Dizziness? Mood swings?"

"No. No. And no." Mateo was smiling at her. "I'm okay. Really. And how about you? You feeling okay?"

"Yes. Much better. Thank you."

There was an awkward silence between them. Mateo was the first to speak. "So, what do you think?"

"About?"

"What we should do next," Mateo said.

"As in?"

*She is not making this easy*, Mateo thought. But he took a leap of faith. "Dinner?"

"Again? Tonight?" Adrian asked.

"Er, well, yeah. I mean yes." He tried not to stammer.

"Alright, but this time, not so fancy." Adrian had enjoyed their dinner the night before but was not interested in another lavish meal so soon.

"I know a little pasta place in the village. Everything is homemade, including the wine."

"Sounds perfect." She watched him roll up his knife apron. "Wait."

He stopped abruptly. "What? You want to go somewhere else?"

"No. Last night." She pointed to his hands. "You were wearing prep gloves last night."

"Yes, I was." Mateo replied. "Why?"

"Don't touch the knives with your bare hands." Adrian pulled on his arm gently.

"I'll be careful," Mateo teased.

"I'm serious. Put on a glove before you put them in the apron. And we should both wash our hands thoroughly. Now." That was an order.

"Okay. If you say so."

They stood next to each other as they scrubbed their hands and between their fingers. Then Mateo walked over to the supply station and donned a pair of gloves. He walked back with his elbows bent and his arms in the air, faking the stance of a surgeon.

"Very funny." Adrian shook her head.

Mateo placed his knives in the apron, and then Adrian showed him how to remove the gloves without touching the exterior by inserting the index finger of one hand under the thumb of the other, then peeling back the glove so they were inside out. He was about to throw them in the trash when she stopped him. "Put them in the bag with the knives."

Normally, Mateo carried his knife apron in a leather sling-type bag with a shoulder strap, but that's not what Nora had handed him. He was in such a hurry to get out of the kitchen, he didn't check the shopping bag until he got back to his apartment. Then he got distracted by the receipt. It hadn't occurred to him to ask Nora about his missing leather bag. He assumed she had left it behind. But why? He went over to his locker and found the leather bag where he usually kept it. It was right there, hanging on a hook. She couldn't have missed it. He shook his head.

"What is it?" Adrian asked.

"Nora. She was very careless with the knives."

Adrian took a step back. "I think you are a little too attached to them."

He gave her a look of surprise. "No. Not really. It's the Nora thing. She's been, I don't know . . . *annoying* would be the best word to describe it."

"And how long has she been working here?"

"A little over two months."

"Huh." Adrian was contemplative. Nora was a nuisance and a distraction. Adrian knew it bothered Mateo that Nora had gotten her job with minimal qualifications. Mateo had made that abundantly clear over dinner last night. His ideology for fairness was evident. Adrian thought Mateo and her father would get along well. Integrity was important to them both. It was how they were raised.

Mateo believed women should never be discouraged or halted from moving ahead with their chosen careers. His mother was a perfect example of someone who had talent and ambition, and she always found a way to figure things out. Now, at this point in his career, he was saddled with working with a woman who was manipulative, with no obvious skills except for social climbing—and she wasn't that good at it, either. She was a poser, and Mateo didn't like anything or anyone that wasn't genuine.

Both drifted off into their own thoughts as Mateo carefully wound the apron tightly and placed it in the leather pouch. Even though they were both feeling fine at the moment, it didn't mean everything *was* fine. Someone could faint in an instant. Adrian didn't want to alarm Mateo, but until they could unearth the cause of this bizarre affliction, they had to focus on the information they had, little as it was.

They checked the kitchen to see if anything else was unusual, then left through the back door, hailed a cab, and went back to Adrian's lab.

Adrian had been sure the mercury was in the fish. Maybe something at the fish market was contaminating everything. "Where do you get your fish and shellfish?"

"A number of purveyors. It depends on who has what and what is the freshest. Obviously." Mateo realized they had been discussing the knives and fish conspiracy for a while. "Do you want to grab dinner?" He actually felt a little agitated, and he didn't know why. Was Dr. Adrian Ardell more interested in his knives than him? Then he realized he was being childish. *Move over, macho man.* She just wanted to help him.

"Yes. I would very much like to have dinner, but there is one more thing I need to do. It should take me a few minutes, and then we can come back here after dinner for the results."

Mateo had no idea what she was talking about. "Fine. Let's go." He held out his hand.

"One more minute, *please.*" She emphasized *please.* She motioned for him to set the leather bag on the counter. She put on a pair of protective gloves. She used forceps to remove the prep gloves Mateo had been wearing, placed them on a clean glass surface, and turned them right-side out. She then removed each knife from the apron, took an eyedropper of something in a brown bottle, and dripped it on the gloves. Then she sprayed the knives with something from a different bottle, this one filled with some blue liquid. When she was finished, she removed her protective gloves in the same manner she had shown Mateo at the restaurant.

She took a deep breath. "Ready. Shall we?"

"I thought you'd never ask."

Once again, they strode past Mildred, who had a gleam in her eye. This time, she gave Dr. Ardell a thumbs-up. Adrian smiled and shook her head.

The pasta restaurant was about five blocks away from the hospital. It was small, quaint, and comfortable, with fresco paintings on the walls depicting scenes from Italy. It looked very traditional.

The smell of roasted garlic wafted through the dining room. A petite Italian woman greeted them and showed them to a table. "Martino will be right with you." She walked to a side bar and returned with a bottle of wine in a straw-covered basket. "We make it ourselves. Please try a glass."

Mateo thanked her and began to pour the wine into what should be water glasses. Adrian asked, "Shouldn't we wait for the wineglasses?"

Mateo laughed. "In this restaurant, these are the wineglasses."

"But what if we don't like it?" Adrian asked.

"The first glass is gratis. If we like it, then we pay for the next round."

"How do they know if we had more than one glass?" Adrian asked.

Mateo nodded over to where the petite woman was standing. "Eyes on the back of her head. She knows where every drop and every crumb goes."

Adrian chuckled. "I'm sure she does. What do you recommend?"

"I love their ravioli. They make two kinds. One is mushroom served with a butter-sage sauce, and the other is three cheese served with a light pomodoro sauce. They'll do half-and-half if you want."

"I'll be honest, I wasn't sure how hungry I was going to be, but as soon as we stepped in here, I became ravenous."

"Glad to see you're feeling more like yourself."

"And I'm glad you are feeling better, in spite of the trace of mercury."

"Maybe I'm developing an immunity," Mateo said as he raised his glass.

"No such thing when it comes to mercury." She clinked her glass against his.

They ordered a less sumptuous dinner than the night before. Salad. Pasta. Hot bread from the oven. They chatted again about their upbringing. Mateo knew Adrian's was more traumatic and challenging than his. Her father was incarcerated; her brother died; they moved to a foreign country and had to reestablish themselves. Then he told her more about his parents' and grandparents' escape from Colombia and how his grandparents decided to stay in Mexico. In some respects, they had a lot in common, the biggest things being family and loyalty.

Not a bad way to start a relationship.

When the check came, Adrian insisted on paying it.

"Now that just makes me feel cheap." Mateo was half serious. "Let me at least leave the tip."

"Sounds fair."

They left the restaurant and walked back to the hospital. The test results should now be complete.

Adrian opened the security doors, and the two walked in. Adrian glanced at the knives lying on the glass plate. "And there you have it." She pointed to the discoloration on the knives and a similar discoloration on the gloves.

"Have what?"

"Mercury." She took a small pointer and indicated the knife handles and the tiny drops on the gloves. "Your knife handles are covered in it."

Mateo was horrified. "How?"

"Whoever is sharpening your knives, perhaps?" Adrian suggested.

"Or whoever else is handling them." Mateo's mind went straight to Nora. "She has the keys to my locker. My knives went missing. She allegedly took them elsewhere, but I don't even think that guy Rupert exists." He had a mischievous look on his face and pulled out his cell phone. After dialing, he said, "Hey, Nora. Sorry to bother you, but I went to Coppola's tonight, and the chef was asking me if there was someone who could do his knives quickly. What was that guy Rupert's last name again?" He knew she never gave it to him in the first place. A few seconds went by, and then Mateo said, "You don't remember? But I thought you said he was a friend." Mateo was growing more suspicious by the second.

"Well, he is," Nora replied. "You know, one of those people you hang out with at a bar."

"Huh. Okay. Never mind. But next time, get his business card, so we can put it on the bulletin board." Mateo knew there would be no business card, just like there was probably no Rupert, either.

"Sure thing," Nora said in her nasal tone. "Gotta go!"

Mateo looked at Adrian. "I think—no, I'm almost certain it's Nora." He dialed another number on his phone. It was Henry again. "Hi, Henry. It's Mateo. Sorry to bother you, but did Nora call and ask if you could sharpen my knives?"

"No," Henry replied. "Like I told ya—I haven't seen anything from your kitchen in weeks. Never talked to nobody, either."

"Thanks, Henry."

"Everything alright?" Henry sounded concerned.

"Everything is fine. We'll see you soon. Have a good evening."

Mateo took a seat on one of the stools and began to put the pieces together. "Nora said she took the knives to some other guy named Rupert, who was supposed to be a friend, but she doesn't even know his last name. She said the reason she took the knives to Rupert was because Henry was busy. Henry just told me he hadn't heard from Nora."

"So Nora was lying."

"Correct," Mateo continued. "And my locker was unlocked twice. The first time, I thought I may have forgotten, which I never do, but I was distracted with all this poisoning stuff. Then the locker was unlocked again. I know I locked it the day before, because I double-checked."

"You told me Nora has a spare key," Adrian added.

"Correct again."

"So she is putting the mercury on your knife handles. But why?"

"I have no idea, and I also don't know how she is doing it." Then he snapped his fingers. "Earlier, when I was about to toss the gloves in the trash can, I noticed an empty box of those squiggly light bulbs, and there was a broken bulb lying on top."

Adrian grabbed her coat. "Come on. We need to retrieve that trash bag."

They bolted out of the hospital and flagged down a cab. "I know everyone says this, but please hurry," Adrian said.

The cab driver looked into the rearview mirror.

"Miss, if I had a dollar for every time someone said that to me, I coulda retired years ago."

"I don't doubt it," Mateo replied.

Adrian leaned close to the Plexiglas divider. She raised her hospital ID lanyard. "I'm a doctor, and I have a patient that needs to see me. We would have called an ambulance, but she is bedridden, and it's faster if I go to her."

The driver looked up again. "Sorry. I'll do my best."

Mateo couldn't resist the temptation to squeeze her knee.

The cab flew through a few lights about to turn red and screeched in front of Le Mer. "She lives in a restaurant?" He was scratching his head.

"Apartment's upstairs. She's been there for years." Mateo embellished the lie. The fare came to ten dollars, but Mateo passed the cabbie a twenty. "Thanks!"

Adrian and Mateo hopped out and scrambled through the front door of the restaurant. There was noise coming from the kitchen. Mateo dashed ahead of Adrian and sprinted into the kitchen. "Forget something?"

Nora was in the process of removing the plastic trash bag. "Uh, yeah. I wanted to be sure nothing was rotting in here."

"Oh, there is something rotten, alright." Mateo grabbed the bag from her and then handed it to Adrian. "I'm sure we will find your fingerprints all over those light bulb boxes."

Nora made a dash for the door, but Mateo was too quick and tackled her. She started screaming expletives and threats. He held her down while Adrian called the police.

"It's over, Nora. Whatever the hell you think you were doing. It's over. O.V.E.R." Mateo was desperately controlling his rage. He was breathing heavily. "Why, Nora? Why me? Why would you want to kill me?"

Nora struggled to get out of his grip, but Mateo wasn't about to let her go. Not without an answer.

"I wasn't trying to kill you. I just wanted you out of the picture for a while."

"But why? I don't understand." Mateo was truly confused.

"Because of Neil."

"Neil wanted me dead?" Mateo was mystified.

"No."

"You need to explain yourself a little better." Adrian was now recording the conversation on her phone.

"Okay, okay! We just wanted to get you sidelined for a while."

"For what reason?"

"Because of the contest. Neil was planning on entering it, and he knew you were probably one of the biggest challengers."

"He wanted to eliminate some of the competition," Mateo huffed. "Were you going to try to poison everyone? That would have been a neat trick." Mateo loosened his grip on her a bit, but not enough for her to get away.

"With you out of the way, he had a chance to be one of the five finalists. They get a lot of exposure, you know."

"And you were going to *kill* Mateo?" Adrian was sure to ask the question for the recording.

"I said we weren't trying to kill him. Just put him out of commission," Nora whined.

"You are lucky I am a good doctor," Adrian stated.

"And why is that?" Nora almost smirked.

"Because I saved his life. Now you'll be tried for attempted murder instead of murder in the first degree."

Nora was sputtering. "But we weren't going to kill him!"

"The levels of mercury that were being introduced into his system would have eventually led to total organ failure, starting with the kidneys, then the liver. Shall I go on? It's a horrible death." Adrian continued in her authoritative tone. "It was rather clever of you to put mercury on the knife handle. The skin is the body's largest organ. When a lethal substance is introduced to the epidermis, it is rapidly absorbed by the dermis, and then the hypodermis, and then into the bloodstream. Ordinarily, the epidermis is supposed to be a protective layer. However, the epidermis is no match for toxic chemicals. Mercury is readily available in many household products, such as thermometers, blood pressure gauges, thermostats, and compact spiral fluorescent light bulbs. Yes, they are energy-saving, but also a hazard. Most people don't know they contain mercury, and they are supposed to be brought to a recycling center. I see you figured out a way to recycle yours." Adrian was laying it on thick.

Mateo kept shaking his head. Never in his life would he have thought that someone would have such disdain as to want to cause him life-threatening harm. "You could have killed me."

"Like I said, that wasn't the plan," Nora insisted.

Mateo was calming down. "Did Neil help you plant the mercury on the knives?"

"Just the first time. He showed me where you normally grip it. And he was the one who showed me how to break the bulb without making it explode."

"You are quite the little criminal, aren't you?" Mateo said incredulously. He looked up at Adrian as she continued to record the confession. She had no idea if it would hold up in court, but it was worth a try.

Several police officers arrived on the scene, and Adrian recounted the entire story to them. "I'm Dr. Ardell. I'm the hematologist who was treating Mr. Castillo for mercury poisoning." Mateo and Adrian both took turns giving the officers information, starting from when Mateo was first admitted into the hospital, his high mercury levels, and then discovering they had been tampered with. Adrian gave them the trash bag, noting they would probably find Nora's fingerprints on the box and the bulbs.

"I'll bring my knives to the police station," Mateo added.

"And I will include my report," said Adrian.

"Thanks," said one of the officers. "If you can bring everything down to the station before noon tomorrow, that would be great. Meanwhile, we'll charge her with assault, and she'll spend the night in jail." The officer took Nora by the arm. "Let's go, Lucrezia Borgia."

Nora gave him a blank look. Obviously, she didn't get the reference to the most notorious poisoner in history.

Adrian leaned against the stainless-steel table. "This has been one very interesting adventure, Mr. Castillo."

*Uh-oh. Mr. Castillo?* Mateo thought that was a hint that they would not be pursuing a romantic relationship.

Seeing Mateo's dismayed reaction to her words, Adrian said, "My apologies. That is your father's name, is it not?" She slipped her arm through his and rested her head on his shoulder. Then a thought came to her, and she jumped up, startling Mateo.

"What is it?" he asked.

"This means you don't need a bone marrow transplant."

"And it also means you are no longer my doctor."

"You are correct. So when can I meet the rest of your family?" Adrian was surprised at her own boldness.

Mateo pulled out his cell phone and dialed, then said, "Mamita? I have some very good news. I do not need a bone marrow transplant. My wonderful doctor discovered what was wrong."

Elena was squealing with joy on the other end of the phone. "My baby! I cannot tell you how happy I am!" She started to cry. Mateo could hear his father's voice in the background, giving a boisterous hoot. "You must come for Sunday dinner," Elena exclaimed. "We have to celebrate."

"Only if I can bring a date." There was that word again. Adrian looked a little confused. She didn't think Mateo had a girlfriend.

"Of course, son. Who is it?" Elena asked eagerly.

"Dr. Adrian Ardell."

# Epilogue

*Ten months later*

The twenty-fifth anniversary of the Colombian Food Festival was on the horizon. Elena and Dante made special arrangements for Sylvia, Gabriel, Yolanda, Rodrigo, and Father Bruno to all come. They paid for their transportation and lodging.

After Nora's trial, where she was found guilty of aggravated assault, Mateo excused himself from the contest and quit Le Mer. He was going to focus on the food festival. When he gave an interview to a local network, he said, "Food should not be about competition. It should be about enjoyment, nourishment, and companionship." This year, the festival would not only benefit Father Bruno's food pantry, it was also going to be the launch of Mateo's new venture, Share a Meal.

When Mateo first told a few people about his idea, he was able to raise enough funds to start an organization that would go into communities and hold events for people to come together to share a meal. Mateo and his team would do a cooking demonstration to show people how to make nutritious and affordable meals, and then everyone would sit together and share the food. He hoped it would be an inspiration for people to think about sharing meals with families and friends.

Adrian continued her research and practice, but she took time from her schedule to have meals with her parents and also with Mateo and his family. She found balance in her life. Surprisingly, she found herself even more productive than before as a result. Perhaps it was because she now spent more time with people. People she cared about. It had a tendency to elevate one's mood.

The evening kickoff party for the festival was bigger this year than before. Speeches needed to be made, acknowledgments noted, but most of all, it was a celebration of fellowship and compassion.

Elena had insisted her parents stay with them. As Elena and Sylvia were getting ready together, they reminisced about their first night at the convent all those years ago and what a wild journey they had been on.

"Mami, come here," Elena said as she ushered her mother into her bedroom. She pulled a garment bag out from the closet. As she zipped it open, Sylvia's eyes began to tear.

"You remembered." Sylvia touched the beautiful beaded dress. She looked lovingly at her daughter. It was like the one at the thrift shop that she had admired decades ago. Only this one was even more beautiful. Elena helped her mother into the dress. It fit her perfectly.

"A promise is a promise," Elena said with a smile.

# RECIPES PROVIDED BY CLAUDIA BASELICE

## Cheese-Stuffed Corn Cakes (Arepas Rellenas de Queso)

**SERVING SIZE**
6 arepas

**INGREDIENTS**
2 cups pre-cooked corn meal
2 cups hot water
¼ teaspoon salt
2 tablespoons soft butter, divided
12 slices mozzarella cheese

**INSTRUCTIONS**
In a medium bowl, mix the water, salt, and pre-cooked corn meal.

Knead with your hands for about 3 minutes, moistening your hands with water as you work.

Form 6 small balls with the dough.

Place each ball between 2 plastic bags or parchment paper, and with a flat pot lid, flatten to about ⅓ inches. The arepas should be about 5 inches in diameter.

Add the butter to a nonstick pan over medium heat. Place the arepas in the pan, and cook about 3 minutes on each side, until a crust forms or until they are golden brown.

Split the arepas using a knife as you would do with an English muffin and stuff with 2 slices of mozzarella cheese.

Place the stuffed arepas back on the skillet over medium-high heat and cook 2 minutes on each side or until the cheese is melted and serve immediately.

# Pan de Queso
# (Colombian-Style Cheese Bread)

**SERVING SIZE**
Serves 6

**INGREDIENTS**
2 cups all-purpose flour
¼ cup warm milk
½ teaspoon sugar
1 tablespoon butter, melted
½ cup queso fresco
½ cup mozzarella cheese
1 beaten egg
1 teaspoon baking powder
Salt to your taste

**INSTRUCTIONS**
Preheat the oven to 350° F.

In a small bowl, dissolve the baking powder in the warm milk. Add 1 tablespoon flour, then the sugar. Stir until well combined. Set aside for 5 minutes.

In a medium bowl, combine the melted butter and milk mixture and stir well. Add the egg, flour, salt, and mozzarella, and queso fresco. Using your hands, mix well. Cover with plastic and let sit at room temperature for about 40 to 50 minutes.

Divide the mixture into 12 equal-size portions, shaping them into balls or a doughnut shape. Cover loosely with plastic wrap and let sit at room temperature for about 30 minutes.

Place on a baking sheet lined with parchment paper and bake for about 25 to 30 minutes or until golden on top. Serve warm.

**Discover the Sisterhood with #1 *NEW YORK TIMES* BESTSELLING AUTHOR FERN MICHAELS!**

**HIDE AND SEEK**
**When it's time for payback, these friends play to win . . .**

*The Sisterhood: a group of women from all walks of life bound by friendship and years of adventure. Armed with vast resources, top-notch expertise, and a loyal network of allies around the globe, the Sisterhood will not rest until every wrong is made right.*

Payback has its price, and the Sisterhood's last assignment almost landed them in jail. Now the women are fugitives with a bounty on their heads, but they're not planning on hiding out for long— not when good friends need the kind of help only they can give.

Mitch Riley, the ruthless assistant director of the FBI, intends to frame Cornelia "Nellie" Easter, the judge who helped the Sisterhood evade prison, and their lawyer, Lizzie Fox, in order to save his own career. He's created a special task force to hunt the Sisters down. Mitch has the entire FBI behind him, but he's about to discover that he's no match for seven formidable women with an unbreakable bond and a wickedly cunning plan to bring the fight right to his door . . .

# SWEET VENGEANCE

*A deeply satisfying and uplifting story of one woman's journey from heartbreak to triumph by #1 New York Times bestselling author Fern Michaels.*

Tessa Jamison couldn't have imagined anything worse than losing her beloved twin girls and husband—until she was convicted of their murder. For ten years, she has counted off the days in Florida's Correctional Center for Women, fully expecting to die behind bars. Fighting to prove her innocence holds little appeal now that her family is gone. But on one extraordinary day, her lawyers announce that Tessa's conviction has been overturned due to a technicality, and she's released on bail to await a new trial.

Hounded by the press, Tessa retreats to the small tropical island owned by her late husband's pharmaceutical company. There, she begins to gather knowledge about her case. For the first time since her nightmare began, Tessa feels a sense of purpose in working to finally expose the truth and avenge her lost family. One by one, the guilty will be led to justice, and Tessa can gain closure. But will she be able to learn the whole truth at last . . . and reclaim her freedom and her future?

Visit our website at
**KensingtonBooks.com**
to sign up for our newsletters, read
more from your favorite authors, see
books by series, view reading group
guides, and more!

**BOOK** **CLUB**

**BETWEEN THE CHAPTERS**

Become a Part of Our
**Between the Chapters Book Club**
Community and Join the Conversation

**Betweenthechapters.net**